A kid they called the Witness . . .

Something funny was going on at Carlo's Pizza. The way they described Carrie Hall's accident, it didn't make any sense. But it wasn't my job to worry about it. My job was to learn to be a pizza driver. There were already three other black-shirted drivers standing at the front counter waiting for deliveries, so I got in line behind them.

The guy standing in front of me was a weird-looking little kid with brown hair sticking out every which way from under his black Carlo's cap. When he copped a look up at me, it seemed like his eyes weren't quite right.

"Who are *you*?" he asked belligerently.

"Terry Saltz," I told him, looking down my chest at him, and trying not to let my voice sound any friendlier than his did. "Who are *you*?"

"Ed Hanus," the kid said nastily. "I suppose you're taking Carrie's place."

"I suppose I am."

He grimaced. "I'd rather have Carrie back."

I shrugged. "People in hell want ice water."

He blinked up at me. "Carrie was pretty. I was gonna ask her out."

I said, "Well, dude, now you got *me*. So, whatcha got in mind? Dinner and a movie?"

He got a horrified look on his face and left with his deliveries.

I was chuckling. "What's that little Ed guy's deal?" I asked the dispatcher.

"Ed?" He gave me a puzzled look. "Oh, you mean the Witness. That's what we call him because he mainly just stands around and watches everyone else work. Ignore him. He's a little creep."

The little creep was about to get himself murdered, but of course we didn't know that then.

COLD SLICE

A WORKING MAN'S MYSTERY

L. T. Fawkes

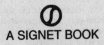

A SIGNET BOOK

SIGNET
Published by New American Library, a division of
Penguin Group (USA) Inc., 375 Hudson Street,
New York, New York 10014, U.S.A.
Penguin Books Ltd, 80 Strand,
London WC2R 0RL, England
Penguin Books Australia Ltd, 250 Camberwell Road,
Camberwell, Victoria 3124, Australia
Penguin Books Canada Ltd, 10 Alcorn Avenue,
Toronto, Ontario, Canada M4V 3B2
Penguin Books (N.Z.) Ltd, Cnr Rosedale and Airborne Roads,
Albany, Auckland 1310, New Zealand

Penguin Books Ltd, Registered Offices:
80 Strand, London WC2R 0RL, England

First published by Signet, an imprint of New American Library,
a division of Penguin Group (USA) Inc.

First Printing, June 2003
10 9 8 7 6 5 4 3 2 1

Copyright © Margo Pierce Dorksen, 2003
All rights reserved

Ⓡ REGISTERED TRADEMARK—MARCA REGISTRADA

Printed in the United States of America

PUBLISHER'S NOTE
This is a work of fiction. Names, characters, places, and incidents either are
the product of the author's imagination or are used fictitiously, and any resem-
blance to actual persons, living or dead, business establishments, events, or
locales is entirely coincidental.

. . . with a little help from my friends . . .

Bob, Aaron, Susan, and Bryan
Frankie, Carol Jane, Anthony, Gayle

to Susanna Einstein, who found me,
to Claire Zion, who remembered me,
to John Paine, who untangled me

Chapter 1

I want to tell you a story. It's about friends, hard work, good love, bad love, and murder. My name's Terry Saltz.

Here's me: Six-five. Twenty-six. Smart-ass. A lot of long black hair, usually tied back with a piece of leather shoelace. Black mustache that tends to turn down at the ends. Plaid flannel shirt with the elbows paper thin or blown out altogether. Old faded jeans. High-tops or work boots.

I'm a carpenter. I like to build things. I like the smell of sawdust. Put me up in the air walking a beam with my hammer in my hand and my tool belt riding low, I'm a happy happy man.

I'm a physical guy. I don't claim to be a writer. So getting this story on paper isn't gonna be the easiest thing I've ever done. But I'm thinking, how hard can it be? Lemme just rock back and fire, like you and me were sitting at my kitchen table, having a cup of coffee, shooting the breeze. I don't see why that wouldn't get the job done.

It started like this. A while ago I hit a rough patch. I guess I let some things pile up on me and I guess I wasn't handling the stress or whatever. I got stoned and drunk in a bar one night, trashed the place, hit some guys, got arrested, pleaded guilty, and went to jail. Besides the jail time, I got a big ol' fine, about a bajillion hours of community service, and a shitload of probation. While I was in jail, I lost my job, my wife, my truck, and my mobile home. Losing that truck was the part that hurt most. It was the first vehicle I ever bought new. I loved that truck.

I felt like I'd fallen down a bottomless well. Sure, I can look back now and realize that getting myself in all that trouble turned out to be the best thing that ever happened to me. Because of my one-man riot, I started over and ended up a lot better off. But at the time, I thought it was pretty much all over for me. I was a busted, divorced, unemployed loser. Sitting in jail. The future looked like a big ugly brick wall.

Danny Gillespie was about the only one of my friends who stuck by me during my trouble. Ol' Danny, he visited me in jail, kept a straight face while he listened to all my trials and tribulations, and eventually asked me what I was gonna do when I got out. Which I said I had no idea. He said he'd be happy to have me move in with him. I said that was really decent of him and I'd think it over.

I'd lived with my wife, Marylou, the party of the first part, hereinafter referred to as the Bitch, in the southernmost tip of Grand County, which is in northeastern Ohio. But the courthouse, and therefore my probation officer, were in Spencer, in the northern part of the county. And Danny lived in Spencer. So I thought about it and decided moving in with Danny was a good idea.

I wasn't gonna have wheels until I got back on my feet, but if I was living with Danny, I'd be in walking distance of my probation officer. Another plus was that I'd be at the other end of the county from the Bitch. So I called him and said if his offer was still good, I'd take him up on it. He said, "Great."

On the day I got released, Danny took off from

work, drove all the way down to what was now the Bitch's trailer, and picked up my hand tools and clothes, which she'd left in a heap in the carport. Then he picked me up at the jail and we cruised up to Spencer, where he had the attic apartment of an un-restored century home on Oak Street, two blocks down the hill from Spencer's town square. I moved into his extra bedroom. It was old, tiny, and grim compared to my ex-trailer, but at that point I was just happy to be with a friend and have a roof over my head.

Once we got my stuff carried up to his apartment, Danny opened his refrigerator door, pulled out a six-pack, and brought it into his living room. He flopped his lanky frame down onto the worst-looking piece-of-shit sofa I ever saw—which I couldn't even tell what color it was supposed to be—pulled a can loose, popped the top, and made to hand the other five cans to me.

I shook my head. "Nope. I'm done with that shit for a while."

He looked at me funny. Then he pulled his bowl out of his vest pocket and started packing it. He looked up at me with his shaggy golden eyebrows raised.

I wanted to help him burn it. I wanted that beer, too. It was a hot day for early June, and his attic apartment was stifling, and I was having the first day of the rest of my life. But I shook my head.

"Done with that, too," I said.

I went into the bathroom, which I couldn't even stand up straight in it, since it was crammed against the sloping attic roof, and splashed cold water on my face. Then, carefully ducking my head to get through the low doorframe, I went into what was now my bedroom and stood there looking at my boxes and bags of hand tools and clothes lined up along one wall.

Twenty-six years, and that was all I had to show for it. Nice.

Since there was no bed, I spread out the ratty extra blanket Danny had set on the floor in there, stretched out on it, and took a nap. His floor was only a little harder than the bunk I'd been sleeping on in jail.

Danny's a big guy, just a little shorter than me, and freckled. Most days he wears his reddish gold hair in a ponytail like me. He's a roofer, same age as me, and has a girl here and there he can call when he feels like it. He's pretty happy with himself, and by the time I moved in with him, he was pretty set in his ways. He likes to start off every working morning with a shower and then breakfast at Brewster's.

Danny likes Brewster's. It's a hometown restaurant, bacon-smelling, holes-in-the-burgundy-vinyl kind of place. It sits at one end of a long strip mall, looking out across a big parking lot at another strip mall. Most of the waitresses know most of the regulars by name, and the menu never changes.

It's a big, wide-open room with windows all across the front, so the retired and unemployed, who like to sit in there all day drinking coffee and trading conspiracy theories, can monitor the comings and goings in the parking lot, which also serves the Thriftway, the hardware store, the hair salon, the bank, the drugstore, and a bunch of other little shops and businesses.

There's a line of booths down each wall, a double row of booths down the middle, a lunch counter in back, and tables down each side of the center booths. You can smoke in there, and talk loud, and hit on the waitresses, and nobody cares.

That first morning, I got up and threw on a pair of jeans while Danny took his shower. While he was still in the bathroom, he yelled for me to come on to Brewster's with him and get some breakfast. What else did I have to do? So I pulled on a flannel shirt, dragged a comb through my hair and tied it back, and tagged along. I hated that he had to pay for my number four, but he said bullshit, I would have done the same for him, and that was true, I would have.

That's how the first week or so went. Every morning we went over to Brewster's and got breakfast. Then Danny went off to his roofing job, and I walked back to the house on Oak Street and spent the day reading the want ads or staring at his crappy little TV, cursing myself for being such a loser asshole that I had lost everything I had, including my employability. Or so I thought.

The walk home from Brewster's took me past Carlo's, a busy little pizza place down in the opposite corner of the same strip mall as Brewster's. Every day I looked at all the little green Carlo's Hyundai delivery cars sitting in their back parking lot, and I looked at the big sign in the window that said HELP WANTED. DRIVERS. WAITRESSES.

Of course, at eight in the morning, Carlo's isn't open yet. But when Tuesday rolled around, I walked up to the courthouse for my scheduled heart-to-heart with my probation officer, which she was out sick and they said I should come back the following Tuesday at ten a.m.

Afterward, I couldn't stand the thought of going back to the house, so I went for an all-day walk. Spencer is a busy little town. Pretty, too. Lots of big old century homes with interesting architecture hunker along the wide tree-lined streets that run in all directions down the hill from the town square.

That day I walked up and down some of those streets, studying the houses. At one point I made use of an old stone water fountain on the town square and then sat at a picnic table for a long time, watching the traffic crawl around the perimeter of the square, and watching the happy lawyers and miserable defendants going in and out of the county courthouse.

After a while I got another drink and went roaming again. In the middle of the afternoon I found myself back down in the little business district near Brewster's. I walked over to Carlo's and more or less wandered inside before I had even thought about what I was doing.

The woman at the front counter was about my age, maybe a few years older. She was attractive, slender, with short brown hair and smart green eyes. She was busy telling a guy to run up to the Thriftway for a bag of onions. Then a phone rang and she took an order for two large pizzas. I stood there long enough to see that she was large and in charge, so I might as well tell her my worst news right up front, because she'd do what she was gonna do, no matter what kind of bullshit I tried to lay on her.

When she looked at me and smiled, signaling me to state my business, I said, "I'd like to apply for a job as a driver, but I just got out of jail."

She blinked and looked me over for a minute, a smirk beginning to show at one corner of her mouth. Then she said, "How's your driving record?"

"Perfect," I said, and I remember being surprised to realize that in all the garbage heap of my life I did have one perfect thing. My driving record. I stood a little straighter. Yeah, right.

"Do you have a car?"

"No. I'd have to drive one of those little Korean pieces of shit you have parked in the back." Then I smiled at her and said, "Heh."

She nodded and thought about me for a bit. Then she said, "How do you take your coffee?"

A few minutes later we were lighting cigarettes, sitting in a booth across from each other with coffee cups in front of us. She said her name was Barb Pannio. Then she asked me what I was in jail for. I told her. She nodded and asked what I did for a living before I went to jail. I told her.

I also told her how I'd been fired as a result of my troubles, filed on for divorce, and fucked in every possible orifice. Figuratively speaking! Don't think I got made into an Alice in jail or anything like that. I'm plenty big enough to take care of myself, and, anyway, it was just little ol' Grand County Jail, with a basketball court, and red geraniums by the front doors. I told her that. She laughed. Then she pushed an application across the table to me. I filled it out.

She said, "How soon can you start?"

"Now?" I said, smiling. Because I was joking, showing that I was gung-ho, expecting her to say, like, Monday will be soon enough, or something.

But she looked at her watch. By then it was just about two. She said, "Good. Let's get you trained. By the time we get busy with the dinner rush you'll be ready to take deliveries. Okay?"

I shrugged. "Sure. Why not?"

She said, "How late can you work tonight?"

I shrugged again, thinking how funny that was. Like I had anything else to do. "Until the place closes?"

She smiled and sipped her coffee and, from out of nowhere, I started to get a funny feeling about Carlo's. I wondered why she was so fucking happy to hire a guy who just got out of jail, and why she was in such a hurry to get me started. If there's one thing I've learned in life, it's this: Whenever something seems too good to be true, it is.

I looked around, wondering what was wrong with the place. I glanced at her. She was watching me.

She said, "You're maybe wondering what's the big hurry?"

"Kind of."

She nodded. "It's like this. I was already hurting for night drivers, and then, night before last, one of my full-timers had an accident."

"Oh. Was it serious?"

"She was shaken up. Bumps and bruises. But the accident means I can't get insurance on her anymore."

"You had to fire her?"

She nodded. "She was lucky the job was *all* she lost. She went into a ditch out on Spencer-Ladonia Road. You know that road?"

I shook my head.

"Well, it's rural, lined by drainage ditches. The speed limit's forty-five, and all the driveways have cement culverts. If she'd hit one of those culverts, it probably would've been fatal."

"Wow."

"Yeah." She shuddered. "God. Anyway, that's why I need you to start right away. Okay?"

After we finished our coffee, Barb led me down the hall that ran off the back end of the dining room, a few steps along that and then to the left, to the waitress station.

She said, "Beverages are free. Grab yourself a Styrofoam cup and write your name on it so nobody throws it away. Make one cup last all shift."

I drew myself a Coke. Then I followed her through the hall, past the office, around past the bathrooms, and into the back room where all the food prep and dough making and stuff was done.

It was pretty obvious to me that the guy she introduced me to was the ass-kicker who rode the vintage Harley I'd noticed in the back parking lot. My first sight of him, he was standing there leaning against the work counter, smoking a cigarette, watching a big blob of pizza dough being badly mistreated in a huge metal bowl by what looked like an outboard motor blade.

Barb told me, "Terry, this is Greg Bellini. We call him Bump."

He was scary looking, lounging there in his black leather vest, black Carlo's T-shirt, and black straight-leg jeans. This is Bump: He's at least six-and-a-half feet tall, has very long blond hair tied with a black leather strap in a wild hit-or-miss ponytail, and wears a mustache but no beard. His pythons bulge like, well, pythons. His face looks like it was carved out of oak with a chain saw.

Bump Bellini makes quite a first impression.

Barb said, "Bump, this is Terry Saltz. He's gonna be a night driver."

We nodded at each other.

Barb said, "Show Terry how to wedge potatoes while you wait for those deliveries to come up, okay?" She turned and started out of the room without waiting for him to nod, then turned back. "Get him started and then I need to talk to you in the office."

"Yup," Bump said. But he didn't move until he had finished his cigarette. When he'd smoked it down to the filter, he slowly raised himself out of his leaning position, slowly walked into the back hallway that led to the back door, and slowly ground it out in an ashtray on one of the shelves that lined the hallway wall.

The wall opposite the shelves was metal, with a big metal door in the middle. He pulled the door open, went inside, and came back out a few seconds later in a frosty cloud, carrying a twenty-five-pound bag of Idahos. He carried it over to a bank of big stainless-steel sinks, emptied it out into one of them, and turned on the cold water. He picked up a potato, rinsed it, turned around to the counter behind him, stood it up in a big wall-mounted tool that worked sort of like a drill press, positioned a tub under it, jerked down the handle and voila! The blade shat out six or seven instamatic potato wedges.

"Knock yourself out," he said. "There's more tubs up there." He jerked his thumb at the shelves above the sinks and walked out of the back room the way I'd come in. I watched him go. He went into the office and closed the door behind him.

I got to work on the potato wedges. You might be thinking I resented having to do that gofer work. How far the mighty carpenter had fallen, something like that? Naw. I was on somebody's time clock again. And I was interested. I'd never stopped to wonder how potato wedges get that way, and it was fun slamming that blade down through the potatoes and watching the wedges squirt out the bottom.

After a while, a guy came walking into the back room from the back door. He stopped by the utility sink and stared at me. I glanced at him and went back to work. But he kept on standing there staring at me, so I looked over again and smiled.

He was a short, strange-looking dude. I made him to be mid-fifties. He was mostly bald, with just a ratty little fringe of gray hair running in a line around the back of his head. He stood there duck-toed with his wilted athletic socks sagging down over black high-tops, baggy black shorts hanging down over skinny, trout-white legs, and a fanny pack strapped tightly around his waist.

He kept standing there, blank-faced, like it was taking him that long to process that there was a guy he didn't know wedging potatoes. I waited for him to say something, or even to develop an expression of some kind on his wide, pasty face, but he didn't. I went back to the wedger.

After a few minutes, I saw peripheral movement and realized the guy was walking toward me. He came up close beside me, so that his ear was touching my arm, and said quietly into my armpit, "Y-y-you're a n-new guy?"

I had to lean forward and duck my head to get a look at his face. "Yeah. Terry Saltz." With him tucked into my armpit like he was, I didn't see any good way to shake his hand, so I didn't try it.

"Y-you're taking C-C-Carrie's place?"

"Carrie? Is that the girl who got in the accident?"

He snorted. "Accident! Is that wh-wh-what they t-t-old you?"

I took a step back from him so I could see him better. "That she accidently put a car in a ditch."

He shook his head scornfully. "Unb-b-believable." He glanced around and then closed up the space between us. "Th-that was n-no accident. S-someone ran her off the r-r-road on p-purpose. Someone tried to *k-k-kill* her!"

Then he gave me a look of exasperation, like he thought *I* was the weird one, and walked away.

Chapter 2

By the time Bump came back from the office, I had a couple tubs of wedges done. When I glanced at him, he gave me a friendly smile, like he had just now met me. He said, "So, you've been away at County, huh?"

What had happened, obviously, was that Barb had called him into the office to tell him about me. Well, good. It saved me from having to explain myself again. And now he was smiling at me.

He said, "I know a guy who's in County now. Louie. You know Louie?"

I laughed. "You know Louie? That poor dumb fuck."

Everybody in the jail knew Louie. He was a seriously deranged, skinny little pothead burnout who couldn't seem to do anything right. I'd never been able to make up my mind whether he was really stupid or just had colossally bad judgment.

Not to get too sidetracked from the story I'm trying to tell here, but Louie was in jail this latest time because he'd robbed an all-night gas station right there in Spencer just as a cop pulled into the parking lot. He got caught trying to run away across a field. See, he'd decided it'd be better if he did the job on foot, and then he wouldn't have to worry that his car would be recognized. But trying to get away in a hurry had put him in kind of a bind because he was on crutches at the time. He had a broken leg.

Bump got busy filling the finished potato wedge tubs with water, putting lids on them, and carrying them into the walk-in cooler that was behind that metal door in the back hall, getting down more empty tubs, and so on.

Pretty soon we were done wedging. We went into the back hall to smoke and wait for the deliveries to be ready.

I said, "There was a guy here a few minutes ago. Weird-looking little . . ."

Bump laughed. "Flute. He's the other day driver."

I took a drag on my smoke. "He mentioned Carrie."

He gave me a sideways look. "Yeah. Carrie Hall. Was a night driver."

I said, "Yeah. What happened to her, exactly?"

"She ran car three into a ditch night before last."

I nodded. "Yeah. I've got that. But was it an accident, or wasn't it? Flute seems to think it wasn't."

Bump snorted. "Listen, do yourself a favor and don't pay any attention to anything Flute tells you. He's one of these guys always wants to make a problem where there isn't one. Gossips like a son-of-a-bitch. That's how he entertains himself."

I said, "Oh."

"Here's the straight shit on Carrie and her accident. She's ditsy to begin with, plus she keeps her cell phone glued to her ear. I warned her a couple of times not to use her cell phone when she's driving for us, and so did Barb. Customers were even calling to complain that she went to their *door* talking on her fuckin' cell phone."

I started to get the idea.

He said, "So, she's out night before last, prolly gabbing away on her cell phone, and drives car three into that ditch. Now she's got a problem. Carlo's insurance won't cover her with points on her license. So she thinks fast and comes up with the story that someone ran her off the road. Thinking, if it's not her fault, she won't get fired."

"Oh, I see."

"Yeah. So she tells the cops that someone in a white car deliberately ran her off the road. Only the cops investigate, and there's no evidence there was another car involved. No skid marks, even. I know one of the cops who was out there. Alan Bushnell. He says they don't buy her story at all. Neither do I."

As he stubbed out his cigarette, a good-looking girl came back to get something out of the walk-in. She had her sand-colored hair twisted around and pinned up in back, but little blond curls had worked their way out here and there around her face. And even though her black Carlo's shirt wasn't tucked in that day, I could tell at a glance that she had a great body.

Bump introduced me and told me her name was Lauren King, but to call her Jackson. She smiled and nodded. Then she turned around and pulled the metal door open. "Nice ass," Bump said, and she said, "Fuck off." The tone of voice they used was the same as they would've used to say, "How ya doin'?" "Fine."

This was when I realized that working at Carlo's was going to be different from being a carpenter. I'd been a carpenter since I was fifteen and my brother brought me into his crew as a gofer. There generally aren't any girls around the job when you're a carpenter.

Jackson came back out of the cooler carrying a tub of grated provolone cheese and hurried around to the front. A few minutes later a female voice from the front yelled, "Driver!" I followed Bump out to the little green Hyundai that was parked just outside the back door. There were big white number twos on the right front fender and on both sides, just under the Carlo's logo, and on the left rear bumper.

There are no front passenger seats in Carlo's delivery cars. They take them out so drivers can stack deliveries on the floor where the front seat used to be. I climbed into the backseat on the passenger side, since Bump had the driver's seat pushed back as far as it would go for legroom and also had the seat back laid down about halfway for headroom. From outside the car, it looked like he was driving from the backseat, which he practically was.

While we rode around to the front of the store, he started explaining things. "Remind me to show you where the car logs are when we get back in. You have to write down your starting and ending mileage. You full-time?"

I shrugged and nodded.

He said, "Full-timers get three Carlo's shirts and one baseball cap. Plus a fanny pack like this to put the money in. Park in back, pick up in front."

I said to myself, Fanny pack? and thought I might have a serious problem with wearing a fanny pack. But as I followed him inside I decided, okay, it's sorta like a tool belt. I watched him pick up the three deliveries that were stacked on the counter and then followed him back to the car.

Once we were out of the big parking lot, he said, "I'll warn you right now, people in this town love narcing on Carlo's drivers. If anyone sees you do anything—hell, they don't even need a reason. They're gonna call and complain."

I nodded.

" 'Course, when someone does call, the managers just fuck with 'em. But they keep track of who's getting called about. If they get a couple of calls on you, they'll talk to you."

I said, "The managers fuck with 'em?"

He said, "Yeah. Like last week, this real old dude called about me."

"Why?"

He chuckled. "I was heading out on a run, along the front of the shopping center, heading down toward Brewster's. I saw him come out of the hardware store." He flipped on his turn signal and started to brake.

"You gotta watch out for people coming out of those stores. Sometimes they'll step off the curb without looking. Anyway, I saw him come out of the True Value and I knew he was gonna walk right out in front of me. He did, and then he looked and saw me coming, and jumped back up on the curb, shaking his fist. Like it was *my* fault he walked right out in front of me. It made me laugh."

"You shouldn'ta laughed. Probably made him mad."

"No shit. By the time I got in from the run, he'd called Barb and given her an earful. Barb goes, 'I'm sorry you were annoyed, sir. I hate to fire him, 'cause he's my best driver, and he's raising those three little kids all by himself since his poor wife died, but that's company policy. He'll be terminated.' "

He chuckled warmly. "They say shit like that. Then the same person usually doesn't call back again."

I said, "You don't have three little kids."

He snorted. "Fuck no." He pulled up to a red light, stopped, and looked back at me.

"I do all the minor maintenance on the cars. I got

a rule. Don't abuse the cars. The managers may go easy on the drivers, but I don't. I can tell when a car's been abused, and I only have to check the log to see who did it. I get irate when someone abuses a car."

"Gotcha." I smiled to myself about his use of the word irate. I enjoy when someone uses a word or a phrase you don't hear every day. I guess I sorta collect them, or something. I decided to add irate to my list and use it when I got the chance.

He lit a cigarette and was taking his first draw on it when the light turned green. He said, "Not allowed to smoke in the cars."

I nodded and tapped out a cigarette from my pack.

He said, "When these cars were delivered, they took all the radios out and put 'em on the shelves in the office. Yeah, right. Like we're really gonna be in one of these cars all day or all night without a radio. As soon as they were gone, me and Gruf put 'em all back in. Gruf's the night manager now. You'll meet him later."

He said, "I scare housewives the first time they see me. Like the last delivery on this run? She's a first timer. They'll be scared of you, too. So you gotta be smiling when they open the door. Then right away you gotta say something friendly. Usually they tip pretty good after that, because they're so relieved you're not gonna kill 'em, or something."

"They tip?" I hadn't realized yet that I'd be getting tips.

Bump looked around at me. "Fuck yeah. That's where you make your money."

We headed north out of town and, at the End Speed Zone sign, Bump stepped on it. He said, "Hey, this is Spencer-Ladonia Road. I'll show you where little Carrie totaled car three." After a few miles, he slowed to a stop. Right in the middle of the road. I looked quickly up and down the road and nothing was coming, but still.

He opened his door, climbed out, and began to walk along the middle of the road, leaving his door hanging wide open. He turned back. "Come on. Have a look."

I climbed out over the stack of stay-warm bags and caught up with him. He pointed. Off to the right I could see the deep parallel tracks of raw black earth that ran along the inner edges of the deep ditch, left by car three's spinning tires. The tracks were a good fifteen feet long. I pointed that out.

Bump said, "And the whole way all four tires are getting pinched in and the axles are getting bent. Fuckin' Carrie."

We turned back to car two. Bump waved at the stretch of road. "And you can see, no skid marks. Nothing whatsoever." I looked carefully on both sides of the road. He was right.

We climbed back into car two and continued on our way. I noticed that the first cement driveway culvert came up less than fifty feet past the end of the tracks. I pointed that out and said, "She *was* lucky."

Bump said, "No shit. And she was lucky the car hit the ditch square, too. If she'd gone in crooked, it coulda flipped. Fuck, for that matter, the front bumper coulda stuck and she coulda gone end-over-end."

I nodded.

Bump said, "But, anyway, car three is totaled and Carrie's ass is fired. End of story."

We made the Spencer-Ladonia delivery. Then Bump drove on down to the next intersection and turned left on 89. After a mile or so, we came into an area of new, widely spaced developments with a lot of woods in between. Huge structures that look more like minor castles than homes, built on winding cul-de-sacs. Bump turned off the highway onto a county road, then off that into one of the new developments, and finally into the driveway of a big new colonial.

This was the home of the first timer he'd mentioned, and he was right. The woman who opened the door got wide-eyed when she saw us standing there like two scruffy miscreants.

But we smiled, and Bump said quickly, "Hi. We're from Carlo's. Dude, your yard looks great! Who's your landscaper?"

"I, ah," she stammered. I saw that the hand holding the wallet was a little unsteady.

He pulled the pizza box out of the stay-warm bag. "What're those little blue flowers? I gotta get some of those for my yard."

She took the box from him and set it on a table by the door. "They're, uh, lobelia. They're pretty, aren't they?"

He looked at the ticket. "It's ten ninety-nine."

She pulled a ten and a five from the wallet and handed them to him.

He said, "Ya want change?"

She shook her head. "No, keep it."

He said, "Lobelia, huh? Gotta get me some of those. Hey, thanks a lot. Have a nice day."

We climbed back into the car.

I said, "You called her dude."

He was backing out of the long driveway by looking in his side mirror. He said, "Huh?"

"That lady. You called her dude."

He chuckled.

Chapter 3

I'm a carpenter. Either a mitered joint fits, or it doesn't. Maybe that's why I kept thinking about Carrie's accident as we drove back to Carlo's. Two things bothered me about it. The first thing was, it happened on a straightaway. I could see if it happened on a curve, but even if this Carrie was the world's biggest airhead, how did she suddenly pull the steering wheel hard to the right and put herself into that ditch on a straight road? It didn't make any sense.

The second thing was, if she was as ditsy as Bump said she was, how did she manage to come up with the story about the other car in time to tell it to the cops? I mean, girls get shaken up by accidents. A lot of girls, even a little fender bender's gonna make 'em cry. Carrie's shaken up, bumped and bruised, according to Barb Pannio, but she's thinking clearly enough to realize that she's gonna get fired, and she makes up a story that rings true enough to get the cops to investigate? Please.

But I was the new guy. Whatever had happened, it wasn't any of my business. My job was to learn to be a pizza driver. Back at Carlo's, Bump got me my Carlo's gear and I went into the men's room and put on one of my three new Carlo's T-shirts and my Carlo's fanny pack, but not my Carlo's baseball cap.

The shirts weren't too bad. They were black, with

a little Carlo's logo on a pocket on the left breast. But the caps sucked rocks. They were the tall, old-style baseball caps, the kind that get worn to, like, Grange meetings or something.

I don't like those old-style high-peaked caps. I like the new low-profile ones that fit your skull. And I don't like new-looking baseball caps, even if they're the right style. A baseball cap should look like you slid into second thirty or forty times in it. Anyway, I noticed that Bump didn't wear a cap, so I decided I wouldn't, either.

After I was in uniform, Bump showed me the big street map on the wall beside the front counter where drivers picked up their deliveries, and he explained the system the drivers used for knowing whose turn it was, who was "up."

He said, "First in, first out. Your next up is right after the driver that came in ahead of you. It's your job to know who you're up after. No one else gives a rat's ass."

By that time there were two more deliveries waiting for us, so we did those and then business died off. It was around four. I followed Bump out to the dining room, where we sat around and drank coffee. After fifteen minutes or so, another guy came walking in wearing a black Carlo's T-shirt and black jeans. He helped himself to a cup of coffee and eased into the booth next to Bump.

He said, "Bump."

Bump said, "Gruf."

I'll tell you about Gruf. The guy is magazine model good-looking. He wears his black hair in a long DA like my dad's was in his high-school yearbook, but on this guy it looks like, well, you think to yourself, *every*body should wear their hair like that. He's as tall as Bump and me, slender, clean-shaven, and about the same age as us. Gruf is one good-looking dude. His eyes are pale blue, almost the color of ice, and he has the kind of long eyelashes most chicks would kill for.

That day, his eyes were also bloodshot. I thought either he was really sensitive to sunlight, or he had just enjoyed a toke. My guess was, toke.

"Hi," he said to me.

"Terry Saltz," I said, reaching across the table to shake his hand. "New driver."

"Joe Ridolfi. Call me Gruf. Night manager."

Bump said, "He trained this afternoon. Should be ready to take deliveries tonight."

Gruf smiled and looked me over. "How late are you working?"

I said, "Uh, Barb didn't say. I can stay as late as you want me to."

"We close at midnight. Can you close?"

I said, "I don't have to be anywhere."

He nodded. "Full-time?"

"Uh, she didn't say. I'd *like* to be full-time." At five bucks an hour, I'd have liked to be all-time.

"Good." His eyes moved past me to the hallway, where Barb had just come around the corner. "Hey, Barb? Do you have Terry scheduled yet?"

She came walking out to the booth and rested a knee on the bench beside me. "Just doing it now. Why?"

He looked back to me. "Can you work Friday and Saturday nights? Will you work overtime?"

"Dude, I can work any hours you let me. The more the better."

He looked meaningfully back to Barb. She said, "I'm on it," and disappeared into the office.

He lit a smoke and took a deep drag. "My problem is, I got too many unreliable young drivers. They're making me nuts. They make me nuts when they don't show up for work, and they make me nuts when they do." He slid out of the booth, walked over to the coffee station, brought a pot back to the table, and topped us all off.

He was just putting the pot back on the burner when a girl wearing a black Carlo's T-shirt walked in the front door and settled herself in a booth near the front of the dining room. She was a scruffy-looking critter. She had little, close-set rodent eyes; her snarled platinum hair was sprayed stiff; and I'd put her weight at right around two hundred, but she dropped herself into that booth like it was closer to three hundred.

The little guy who was with her wasn't wearing a Carlo's shirt. He looked like the nervous type, all twitchy and loose eyed. He was cave shouldered, pale and thin, with a sparse Vandyke and dirty, thinning blond hair.

I glanced at Bump and Gruf and saw that they were watching the new arrivals, too.

Gruf told me, "That's Sheila Werbel. Night waitress. She started last week. We're not sure who the guy is yet. Possibly her husband."

"He doesn't look like man enough for the lovely Sheila, does he?" Bump said.

She glanced at us, saw us watching her, and treated us to one of the sleazier smiles I've ever seen. I looked away quickly and saw that Gruf and Bump did the same. They looked at each other and rolled their eyes.

Gruf said, "She's messed up, huh?"

Bump was stirring sugar into his coffee. "Where does Barb find these Sasquatches?"

Gruf said, "She won't last two weeks. She doesn't like having to mop the entryway at the end of shift."

Bump said, "Why don't you just make Jackson a night waitress? She's great at waitressing."

Gruf said, "I know, but she won't do it. Tips are better driving. Anyway, she doesn't like waitressing."

Someone yelled, "Driver!" from the front area on the far side of the dining room, on the other side of the big room-dividing planter with fake flowers on top.

Bump looked at me. "Ready to lose your virginity?"

I gave him a stern look. "You didn't even say you liked my dress."

Bump said, "Fuck you," but he was laughing.

I started across the dining room for the front counter, but Bump stopped me. "Dude. Go through the back and get your car and drive it around to the front door first, like I showed you."

I said, "Oh, yeah." I felt irate with myself. As I walked through the hall to the back door, I wondered if they were rolling their eyes about me now.

My first time out I had a triple, which means three deliveries. I didn't get lost, and I got eight dollars and change in tips. By the time I got back, Bump and Barb and the rest of the day shifters were gone, and the night shift was working.

Whole different ball game there, Chief. People weren't walking, they were practically running. The phones were ringing off the hook, all four of them. Working the phones were three front girls—silly, squirmy, giggly little teenagers—and Gruf. There were three more front girls standing at the pizza counter making pizzas, and two cooks bumping into each other in the small kitchen. There were already three other black-shirted drivers standing at the front counter waiting for deliveries, so I got in line behind them.

The guy standing in front of me turned around, took my empty pizza bags from me, and stacked them on the pile of empty bags that was sitting on the far left of the counter. He was a weird-looking little kid, maybe nineteen, twenty, skinny, with brown hair sticking out

every which way from under his black Carlo's cap.
When he copped a look up at me, checking out the
new guy, it seemed like his eyes weren't quite right.

Goofy son of a bitch was about to get himself murdered, but of course I didn't know that then.

"Who are *you?*" he asked belligerently.

"Terry Saltz," I told him, looking down my chest
at him, and trying not to let my voice sound any
friendlier than his did. "Who are *you?*"

The driver at the counter picked up a stack of bulg-
ing red stay-warm bags and squeezed past us, heading
toward the front door. The rest of us all moved a few
steps closer to the counter.

"Ed Hanus," the kid said nastily. "I suppose you're
taking Carrie's place."

"I suppose I am."

He grimaced. "I'd rather have Carrie back."

I shrugged. "People in hell want ice water."

He blinked up at me. "Carrie was pretty. I was
gonna ask her out."

I said, "Well, dude, now you got *me*. So, whatcha
got in mind? Dinner and a movie?"

He got a horrified look on his face and snapped
around to face the counter. The driver in front of him
was just moving away with his stack of deliveries. Ed
stepped up to the counter.

The way the system worked, finished food was
brought to Gruf and he put it into stay-warm bags and
organized it into trips. He quickly dispatched Ed,
who edged past me cautiously with his stay-warm bags,
and I stepped up.

I was chuckling. "What's that little Ed guy's deal?"

"Ed?" He gave me a puzzled look. "Oh, you mean
the Witness. That's what we call him because he
mainly just stands around and watches everyone else

work. Ignore him. He's a little creep. Okay, this trip's pretty easy. . . ." With a little help from Gruf, I found the streets on the wall map and I was gone again.

The next time I went in, there were a lot of orders already in delivery bags and stacked on the five-shelf wire rack next to where Gruf was working, but I was the only driver in. Gruf was flying around the front area so fast he looked like a blur. He came up to the counter and lifted a stack of deliveries over to me.

He said, "Hey, what time did you start today?"

"Uh, around two?"

"Nobody clocked you in. I'll do it for you. Remind me to show you how to clock out tonight. Have you eaten?"

"No."

"You get food half price. I'll try to give you a meal break when you get back from this trip. Business should start tapering off in another hour or so."

I didn't get my meal break until after eight, but that was okay. I was happy sticking out my hand and getting cold, hard cash put in it. When I did get my break, I ordered a sub and a salad, ate fast, and went right back to delivering pizzas.

Meanwhile, the number of people working was rapidly diminishing. As business slowed down, Gruf started sending people home. By ten, there were just me and two other drivers—the Witness and that cute little girl, Jackson, who apparently had worked on through day shift and was now a night driver. Gruf was working the front with one girl, and there was one cook and one waitress left that I could see.

I finished my last delivery and Gruf sent me out to park my car in the back parking lot. I filled out the car log and locked up the car. When I came into the back room, everybody there was busting ass.

"You caught a break tonight, Terry," Gruf told me

as I walked in. He was standing at the stainless-steel sinks, running dishes through the giant dishwasher that was bolted onto the middle one. The counter behind him, where I had been wedging potatoes earlier, was stacked halfway to the ceiling with dirty dishes. He was wet from his neck to his knees, and he never broke stride working while he talked to me.

He said, "The Witness was supposed to close with you tonight, but he's about useless as a closing driver, so Jackson volunteered to stay. As soon as he comes in from his run, I'll send him home. Closing jobs are to do the dishes, food prep for tomorrow, trash, clean, sweep, and mop. Hey, Jackson, check if anybody made up the ham-and-cheese subs. And check if the bread got sliced."

He turned back to me. "Believe me, a lot of nights, this back area looks like a tornado hit it." Raising his voice, he yelled, "Hey, Hammer, I need your dirty pans from the kitchen."

A voice from the kitchen yelled, "I'm workin' on it. It's only eleven-fifteen."

"You better have 'em back here by eleven-sixteen or you can fuckin' wash 'em yourself. Anyways, Terry, you can do trash first. Go around and police the work surfaces and shelves, throw away the trash and scraps, people's leftover Styrofoam cups and shit. Then pull the trash from the office and the rest rooms and these cans back here, and carry it all out to the Dumpster. Then you can grab that bucket under the utility sink and make yourself some soapy water. Soap dispensers are above the sink. Then just start washing everything down."

As he talked, I started clearing off the countertops and picking up leftover trash. There was a lot of it. I picked up a Styrofoam cup and saw that it was covered with crude drawings. I did a double take. All the way around the thing there were disgusting drawings in black ink of stick figures engaged in the most violent acts you could think of. Little stick people were being beaten, stabbed, and tortured. Big black teardrops of blood flew from all the wounds. It creeped me out.

"Jeez!" I said. "Who did this?" I held it up for Gruf to see.

Gruf groaned. "That's the Witness's artwork. Instead of writing his name he always does that on his cups."

I turned the cup around in my hand. "Man. That's messed up."

Shaking my head, I tossed the nasty-looking cup into the trash and went on with clearing off the work surfaces.

Jackson came hurrying by carrying two empty plate trays. She stacked them next to the dishwasher so Gruf could fill them again. Gruf asked her, "Is everybody out of the dining room?"

She said, "I'll check," and went bouncing back out the front hall.

Gruf watched her go, then shook his head. "I oughtta be in jail for what I'm thinking."

"She's cute," I agreed.

"She's only seventeen," he said sadly.

She was gone for a few seconds, then she came bouncing back. "Dining room's empty." She grinned and held out her hand.

Gruf lifted his wet apron with his wet hands and twisted his hip toward her. She reached into his jeans pocket and came out with a handful of quarters. While her hand was in his pants, he gave me a wink and an eye-brow-bouncing grin.

He told her, "You know the three I want. And crank it up."

She was off again. Gruf turned to me, shaking his head. "She's the best person I've ever known. One in a million."

Jukebox music suddenly filled the air. Stevie Ray Vaughan's magical guitar playing "Brothers." Loud? Wow. You could feel the vibrating bass through the linoleum. I looked at Gruf in surprise. He grinned, put his hands in the air, and did a slow grind.

I got back to work. Once I had all the trash off the back room counters, I went looking for the other trash cans. I pulled the full bags and replaced them with new ones. Then I condensed all the individual trash bags into two big ones and headed out to the Dumpster with them. The Witness was just coming in the back door as I went out.

When I came back in, the first thing I heard was Jackson's angry voice. I walked into the back room and saw her standing in the front hallway with her hands on her hips, yelling and sputtering at the Witness, who was standing with his back to me. Sheila the Enchanting was standing right behind Jackson.

"I swear to God, Ed, if you *ever* touch me again I'll turn you into a soprano so fast you won't *even* have time to, to . . . And *don't* follow me around anymore, either. I'm sick and *tired* of you. . . ."

I quickly headed toward them. As she kept on yelling, fuck me if I didn't see the little turd square off like he was gonna swing on her. I took hold of his ear from behind, which made him give out a little squeal, turned him around, and marched him back to the utility sink.

I bent him over it, so that his head was halfway down in it, reached under the sink, and pulled out one of the scrub buckets. I put it in his hand and said in his ear, "Fill this up with soapy water and start washing stuff."

He squirmed a little like he was trying to get loose, so I squeezed a little tighter. "Unless you'd rather drink it."

All of a sudden he went limp and began to tremble. He spoke into the sink, which gave his voice an eerie, amplified quality. "Don't hurt me. Please don't hurt me."

I felt a little sick. This guy wasn't normal. By that time Gruf and Jackson and the night cook were all standing there, watching.

I can still see that scene so clearly in my mind, like I was somebody else standing off to the side. Me holding the Witness by his ear, him spending precious seconds of one of his last nights in this world with his head in a sink.

I let go of him. He stood up, blinking back tears. Under my supervision, he filled his bucket with soapy water, and the two of us got busy washing down the counters.

I picked up a Styrofoam cup I'd missed earlier and saw by the demented artwork all over it that it was his. "Done with this?"

He nodded sullenly. I held it up and examined it. It was pretty much like the other one I'd seen, with black ink drawings of sick and disgusting acts all the way around, blood flying in all directions.

I said, "Why do you draw this sick stuff all over your cups, dude?"

A disturbing smile crawled and twisted across his face. I just shook my head at him.

When we were finished washing everything down, Gruf called him up front to cash out, which means he totaled up how much of the money in the Witness's fanny pack had to be paid to the company, and how much was tips he got to keep. I started sweeping. I was just finishing when the Witness walked through the back room, down the hall, and out the back door. A minute later his little Jeep rattled out of the parking lot.

Jackson appeared at my elbow. "Hey, Terry? Thank you."

I smiled at her. She really was cute. I said, "You mean about the Witness?"

"He drives us all nuts. He's always bumping into you, brushing up against you. You turn around, he's standing there watching you. You give him a dirty look and he doesn't stop, you know? You say something nasty to him and he just smiles. He's so weird."

Gruf had come walking back from the front, and the young guy they called Hammer, who was the main night cook, came around the corner from the kitchen. Hammer wadded up his apron, threw it into the laundry basket by the back hall, and ran his hands through his damp red hair. "Talking about the Witness?"

"We haven't really met," I said. "I'm Terry Saltz."

"Jeez! I know that!" He was a redheaded, freckled, skinny, goofy teenager. His black pants were too small for him, the kind a girl I used to know called nuthuggers.

I already knew he was the clown of the operation. Earlier that night, I'd seen him flying around through the back room with his apron tied around his shoulders like a cape and a hastily made aluminum foil crown on his head, yelling, *"I'm Pizza Man!"*

I had an idea he might be the Romeo of the operation, too. Earlier, when I'd gone to the waitress station to get more Coke, I'd caught him in there caressing Sheila Werbel's ample butt.

I said, "Yeah, so, what's *your* name?"

"Oh." He laughed. "Boyd Chesnik. Call me Hammer."

"Why do they call you Hammer?"

Jackson laughed. "Don't *even* ask him why. He'd probably tell you."

Gruf said, "All right, boys and girl. Let's close this pop stand."

For the next half hour we worked our asses off, dancing like fools to the loud music the whole time. We got all the rest of the dishes washed and put away and we got the place detailed, everything set up, shining and ready to go in the morning.

No sooner had Gruf cashed Jackson out than a car pulled up beside the open back door. We saw the flash of headlights and heard the engine idling through the screen. Lynnard Skynnard music blasted into the back hall. *"Nobody left to run with anymore. . . ."*

Jackson said, "There's my brother. I'm outa here."

Hammer, Gruf, and I stood shoulder to shoulder and watched her walk down the back hall and out the back door. Her shirt had gotten tucked into the waistband of her black jeans a little bit in back so you could see the outline of her cute little ass very clearly.

"Shit," said Joe "Gruf" Ridolfi.

"Me, too," said Boyd "Hammer" Chesnik.

"Me, too," said Terry Saltz.

Gruf called me up to the computer in front and cashed me out. I cleared thirty-five dollars and change. Then he showed me how to log out on the computer.

He shook my hand and said, "You did good tonight, Terry. See you tomorrow."

I walked home to Oak Street along the shadowy, sleepy sidewalks, whistling like a happy boy. Ah, a breezy summer night in northeastern Ohio, with loose change jingling in your pocket. Nothing else like it.

The next morning, I bought my own pack of Marlboros, and at Brewster's, I took the bill away from Danny and paid it myself.

Chapter 4

I settled into driving for Carlo's pretty smoothly. I took all the overtime they wanted to give me, which was a lot, and that was good, because I wanted the money. I usually got there around four-thirty every day, sat down with Bump and Gruf, and had a cup of coffee. Listened to them shoot the shit. Went to work. Closed up. Cashed out. Went home.

Other than Bump and Gruf, I didn't really make an effort to get to know anybody. The place was busy. I was new. I was mainly interested in doing my job and making money. Really, it seemed like most of the people were half scared of me. I assumed they all knew I'd been in jail, and I assumed they all knew about how I'd stuck the Witness's head in the sink. And I am a little scary looking, when you put my size together with my black mustache and my scruffy black ponytail. Fuck, I look like a bad-ass. From time to time I'd say something funny and make someone laugh, or vice versa, but mainly it was just a job.

Things went along like this for a few weeks, until one day I went in real early. Barb had scheduled me to start at five as usual, but I was antsy sitting around in that hot, stuffy attic, so I walked down to Carlo's a little before two, figuring I'd pass the time drinking coffee and talking to Bump when he didn't have deliveries.

Barb was standing at the front counter and looked surprised to see me. She said, "What're *you* doing here?"

I shrugged. "Nothing else to do. Figured I'd have a cup of coffee."

She nodded. "Well, we're slammed. Ya wanna start now?"

"Sure."

I didn't see Bump for the next hour or so. He was on the road when I came in for the next deliveries, and vice versa. But around three-thirty, I came back from a run and Barb said to go around, she didn't have anything. Bump was sitting in the dining room with a cup of coffee in front of him. He saw me coming away from the counter and told me to park the car and grab a cup of my own.

"Whassup?" he said as I sat down in the booth across from him.

I said, "Same shit, different day. You?"

He made an explosive sound by blowing air through his lips. He was scowling, watching Sheila Werbel, who was leaning against a far booth, daydreaming and trying to pretend that she wasn't scratching herself.

Bump said, "What do you drive, dude? You parking up in the grocery store parking lot, or what?"

I said, "I walk. The Bitch got my truck when she dumped me."

He shook his head sadly. "That ain't right."

I said, "Oh de well."

He laughed. "Seems like you shoulda got to keep your truck. Who's your lawyer?"

"Don't have one," I said, slurping the coffee because it was hot. It also was very good. Fresh. I said, "This is good. You make it?"

He snorted. "Sure as hell wasn't her." He jerked his chin in Sheila's direction.

He said, "No lawyer? What're ya, fuckin' stupid?"

I shrugged. "The Bitch is a ruthless and heartless human being. I figured she was gonna get everything anyway, so I figured, let her have it. At least I'm not trying to pay a bunch of lawyer bills now on top of everything else."

He shrugged. "What kind of truck was it?"

I sighed. "Big black Toyota Tacoma, man. Brand-new. Extended cab, custom sound system, moonroof, four-wheel drive. Loaded. Cherry."

He said, "Ow."

"Yeah. I loved that truck. Well, fuck it. I like your Harley, dude."

"Yeah. Got her running pretty smooth." He sipped his coffee and lit a cigarette. "I got a truck, too. Old Chevy. Use it for my business. Beat on it. No sense beating on something new and shiny."

I nodded and lit up. Sheila dragged herself out of her lean and waddled across the dining room and down the hall toward the bathrooms. Bump watched her go.

"Uh-oh," he said. "Time out for a potty break."

I snickered.

He said, "Hey, I know what I wanted to ask you. You're a carpenter, right?"

"Was."

"Still got your tools?"

"Oh, hail yeah."

"Know anything about building decks?"

I said, "Decks? Fuck. I could drive you around this county and show you a hundred decks I built."

His eyes lit up. "Really! 'Cause I been thinkin' I'd like a deck built onto the back of my house. Got these sliding doors from the dining room. Put a hot tub out there. Ya know?"

I said, "Deck adds a lot to a house."

"Yeah. It'd be tits and ass. Whad'ya think it'd cost me?"

"It depends. Size. Materials. I could measure, give you a ballpark. . . ."

He stood up. Which I just looked at him.

"Let's go," he said.

I hesitated. "I'm on the clock."

"Fuck the clock."

I followed him around to the back room, where Barb was slicing onions. Bump said, "Barb, got anything?"

"Nothing."

"We're running over my house for a few minutes."

"Have fun." She never even looked up from her work.

Bump lived about a mile out of town on Carlson's Mill Road. His house surprised me. "You own this, man?" I climbed off the back of the Harley and followed him across the front yard.

"Free and clear."

It was a fifties ranch, three bedrooms, bath and a half, nicely furnished, a little rough here and there maintenance-wise, but still a very cool house for a single guy. We went through to the kitchen, where he pulled two Cokes out of the refrigerator and flipped me one. Then he led the way around the dining room table, through the sliding-glass doors, and into the backyard.

While I ran my eyes over the back of the house, I wondered how a pizza driver could own a house like this. I figured SuperLotto or crime. Something stopped my eye. "Uh-oh."

"What?"

"How long's your roof been leaking?"

He squinted at me. "Roof's all good, dude. Just got a new one put on two years ago."

I shook my head. "No. It's leaking." I pointed. "Follow the left side of your kitchen window straight up the wall, straight up the roof. Three rows down from the peak. See those buckled shingles? That means water."

He squinted, looked, shook his head. "No, I don't think so, dude. I haven't seen anything leaking inside. . . ."

He followed me back into the kitchen. The leak was going into the attic, but it had to be coming down somewhere or I didn't have a clear understanding of gravity. I scoped it out for a minute, then unplugged the refrigerator and gently began to work it out away from the wall.

He leaned over my shoulder. "Shit. Shit!" Big brown stains streaked all down the wall where the water'd been running behind the refrigerator.

I looked at the floor where the refrigerator had been. A section of it was rotted pretty good. We moved the refrigerator out into the middle of the kitchen, and I pulled up one of the buckled tiles to show him how his subfloor had rotted. A bunch of carpenter ants came swarming up and out across the floor.

"Shit!" he yelled again, stomping them with his black engineer boots. "Dammit! Well, there goes my deck, time I finish paying to fix this mess!"

I said, "Naw, this won't cost anything. Couple pieces of wood to replace the rotted part of the subfloor, couple shingles to replace the buckled ones, maybe another board or two if the subroof needs reinforced. It ain't no thang."

He blinked at me. "Really? Can you do it?"

"Fuck."

"But then there's your labor."

"Shit. I wouldn't charge you for this. Now, if you

want me to build you a deck, you'll pay for that.
That's business. But fixing this mess is just a favor for
a friend."

"Wow. I mean, that's really . . . When can you
do it?"

I said, "You got a ladder? Hammer and some nails
or screws? A little scrap wood?"

He said, "Prolly. Let's go look in the garage."

"If you've got the stuff, I can fix it right now."

He pushed the refrigerator close enough to another
wall to plug it in. Then he pulled his cell phone out
of his shirt pocket and punched in a number. He said,
"Barb. Got anything? Good. We're still at my house.
Terry found a leak in my roof that's rotting my whole
kitchen floor. I didn't even know about it. Yeah, call
me if you get anything."

I followed him out to the driveway, past the Harley,
past a beat-up blue Chevy pickup, to his garage. The
doors were padlocked, and when he raised one of
them, I could see why. Three-fourths of his garage was
loaded with all kinds of sound equipment, furniture,
televisions, a little bit of everything.

"Holy crap!" I laughed. "What are you doing, fenc-
ing stolen goods or something?"

He glanced disinterestedly at the piles of merchan-
dise and snorted. "I buy stuff. I sell stuff." He turned
to the floor-to-ceiling shelves on the other wall of the
garage and began to search for the leftover boxes of
shingles.

I said, "You buy and sell a lot of stuff."

He said, "I know a lot of people. Here they are."
He lifted a box of shingles out from under a shoe box
and blew the dust off it. "What else did you say?
Hammer, nails . . ."

". . . and some scrap wood." I couldn't tear my eyes
away from the piles and piles of stuff.

He saw me gaping at it. "You didn't think I supported myself delivering pizza, didya? I got a lot of things going on."

"Yeah. I guess you do." Then I saw the mattresses and box springs leaning in rows against the back wall. I said, "Hey, you sell beds, too?"

"Dude, you need a bed? What size ya need?"

I said, "Full, I guess. I don't think the little room I'm in right now will hold anything bigger than a full."

"Where do you live?"

"Attic of a little house over on Oak."

He screwed up his nose. "Attic?"

I shrugged. "Danny, my roommate, he was already living there. He was nice enough to take me in. . . ."

"Here, hold this." He handed me the heavy box of shingles and began to plow his way through, moving stacks of stuff to clear a path back to the mattresses. "Full mattress," he said, dragging it out into the open garage. "Full box spring. Need bedding?"

"You got bedding, too?"

He chuckled as he finished dragging the box spring out next to the mattress. "I got some bedding." He made his way over to a stack of trunks. "King, queen, full . . ." He dragged out a trunk with "full" written on masking tape and opened it. "White fitted, white top, white cases. Yeah, here's a plaid. Fitted, top, cases. Here's a thermal blanket. That oughtta hook you up for a while."

I was pretty much speechless. We loaded the mattress and box spring into the bed of his truck. Then we gathered up the shit I needed to fix his roof and I got to work. It took less than an hour to replace his buckled shingles and repair his floor enough to support his refrigerator. I told him if I was gonna build him a deck, then I could do a proper job fixing his kitchen floor at the same time.

While I washed up, he pulled a magazine from a kitchen drawer and thumbed to the page that had a picture of the deck he liked. Then he found the page that had a picture of the hot tub he liked. I tucked the magazine under my arm. He scrounged up an ancient measuring tape and we took some basic measurements for his deck. We carried the ladder back into his garage; then he called Barb again. It was still dead at Carlo's, so we hopped into Bump's truck and drove my new bed over to Oak Street.

But he didn't like the looks of the house on Oak Street. He made a snorting noise when he pulled into the driveway, and said he wanted to look the place over before we started carrying stuff up.

He stood in the doorway to my bedroom, his head ducked low, the back of his neck almost touching the top of the doorjamb.

"This is bullshit." He wiped sweat and damp blond curls off his forehead. It was stuffy up there in the late afternoon.

I said, "It's not so bad. It'll do for a while."

He said, "No, it won't. What does Danny pay for this rathole?"

"Two-fifty. I'm picking up half of it now."

"That's bullshit," he said. "Come on."

We clumped back down the stairs to his truck. As he backed out, he said, "I got a mobile home over in Chandler's. It's a nice trailer park. I've only held title on it for a week, week and a half. I'll show it to you."

I'd already been in Chandler's. I'd delivered pizza there. It was a nice park less than ten minutes out of town. And Bump's trailer was beautiful. Double-wide, way nicer than the one the Bitch now had all to herself.

I stood in the living room, checking out the new-looking colonial blue carpeting, the new-looking khaki sofa and recliner, the oak coffee table and end tables.

I said, "This is a beauty, Bump, but I can't afford it."

Bump was walking through the kitchen, talking over his shoulder. "Kitchen's fully equipped, living room and dining room furniture, washer and dryer, all come with. Three bedrooms, unfurnished, two baths. I only need to get two-fifty a month out of it for now. You and Danny'll have to take care of the utilities and the trailer-park fees. Later, if you wanna buy it, I'll give you a deal."

"What kind of deal?"

He pulled a notebook out of his inside vest pocket and thumbed some pages. "I paid twenty for it. Dude needed cash fast. I could sell it for fifty, but if you and Danny want to buy it down the road, I'll sell it to you for thirty."

"Thirty? Jeez, that's a great price, but . . ."

"No shit."

I said, "But there's another problem. I can walk to work from Oak Street. How'm I gonna—"

"Not a prom. I'll get you where you need to go. Gruf'll drive you home after work. You'll have your own wheels before long."

I shrugged. "I'm not gonna argue. We'll take it."

He grinned and flipped me the front-door key.

I said, "All right! Let's bring in my new bed."

Bump was right. He said that the slow day meant we'd get slammed that night, and we did. Which was okay with me because if you're going out with two, usually three deliveries every trip, you can make some serious tip money. Gruf gave me a choice of taking a meal break or working on through. I chose working on through.

One of the times I came in from a trip, Danny was sitting in the dining room scarfing down a meatball sub. By that time he was stopping in Carlo's for supper a few nights a week. Say hi. Eat. I told him about the trailer and gave him the key so he could go take a look at it.

Next time in, he was standing by the front counter, grinning, and said he was gonna start moving in. He said he'd come back over to pick me up after work, but Gruf overheard him and said, don't worry about it, he'd bring me home, because he wanted to see the trailer.

By the time Gruf drove me out to the trailer park, Danny had us all moved in, beer and Coke in the refrigerator, and the TV on. He was majorly happy. He was fully extended on the La-Z-Boy, his toes clicking, a beer in his hand.

He said, "This place even has AC, dude. This is fucking great!"

Gruf stood in the doorway looking around. "Nice," he said, nodding.

"Wanna beer?" I asked him, heading for the refrigerator.

"Yeah, great."

I got a can of Coke for myself and brought Gruf a Bud and we sat down on the sofa.

The big TV that came with the place even had working cable. Gruf grinned as Danny packed a bowl. They passed it back and forth as they got to know each other, and Gruf and I watched Danny surf the channels for a while until Gruf's beer was gone. Then Gruf said he knew we usually got up early so he'd split.

I walked outside with him. It was a hot, muggy night and the mosquitoes were hungry. We stood on the street near his Jeep for a few minutes looking around and swatting the nasty little bloodsuckers away from our faces. A guy walked past carrying a leash attached to the ugliest little pig-faced dog I ever saw.

Gruf said, "So, how's it going? You like working at Carlo's?"

I said, "It's all good. Seriously. It's a lot of fun."

Gruf nodded. He cleared his throat and looked up the street. A baby in a trailer a few doors down began to wail. He said, "Has anything, I don't know, unusual? Ever happened at night while you were driving?"

I looked at him, baffled. "Unusual how?"

He shrugged. "I still think about that girl you replaced. Carrie. And her accident. I guess somebody probably told you about that."

I nodded. I'd almost forgotten about it by that time.

"Barb and Bump are both sure it was an accident, but I went out there and looked the day after it happened, and it didn't make sense to me."

I said, "I know. Bump and I looked at it, too. It doesn't make sense to me, either."

He nodded. "You never met Carrie, did you?"

I shook my head.

"She finally came in tonight to pick up her last paycheck, and she still tells the same story. White car deliberately ran her right into the ditch. I kinda believe her. She's a cute girl, but she's pretty much brain-dead. I can't see her making it up."

I said, "But her story doesn't make any sense, either, when you think about it. I mean, if somebody *did* run her off the road, why? She wasn't robbed. What would've been the point?"

He nodded. "I know." But he was wrong. He didn't know. Nobody did, yet.

Chapter 5

The next day was Sunday. Danny and I caught a late breakfast at Brewster's. Then we went to the Thriftway and bought some big-ass New York strip steaks, along with a hundred-forty dollars worth of other stuff. Then we ran over to the hardware store and bought a cheap little hand-push lawn mower and a cheap little outdoor grill, charcoal, and lighter fluid.

I cut the little bit of grass around the trailer and we grilled in the middle of the afternoon. We stuffed ourselves with steak, baked potatoes, and a massive tossed salad with sliced tomatoes, radishes, onions, shrooms and shredded mozzarella. Then we walked up and down the narrow streets of Chandler's Trailer Park at a leisurely pace, belching, feeling fat and phat, saying hi to any neighbors that happened to be outside. When we got back home, I jumped in the shower and quick got ready for work. Then Danny gave me a ride into town.

I walked into Carlo's around ten of five. Gruf and Bump were swilling coffee in their usual booth in the dining room. I could tell by the merriment in their eyes that something was up. As I walked through the dining room, I glanced at the other diners and saw right away what gave.

Sheila Werbel was sitting in a booth by the front windows, deep in conversation with one of the uglier men I'd ever seen in my life, and it wasn't the nervous little translucent guy she usually sat with. This one was dark, large, and gross looking. He had only the suggestion of a forehead, and heavy black eyebrows that pretty much flowed together like a single big hairy caterpiller. His lower lip was so large it was almost embarrassing to look at.

I grabbed a Styrofoam cup, sloshed coffee in it, and slouched into the booth next to Bump.

I said, "Who's the missing link?" I jerked my head in the direction of the couple in the front booth.

"That's what we were wondering," Bump drawled.

I said, "Is she, like, torn between two lovers, do you think?"

Gruf said, "I'm gonna try really hard *not* to think about it."

I pulled a piece of paper from my shirt pocket, unfolded it, and passed it over to Bump. It was my estimate for his deck, all itemized for materials and labor. He barely glanced at it before he folded it up and shoved it into a pocket of the black leather vest he wore over his Carlo's T-shirt.

He said, "That's a lot cheaper than I thought it'd be. Let's do it."

I said, "The only thing I forgot is the cost of renting a backhoe."

He grinned at me. "I can get you a backhoe. When can you start?"

"You'll have to pay for the materials up front."

"No prom."

"You'll need a building permit."

"I'll get my lawyer on it."

His lawyer. I loved this guy. "As soon as you've got a backhoe and a building permit, we're good to go."

"Tomorrow good for you?"

I laughed. "That soon? Okay. I need a ride down

to my brother's so I can pick up my power tools. It's about a half-hour drive."

He nodded.

"How 'bout this? Meet me and Danny at Brewster's in the morning. We usually get there around seven. After breakfast we can go get my tools."

"Sounds good."

I clocked in at five and went around to the back room. Flute was there, loitering, waiting for an ear to gossip into. He was all over Sheila Werbel's sex life, and now he must share or die.

He tucked his face into my armpit and whispered, "Sheila W-Werbel's a s-s-slut!"

I took a step back from him. "Now, how do you know that, Flute?"

He drew back, indignant. Then he zeroed right back in on my armpit. "She's m-married, b-b-but she lets H-Hammer feel her up, and n-now she's s-s-sitting out th-th-there with *another* b-boyfriend! How do you think th-that's gonna l-l-look?"

"What. You think she's gonna sully Carlo's good name?"

"Oh. I g-g-guess you think it's p-perfectly all right."

"I must be dense, because I don't see how it's any of *your* business."

He came out of my armpit to give me a scornful look. "I g-g-guess you *are* dense. What h-h-happens when they all f-f-find out about each other?"

I suddenly got a vivid mental picture of the three of them, beasts that they were, and Hammer, involved in a furry free-for-all in the dining room, and burst out laughing. "Oh my God, Flute. Get the hell away from me."

Fortunately, at that moment Gruf yelled, "Dispatch!" and I was able to escape.

*   *   *

It was a slow night, delivery-wise, for a Sunday. At around eight-thirty, I came in from a run and Gruf said, "Want a meal break?"

I just looked at him. Duh.

I stuck my head around the kitchen doorway to give Hammer my meal order, but he wasn't there. I had the grumbellies so I went looking for him. There wasn't anyone in the waitress station, either. The dining room was nearly empty, but Hammer was out there. He was sitting in a booth, his back to me, all cuddled up with Sheila Werbel.

He had his arm up over the back of the booth behind her and was whispering through her stiff platinum hair into her ear, his skinny immature body all zigging and zagging to fit around her largish curves. I stood there for a minute, blinking at the sight. There was no sign of Neanderthal Man.

I stepped back into the hallway where they wouldn't be able to see me and yelled, "Hey, Hammer? Where are you, dude? I'm hungry."

"Out here," he yelled.

I turned around and stepped out into the dining room. Now he was sitting casually across the table from her, beaming happily at me. "Whatcha want?"

"Grilled cheese and fries."

He hustled out of the booth and rushed past me, heading for his kitchen. I started after him and then I thought, you know, like, What's she got? Like maybe I missed something and ought to take another look at that, you know? So I did. Nope, she was definitely a mess. I chalked up all the randy activity under the column: Guys So Horny They'd Go For Anything, subcolumn: If I'm Ever That Desperate, Shoot Me in the Head, and let it go at that.

Before long, Hammer had my supper ready. By that time there were a few more customers sitting at tables.

Gruf came out and smoked a cigarette with me while I ate.

Sheila was bussing a nearby table. I coulda *built* the fucking thing faster than she cleared it off, but she finally walked away carrying a stack of dirty plates. A few minutes later we heard loud laughter coming from around the corner in the waitress station. Then a female voice shouted, "Fuckeen A!" Several customers looked up from their plates, frowning.

Gruf turned around to look down the hall. I could tell he was annoyed. Jackson appeared in the hallway outside the waitress station, shaking her head and frowning. She came out to our table.

Gruf said quietly, "What the hell's going on in there?"

Jackson said, "I keep telling her she's got to quiet down."

"I'm not blaming *you*. Send Sheila out here."

"Can you wait a few minutes? I've actually got her working for once."

"Better yet, *you* yell at her. In fact, I hereby authorize you to fire her ass if you need to."

She started to turn away, then came back. "Oh, Terry. I almost forgot. Would you mind closing with the Witness tonight? My sister-in-law wants me to watch her kids so she can go to a baby shower."

I said, "Sure. No problem."

"It started at seven, but she thought if I could come over, she could go catch the end of it."

I smiled at her. "Sure. Me and the Witness'll get along fine."

"Thanks, Terry. I owe you one."

Gruf said, "I already cashed you out, didn't I?"

She nodded.

"Okay. Tell Sheila to shut her fat mouth and then you can take off."

She smiled, waved, squared her shoulders, and marched back toward the waitress station.

Gruf turned back to me, shaking his head. "I gotta find some new waitresses. Hey. I wonder if any of the old ones who used to work here could be talked into coming back. Like Debby Duncan. I wonder if she'd come back."

He stared at me absently for a minute, then stubbed out his smoke and hurried off to the office. I finished eating and went back to work.

The back wasn't in too bad of a condition at closing time. Gruf and the front girls had been able to keep up with the mess pretty well. So I decided, since I had the Witness at my disposal, this would be a good night to clean out the shelves in the back hall.

The whole side of the hallway to the back door was shelves, floor to ceiling, and I knew for a fact that they'd never been cleaned off and washed down since I'd been working at Carlo's. I got the stepladder from the office and went through the shelves, pulling everything off, and had the Witness follow behind me washing them down. He worked slowly, and he was shy and flinchy, but from what I saw he didn't let his attention stray very far from his work.

The shelves were mainly used to store pizza boxes. Big plastic-wrapped packs of boxes that hadn't been folded yet, and folded boxes that were stacked there until they could be moved to the high shelves up front.

But all wedged in among and behind the pizza boxes was every type of thing you could possibly imagine that people had stashed there. Everything from all over the store that people didn't know what to do with had been crammed in there and then been shoved to the back when new packs of pizza boxes had been brought in.

As I pulled out the pizza boxes, I found brake fluid, flashlights, fuses, trash of every imaginable description, dirty plates and silverware, a hairbrush, a tube of lip gloss, old Styrofoam cups with mold growing in them, including three of the Witness's works of art, articles of clothing including shirts, gloves, hats, even a sock. It was unbelievable what had been crammed onto those shelves and forgotten there.

It was a time-consuming job, but even so, we got those shelves cleaned, and did most of the other closing work, and still finished earlier than on a normal night. The Witness dumped his dirty water in the sink, then turned around and looked over at me, frowning.

He cleared his throat. "You shouldn'ta put my head in the sink that one time."

I looked at him. "I thought you were gonna swing on Jackson. We can't have that."

He said, "I thought *she* was gonna swing on *me.* But you *still* shouldn'ta done it. Sheila thinks so, too."

I thought about mentioning how greatly I valued Sheila's opinion on anything, but I settled for saying, "Maybe you're right. Tell you what. You don't bother the girls anymore, and I won't put your head in the sink again. Deal?"

He nodded.

I told him he could go ask Gruf to cash him out if he wanted to, that I'd finish up the sweeping and mopping. Gruf cashed him out, and I didn't see him around anymore, so I thought he was gone.

I got the office, back hall, rest rooms, and back room all swept, and was just starting to fix my mop water when there was a loud crash in the kitchen. I looked over in time to see Hammer come stomping toward me.

He stopped short when he saw me staring at him.

He said, "I swear to God I'm gonna kill that little bastard," and went slamming out the back door. I got to the doorway in time to see him peel out of the parking lot in his little red Mitsubishi truck.

Gruf came walking up behind me. "That better not've been Hammer."

"It was. What the hell happened?"

"I don't know, but he better be right back."

We went to the kitchen and stuck our heads in. Nobody was there, of course, just a couple of pans on the floor where he'd thrown them, and the kitchen looking like a disaster area because he hadn't even started to clean it yet. Then we went around the corner and looked in the waitress station. Nobody was there, either. Which the lovely Sheila was supposed to be there, closing it out.

So then we went on out to the dining room and guess what? Sheila was sitting in a booth, her back to us, and the Witness was standing behind her, rubbing her shoulders, leaning over her neck.

I thought Gruf was gonna have a stroke. He yelled, "Witness! Get the fuck out of here! Sheila! Get in the waitress station and start closing it out! Terry! Office!"

He ushered me into the office ahead of him and slammed the door behind us. He leaned his arm high on the door and his head on his arm. He groaned. "What the fuck's going on around here?"

"You took the words right outa my mouth."

He took his cigs out of his shirt pocket, tapped one out, and flipped the pack to me. We lit up and puffed.

I said, "Sheila reminds me of that type of bar slut that's always trying to get a fight started. You know the kind? She's got troublemaker written all over her."

"*All* over her. I can't wait to get rid of her. I can't

wait to get rid of the Witness. I gotta get Hammer back. Do you know how screwed we are if we lose Hammer?"

"Pretty screwed?"

"All the way up and all the way back down. The only other people who can handle the kitchen on night shift are me and Jackson. And Jackson won't do it. And neither one of us is as good as Hammer. Let's get this pop stand closed down and then I gotta go looking for him."

Sheila was vacuuming the dining room when Gruf and I left the office. We went to work closing up the kitchen, and as we worked I was vaguely aware of her moving around in the waitress station. Then she told Gruf she was finished. He went to check her work and she clocked out and left. I finished sweeping and mopping the kitchen and the drivers' areas and Gruf cashed me out.

He carried his paperwork back to the office. I stepped out the back door to have a smoke and enjoy the night air while I waited for him to finish and give me a ride out to the trailer.

The next morning I was starting Bump's deck, so I was gonna use the fresh air and quiet time to think through the beginning stages, take a mental walk through the next morning's job. But it didn't work out that way. I was surprised to see the Witness's little Jeep still parked in the back parking lot.

He was surprised to see me, too. In the shadowy light, I saw the black bill of his Carlo's cap snap around in my direction. He instantly reached forward and turned the key in the ignition and his Jeep roared to life. Then Sheila Werbel's platinum head popped up out of his lap and into view. She'd been giving him head, right there in the parking lot.

The Witness quickly backed the Jeep out of its spot

and squealed it away out of the parking lot. I stood there, disgusted, shaking my head, glad that Gruf was fired up to get rid of the two of them as soon as possible, thinking that it couldn't happen soon enough for me. As it turned out, it didn't happen soon enough for the Witness, either.

Chapter 6

Monday morning, Bump came walking into Brewster's just as me and Danny were getting our coffee poured. "Hey, Bump." I slid over in the booth to make room for him. "Whassup?"

"Coffee, Bump?" our sweet little waitress of the morning asked him. I was surprised that she knew him. I hadn't discovered yet that everyone in Spencer knew everyone else in Spencer.

Bump said, "Yeah. Thanks, Mary."

I watched her pour, wondering how old she was. I knew she had a kid in middle school. Several mornings a week he bussed tables there at Brewster's. He was a skinny, chipmunk-cheeked kid who seemed to live in that middle school hell of bad hair days and zits and awkwardness. He always wore huge shorts that rode halfway down his butt and seemed to trip him when he walked, which his enormous high-tops didn't help his walking much, either. Little, small-town gangsta wanna-be who always grinned shyly and said "Yes, sir" when one of the customers teased him.

Bump said, "Oh, and Mary. Tell your brother I have the TV he wanted. He can come over and pick it up tonight if he wants to."

"Great," she said. "I'll call him right now." She hurried away.

"That reminds me," I said. "I never asked what I owe you for my bed."

He pulled out his notebook and thumbed pages. "The sheets and shit are free," he said as he thumbed. "Thanks for fixin' my roof. The mattress and box spring, um"—he found the page he was looking for and did some calculating—"two hundred'll cover it."

I pulled out my wallet and gave him ten twenties. "Cheap at half the price."

Danny pulled out his wallet, too. "Long as we're throwing money atcha, lemme catch the first month's rent." He peeled off five fifties and handed them over to Bump, who pulled a fat money clip out of his inside vest pocket and folded all the bills onto it.

If you're not a working man, you might think it's odd how we were all carrying cash around. It seems to me most of us do that, especially if we're single. I think it's because we feel like it's safer with us. *Anything* could happen to it in a bank.

Danny and Bump had met in passing before, but this was the first time they'd had anything like a conversation. They discovered almost right away that they had friends in common. I listened to them talk. You could tell Bump liked Danny. Well, hell, everybody always likes Danny. He's that kind of guy. It's when Danny likes 'em back that you know you've got something. You could tell Danny liked Bump, too. Listening to them, how they started to mildly rip on each other, I felt happier and happier.

Mary came back to the table. "Bennie'll be over tonight, Bump. Did you want to order breakfast?"

He certainly did. He ordered a big breakfast and hit on Mary the whole time he ate it. Then Danny went off to work and me and Bump headed south to my brother's. Nobody was home there, so I popped the screen in his family room, which was how I'd been breaking into his house for the nine-and-a-half years he'd lived there. We carried all my power tools out of his basement, I left him a note, and we went back to Bump's to drop off the tools. Then we went to the lumberyard for some stuff like framing wood, string, and stakes, and we were back at Bump's by ten. Not bad.

The backhoe was sitting in the middle of the backyard, sparkling in the sunlight. I quickly measured, sighted, and staked the deck and the footer holes. Then I started grading and digging. The work went easy because the backhoe was a brand-spanking-new John Deere.

Half an hour later, a big, shiny red Caddy came rolling into Bump's driveway. The guy driving it was wearing a navy blue suit that was already rumpled and it wasn't even midday yet. He had a narrow ring of brown hair left around his shiny, sunburned head and about a gut-and-a-half hanging over his belt. He walked like his shoulders were doing all the work. He waved at me and walked into the house using the sliding door.

A few minutes later he and Bump walked outside, grinning. Bump shouted, "Terry. Come on over here and meet a friend of mine."

I shut off the engine and hopped down.

"This is Terry Saltz, dude," Bump said to the man as I came up to them.

The man's big face split into a cheerful grin and he stuck out a pudgy hand. "Alfred 'Bud' Hanratty, Terry. Good to meetcha."

This amused me. I shook his hand.

Bump said, "Bud's my lawyer. He brought over the building permit."

The guy had a lawyer hand delivering his building permit. It cracked me up.

Bump said, "I got a few minutes before I hafta leave for work. Let's go get a Coke. Hey, Bud, I'll show you the pictures how the deck's gonna look."

Bud and I sat at the kitchen table while Bump got Cokes out of the refrigerator. Then he walked out into his living room to handle a call on his cell phone.

Bud said, "So, Terry. Bump tells me you recently went through a divorce."

I nodded. Funny, but I don't have much of anything to say to guys in suits. Oh, I'm talkative enough around guys who do physical labor like me. On a good day, I can be chatty, even. But sit me down with a guy in a suit, and I'm pretty much a silent spectator. I've noticed over the years that a lot of working men are the same way. I've got a theory about this, but now's not the time.

Bud said, "Didn't get yourself a lawyer, huh?"

His brown eyes, when they were looking directly at you, were like sharp little ice picks. I saw that this guy could quite possibly be hell on wheels in a courtroom.

I shrugged. "No."

"That's a mistake."

I said, "Seemed like a good idea at the time."

I laughed.

He didn't.

I said, "Hell, I shoulda known *you* then."

I laughed again. This time, so did he.

He asked me where I'd been living at the time of the divorce and I told him, but I swear that was all there was to the conversation. For the life of me, I can't remember another word being said about my divorce by any of us. What I didn't know at the time was that the two of *them* had discussed it.

Bump came back into the kitchen, set his cell phone on the counter, twirled an empty chair around backward, and straddled it, leaning his forearms up over the top. Taking a big slug of Coke, he pushed one of his deck magazines over to Bud. It was folded open to the deck we had settled on.

Bud studied it. "Nice," he said thoughtfully. "Very nice."

Bump said, "No shit."

We all sipped on our Cokes for a few minutes while Bud looked through another one of the deck magazines. Then Bud said, "Listen, Terry, I think I'll do a deck on my place. When you're done here, can you build me one?"

Just like that, the guy decides to get a deck built? I stared at him for a second to make sure he wasn't kidding. He wasn't.

I said, "Sure. Of course." It was my first thrill as a self-employed carpenter. Still working on one job with the next one already lined up and waiting. "Where do you live?"

Bud said, "It's about fifteen miles north of here. In the Pheasant Trails area. You know it?"

"No. Well, I think I've heard of it. Uh, the reason I asked is that I don't have my own wheels right now . . ."

Bump and Bud made eye contact. There was a certain eye-twinkling thing that happened between them that I didn't understand.

". . . so getting up to your place will be a problem."

Bud winked at Bump and they grinned at each other. Bud said, "No, I don't think it will."

I didn't understand that at all, but I let it go. There'd be time to work things out later.

After a few minutes, Bump left for work and Bud left carrying the stack of Bump's deck magazines.

I got all the footers dug and the swale graded and for once I'd timed my call for the cement truck right. The truck came backing up the driveway just about the time I needed it.

I knew the cement guy, Billy Grabowski, from when I was working in the southern part of the county. We'd passed a bowl a time or two on jobs and had some laughs. After we got all the pouring done, he pulled his bowl from his hip pocket and held it up.

"Got time for a safety meeting?"

I told him I was still on probation. It was easier than explaining that I'd changed my ways. "You go ahead, though. I'll smoke a legal one, keep ya company."

He packed the bowl and lit it. "Gone into business for yourself, then, huh?"

I said, "Yeah, it's starting to look like it."

He was a friendly, stocky little wide-faced guy. He grinned at me. "Well, good for you. Red Perkins is a jerk."

Red Perkins, owner, Perkins Construction, used to be my boss.

I said, "Yes, he is."

When the footers were all done, I finished the job of repairing Bump's rotting kitchen floor. Then I used his shower, put on my black Carlo's T-shirt and fresh black jeans, and ate the lunch I'd packed. After a while, Bump came by to pick me up and we went on to Carlo's.

We got two new employees that night. Sheila Werbel was off. A new waitress took her place. She wasn't new to Carlo's. I got the impression that she'd worked there off and on for years. She was just new to me. Gruf had called her and begged her to come back to help us out. Her name was Debby Duncan, and she looked to be mid-thirties. She had shortish brown hair, super layered and curly; wore big hoop earrings; was large, knowing, and earthy; and made very funny and outrageous remarks in her whiskey voice. She reminded me of about eighty percent of all the biker chicks I'd ever known. She was great with the customers. Most of the night, people were laughing all over the dining room.

The other new employee was an older woman who'd been hired as a driver. She came in at about five-thirty wearing a black blazer and a long black skirt, went into the ladies' john, and came back out wearing her black Carlo's T-shirt and a pair of black sweatpants. She had short graying hair and she was overweight. Somebody said she was gonna moonlight, coming straight to Carlo's from a full-time office job. She looked tired. I didn't think to ask her name, because I didn't think she was gonna last long, which was okay with me, because I didn't think I was gonna like her, anyway.

There were a lot of deliveries that night, which was why I wasn't there when things got interesting. Sheila's pale little husband came walking in around nine and slouched into his usual booth up front. He was surprised and not a little pissed off when Debby told him that Sheila wasn't there. Hubby left his full cup of coffee on the table and went away mumbling to himself.

Gruf told me about it later, while I busted up wings for wingdings, and then, about an hour and a half after Debby had to disappoint Sheila Werbel's hubby, she also had to disappoint the Neanderthal boyfriend. The husband didn't take it well. The boyfriend took it worse.

I was washing dishes when Debby gave the boyfriend the bad news. All of a sudden I heard a lot of yelling in the front. I looked through the doorway in time to see Gruf going right over the top of the front counter. Not one to be left behind, I hit the counter on the run and went over it right behind him. He landed on one side of Big Deb and I landed on the other side. We found ourselves face-to-face with an unhappy big ol' boyfriend.

"Where the hell *is* she?" he yelled again.

"How the *fuck* should I know?" Debby yelled just as loud, getting in his face. "It ain't *my* day to watch her!"

They squared off to each other, and for a giddy split second I considered stepping back to watch. But that wouldn't have been right. Like a mirror image, Gruf and I closed in front of Debby, pushing her back behind us.

Gruf said calmly, "Dude, this is a place of business. I don't want any trouble, and I know you don't, either."

The boyfriend looked like maybe he did want some trouble.

I said, "Can we do something for ya? Want a cup of coffee?"

"No I do *not* want any coffee."

Gruf said, "Well, then, I think the best thing at this point would be for you to leave."

He stood there breathing hard for a few more seconds. Then he turned and walked out the door. Almost immediately we heard a crash outside. We ran outside and saw that he had knocked over the *Plain Dealer* vending machine, and was now slamming his car door. He started up his engine, backed out, and peeled across the parking lot. We stood there and watched him go.

As we righted the vending machine, I said, "That went well."

Debby was waiting by the door. "Thanks, guys," she said as we came back in, "but I coulda handled him, the pussy."

I tended to think maybe she could have.

She started laughing. She said, "I haven't met this Sheila chick yet. She must be a piece of work."

Gruf said, "Deb, I gotta get rid of that bitch."

She nodded. "I'll say."

"But I can't fire her until I have someone to replace her."

A suspicious look crawled across Debby's face.

Gruf said, "I know you don't wanna work full-time. But is there any chance you could do it, just until I can find someone?"

She screwed up her face for a minute, but then she smiled at him. I think I've already mentioned what a good-looking guy Gruf is.

She said, "All right, I'll do it."

He said, "*Yes!* Sheila and the Witness are both on the schedule for tomorrow night. At the end of shift I can fire both of 'em."

Chapter 7

Tuesday morning, Bump was already in Brewster's when me and Danny walked in, and he was wired about his deck. He could barely sit still. I think he downed a pot of coffee all by himself. I ate too fast because of his impatience, and let go with a big sausage belch as I climbed into his truck.

We went to pick up the first batch of wood and we unloaded it all in a heap in his backyard. Then it was time for me to go to the courthouse and try once again to have a meeting with my probation officer. Bump drove me up to the square and dropped me off. He said he'd swing up around eleven to give me a ride back to his house, but I said, Don't even bother, it isn't that long of a walk.

I knew my probation officer's name was Nelma Wolfert, and I knew that she'd been suffering from some sort of illness these past weeks, because every Tuesday when I went to her office, they told me she was out sick and to come back next Tuesday.

I pictured her as a youngish, neurotic, hypochondriac, stringy, angry, chain-smoking bitch, who'd want to give me an extremely unpleasant hour per week while she got even for every time in her life a guy had said he'd call and then didn't. Something to that effect. You could say I still had some residual issues left over from my divorce, chick-wise. Whatever. Anyway, I was expecting the worst.

But Nelma Wolfert turned out to be a big ol' lady in her early sixties, with thinning curly hair that was orange losing to gray, dramatic brown eyes, a voice like a clock-tower gong, and smart? This lady had been around the block a time or two, Champ. She knew what was what. You took one look in those big brown eyes and you knew that.

I knocked on her open office door and stepped inside. She looked up and her eyes went from my eyes to my toes and back again. Slowly. I was an open book.

"Mr. Saltz," she said. "How's it going?" She pointed to the chair in front of her desk. I pulled it back a little to make room for my legs and sat down.

She shuffled through the stack of backed-up files on the far corner of her desk, found mine, and opened it. "Terrence William Saltz. Carpenter?" She looked up at me.

"Yes, ma'am."

"Hmm. Carpenter." She looked at me again. She didn't just look. She scrutinized.

She said, "You know, I do a little woodworking myself. I like to make little shelves and benches and things for my family and friends."

"You do?"

"Oh my, yes. I have a table saw, a band saw, and a router. And a drill. And a sander."

I didn't know how I was supposed to respond to this. I just said the first thing that came to mind. "How'd you happen to get interested in woodworking?"

She pursed her lips and thought about it, but her eyes never left mine. "Now that's a good question. I don't know. I was walking through Sears one day, and there was a big display out in the middle of the aisle. Table saws that were on sale. I looked at the things, but I went on by. What's an old lady like me going to do with a table saw? Then the next day I went back and bought one." She laughed. "That was, um, two years ago."

She stopped talking and stared at me. I tried not to squirm. She said, "What do you think about that?"

"Uh, I think it's pretty cool. But how'd you learn how to use it?"

She grinned. "Just watched that Norm guy on *The New Yankee Workshop*."

I had to laugh. "Norm. That dude has every power tool ever invented. Don't you lust for his workshop?"

"His *workshop?* Hell, I lust for Norm!"

We both burst out laughing. The last thing I expected to hear out of a probation officer's mouth was that she lusted for Norm Abram.

"Hey," she said. "You want some coffee?"

"Sure. Yes, please."

I thought she meant to produce a coffeepot and pour us coffee into some Styrofoam cups, or something, but she pushed herself up out of her chair, pulled her big loose green jacket thing together across her broad chest, and heaved an enormous tapestry bag up over her shoulder.

She said, "Me, too. Come on."

She led me out the office door, down the hall, out the front doors, down the sidewalk, and across the street to a coffee shop. I noticed she walked with a limp. We gave our orders at the back counter—she insisted on paying—and we took our cappuccinos to a little table up in the window. The chairs in the place were those little old-fashioned soda chairs, and I wondered how she was going to balance her large you-know-what on hers, but she managed okay.

She sat there smiling and looking around for a while. I felt uncomfortable sitting there in silence, so I said, "You've been sick, huh?"

"Foot surgery. Kept me laid up for, what? Five, six weeks."

I nodded, not really having any comments handy on the subject of foot surgery. We sipped for a while. Then she said, "So, how's it going?"

"A lot better than I thought it would when I was coolin' my heels in jail."

"Yeah?" She smiled and waited.

I explained how everything in my life had changed. How I'd come out of jail thinking I had nothing going for me at all. How Danny had taken me in, how I'd gotten the job at Carlo's, and how Bump had rented us the trailer. How I was even back into carpentry again, but as my own man this time, thanks to Bump.

She smiled and said, "Good ol' Bump. Greg Bellini. I know him very well."

"You do?" I was astonished.

"Oh, yes. I'm very fond of Bump. Known him since he was fourteen years old."

"He cracks me up. I've never met anyone like him."

She nodded. "He's one of a kind."

We sat quietly for a while. Then she said, "So. Why'd you trash that bar?"

I wasn't expecting the question. I swear to you, by that time I had pretty much forgotten I was talking to my probation officer. Just in that short time I'd come to like her so much, it was like I was talking to a favorite aunt I never had, or somebody.

I shrugged. "Because I was loaded, I guess."

She nodded, thinking. "But why were you loaded?"

I just looked at her. Because that was the real question, wasn't it? Nobody had asked me that.

I said, "That's a good question."

She said, "Of course it is. That's why they pay me the big bucks." We laughed, and then she waited for my answer.

Now I did squirm. I looked out the front windows at the big redbrick courthouse across the street, I looked back at the service counter, I looked down at the fake brick floor, I looked at the fake plants, but wherever I looked, her intelligent brown eyes were right in the middle of the picture, waiting.

I folded my hands on the table and scraped a busted fingernail across the callus on the inside of my thumb. I said, "I never used to do shots. Just beer. But that night I did shots. A lot of shots. I don't know why."

She said, "Sure you do."

I looked up at her. She gestured, like, Come on. Out with it.

I shrugged. "I'm not gonna sit here and make excuses. I fucked up. End of story."

She grinned at me. "Oh, okay. You're a big tough guy. Bite the bullet and set the bone yourself, huh? Whoop-de-doo. Call 'em excuses or call 'em reasons, but one or more matches lit your fuse that night, and I wanna know what those matches were."

"Jeez, Mrs. Wolfert."

She looked horrified. "Mrs. Wolfert is still my mother-in-law to me. My friends call me Nelma."

I went back to work on that callus, thinking, Her *friends?* Huh.

After a while I managed to say, "Okay. I was trying to hold my marriage together, even though I knew it wasn't gonna work. I was stuck working for a guy I didn't, uh, respect. There was other stuff, but those were the big two. I was trapped. I guess I was trying to obliterate everything. Wipe everything out." I looked up at her and shrugged. "That's the best I can do."

She was nodding. "And now it is, isn't it? Wiped out. Your life, the way it was then. Is that a good thing? Or a bad thing?"

That was a question I *did* know the answer to. "Oh, it's a good thing."

Once we were back in her office, she went down a checklist for my file. She got my new address, she told me to start bringing her my Carlo's pay stubs, she reminded me about the fines and payments I owed, and she reminded me to stay away from alcohol and drugs.

Then she said she'd see me next week, same time, same place, and told me to say hi to Bump for her. I said thanks, and it was really nice talking with her. That seemed to please her. We shook hands and I was done.

I started off walking toward Bump's, but I hadn't gotten very far before he pulled his beat-up blue truck over to the curb and picked me up. I told him Nelma said hi and he grinned.

He said, "Nelma Wolfert's your probation officer?"

I nodded.

He laughed. "Fuckin' Nelma," he said.

Back at Bump's house, I started setting up a work surface in the backyard with a couple of sawhorses and a piece of plywood. Bump brought out a radio and turned it on. Then he said he had an errand to run and took off.

It was a brisk, clear day. Low seventies. I started sorting the wood and stacking it on pallets with spacers so it would dry out and not warp. The sun got hot. I took off my T-shirt and wiped my face with it. Gotta remember to bring a dew rag tomorrow, I told myself. After a while I went inside, got myself a cold Coke, sat on a stack of wood, and listened to "Freebird" on

Bump's radio. When it swung into the fast part, the beat got me bouncing. I was back up, finishing sorting the wood, when I heard a couple of vehicles turn in off the street.

A shiny black Toyota Tacoma pickup truck came crawling up the driveway, Bud Hanratty driving, followed by Bump's truck. They were both grinning through the windshields like idiots.

"Hey," I said as they climbed out and came toward me. "That looks exactly like the truck I had."

"Probably because it *is* the truck you had, you silly son of a bitch," Bud yelled, and flipped me the keys. Which I grabbed for them too late and had to bend over and pick them up out of the grass. Then I saw my license plate and my mouth dropped open.

"My *truck?*" I must have sounded like an idiot. "How did you . . . ?"

"Lawyer magic, my boy. It's all yours, free and clear. Now, I gotta get back to the office. Come on, Bump, drive me back. I got a hearing this afternoon."

"Thank you. How . . . ? Thank you."

They were already walking to Bump's truck. Bud waved a hand at me over his shoulder. "Glad I could help."

I musta sat in my truck for ten minutes, bouncing on the seat and looking at the dashboard controls like a thirteen-year-old kid whose dad left the keys lying around.

When Bump came back a while later, I was cutting the first lengths of wood for the frame. I was singin' along to the tune on the radio. *"Boom boom! Out go the lights!"*

Bump came strutting across the grass with a shit-eating grin on his face.

I set down my circular saw and said, "How the hell did you guys bust my truck loose?"

He shrugged nonchalantly. "Ol' Bud made a few calls yesterday to find out the status of your case. Then this morning, he called your, uh, bitch, introduced himself, and told her to leave it unlocked and the keys in it, that we'd be coming down to pick it up. Plain and simple."

I just stared at him.

He said, "Hey, did you know your divorce hasn't gone through yet?"

"It hasn't?" I thought about this a second, then shrugged. "Well, but it will."

"Anyways, Bud thinks he can get your community service reduced, too. He's gonna look into it this afternoon while he's at the courthouse."

Oh, yeah. Community service. I'd forgotten to ask Nelma about that.

He reached into his vest pocket and pulled out an envelope with a whole bunch of cash in it. It turned out to be half my labor charge for building the deck. Then his kitchen phone started ringing. I was still standing there staring at the money after he'd disappeared inside.

At four I put my tools away in his dining room, jumped in my truck, and took a little joy ride back to the trailer. I had the window down, the moonroof open and the CD player cranked. Did I mention how much I love my truck?

It's a funny thing about life. When things are bad, hang on. Something good might come around the corner any minute. 'Course, there's a flip side to that coin, as I was about to be reminded.

Carlo's was busy that night. Most of the night I was in car two making deliveries. Finally, around eleven-thirty, I came in from a trip and Gruf said, "You can go around. I sent the Witness out with the last delivery. He should be back any minute."

By the time I pulled my car around, locked it, and logged it back in, Gruf was already at the sinks washing dishes. The back room looked about how I expected it to look after a night like we'd had. It was trashed.

Gruf said, "You never got a meal break. You want me to make you something, or you wanna just bust hump and get this place closed?"

"Let's just get it closed."

"Good."

I picked up a tray of clean dishes and started for the waitress station to put them away. Gruf said, "Tell Sheila to bust a move out there so we can close up and go home."

Sheila, looking really pissed about something, was leaning against the salad counter in the waitress station. She had a cup of coffee in one hand and a lit cigarette in the other. She had her cigarette hand up to her sneering mouth and was gnawing on her thumbnail while the cigarette smoke wrapped itself around her head.

I stood there holding the tray of dishes and stared at her in disbelief.

"What are you doing? You know you're not supposed to be smoking in here."

She stiffened and gave me a hostile glare. "Oh, go fuck yourself."

"Sheila . . ."

"All right. All right." She held the cigarette under the faucet and dropped it into the trash, muttering about limp-dicked, brownnosing, asshole drivers.

I told her Gruf wanted everybody to bust ass so we could get out of there as soon as possible. She was

real receptive to that suggestion, too. I walked away
shaking my head. I knew Gruf's plan was to fire her
as soon as her closing work was done. I couldn't wait
to see her walk out the door for the last time.

Gruf said, "There wasn't any sign of the Witness
out in the dining room, was there? He shoulda been
back by now."

"No, I didn't see him."

"Check the men's room. See if he's hiding."

"Naw, it's unoccupied. I just emptied the trash in
there." I pulled a bag of trash out of one of the big
back room trash cans, dropped the men's room trash
bag in on top, and tied the bag in a knot. I tossed it
in the direction of the back hall and started pulling
the bag out of the next can.

I said, "Did he ever come back from his last
delivery?"

He shook his head and slammed another tray of
dirty dishes into the dishwasher.

"Haven't seen him. I'm gonna kill that little bastard.
He knows the back's trashed and he's hiding somewhere. He'll do anything to get out of work."

Hammer came out of the kitchen with an armload
of his dirty pans and skillets. "Who?" he asked defen-
sively, like he thought Gruf was talking about him.

Gruf said, "The Witness. Who do you think?"

"Oh," he said. "Well, when you kill him, can I
watch?"

"You just get back to your business and don't be
sticking your nose in mine. We're getting out of here
as soon as we can tonight."

I carried a tray of clean dishes to the waitress station, put them away, and got the last cart of dirty
dishes from the office. Sheila was out in the dining
room turning chairs upside down on the tables, getting
ready to vacuum. I pushed the cart back to Gruf and

went on carrying trays of clean dishes out and putting them away.

I forgot all about cranking up the jukebox and I guess Gruf did, too. We just busted ass in silence for a long time, until finally, while I was mopping the back room floor, Gruf came up behind me and said, "That little shit still isn't back. I wonder what time I dispatched him on that last delivery."

He went around to the computer on the front counter and was back a minute later. "I sent him out fuckin' two hours ago. Shit. I better make sure he made the delivery."

He went out to the front counter and I could hear him talking on the phone right before I dumped out the mop water. "Okay, thanks. Sorry to have bothered you so late."

When he came back I was standing in the back hall lighting up a cigarette. He said, "Everything finished?"

"Yep."

"Okay. I'll cash you out as soon as you're done with your smoke."

He tapped one out of his own pack and lit up. "The Witness made that last delivery about twenty, twenty-five minutes after they called it in. So he left their house way over an hour ago."

Hammer came toward the back hall from the kitchen carrying his grease bucket, heading for the back door. The cooks dump their grease in a special Dumpster out on the far side of the back parking lot.

"What," Hammer said. "He's still not back?"

"No," Gruf said, and his voice had a sharp edge to it. We made room for Hammer to pass through the hall, and Gruf held the back door open for him. He started down across the dark parking lot toward the grease Dumpster.

Gruf turned toward me. "I wonder—remember what happened to Carrie Hall? Maybe I should call the cops."

Outside, in the dark parking lot, we heard Hammer say, "Oh my God."

A second later the back door opened. Hammer stepped up into the dim light of the hallway. He wasn't carrying the empty grease bucket, and he hadn't been out there long enough to have dumped it. His face was white as a sheet and he was shaking from head to toe.

"Uh, guys?" he said in a high, odd voice.

Gruf looked at him. "What?"

Hammer said, "The Witness is back."

He turned and pointed out across the dark parking lot. I followed Gruf out the door and came up beside him when he stopped a few feet short of the Dumpster. It was dark, but I could see Hammer's white bucket over by the grease Dumpster, lying on its side right where he'd dropped it. And I could see the shiny black grease pool all around it.

I took all that in somehow, but that wasn't the main thing out there that night. The main thing was the shadowy body lying spread-eagled and faceup on the pavement. It was the Witness. His head was at a funny angle, and his throat had been cut. There was big pool of shiny blood under his head, spreading down to the edge of the parking lot and off into the weeds. In the dark parking lot, it looked as black as the blood he'd always drawn on his Styrofoam cups.

Chapter 8

I stared at the Witness's body, trying to think what could've happened. Had he and Hammer mixed it up? But Hammer'd only been outside a few seconds. No way he was outside long enough to have done this. Then I thought to wonder if the guy who *had* done it was still around somewhere. I did a quick three-sixty and ended up face-to-face with Gruf, who had just turned in his own circle.

We heard sirens and looked toward the back door. Hammer was standing there.

"I called the cops," he said.

Neither one of us had spoken, but now Gruf said, "Shit. I gotta call Kenny Carlo."

We hurried back inside. Gruf told Hammer to go sit in the dining room and we went to the front counter. Gruf stared at the list of phone numbers taped to the wall, muttering to himself.

"He'll probably still be in his office at the Fairfield store. Shit. I hate trying to call him up there. The phone girls always wanna fuck around, waste my time. . . ." He dialed, and when he had his connection, he asked for Kenny. "This is Joe Ridolfi at store six. It's an emergency."

He waited. Then he said, "Stop it. I need to talk to Kenny. It's urgent." He listened for a second. "Marlene, if I wanted to talk to *you*, I'da asked for you.

This is a fucking emergency. Is Kenny still there or not?"

He waited a minute and finally let go a relieved breath. "Kenny, this is Joe Ridolfi at store six. One of my drivers was just murdered in the back parking lot."

He listened. "They're on the way. We can hear the sirens." He listened. "Shit no, Kenny. Nobody who works here would've done *that*." He listened again, then looked up at me. "Go see if his fanny pack is still on him."

I hustled out to the parking lot. The closest siren sounded like it was less than a block away. I got just close enough to see the Witness's body, squinted at his waist area, and ran back inside. "No."

"Fanny pack's gone," he reported into the mouthpiece. He listened again, then said to me, "Go see which car he logged out, and see if it's in the parking lot."

But I was ahead of him on that one, because while he was talking I happened to look out the side windows. Car four was parked sideways at the front corner of the building, the way we parked when we ran in for another delivery and expected to go right back out. The headlights were on.

I pointed. "It's right out there with the motor still running."

Gruf said, "The car's here." Then he listened into the phone. "Okay. All right." He hung up. "He's on his way here. He's bringing his lawyer."

That was when I realized it was going to be a long night.

Two cops came walking in the front door.

Gruf said, "Hey, Alan. Keith."

The cops, both big, burly men, said hi.

Gruf said, "He's out back, by the Dumpster. His

money bag's gone. The car he was driving is parked up front, motor still running. What do you want us to do?"

The older one, who wore metal-framed glasses and had longer-than-regulation gray hair, thought about it and said, "Who's still here?"

Gruf said, "Waitress, cook, driver, and me."

"Have a cup of coffee. Nobody leaves."

"Okay."

The cops hurried out the front door. Gruf and I walked around through the back to the dining room, picking up Hammer on the way. He'd been standing at the back door, watching the cop cars pull around. We walked out into the darkened dining room.

Gruf turned the lights back on and started a pot of coffee. I stopped beside him at the coffee station and put together another pot. He looked over at me. "Cops'll want some," I explained.

"Yeah. Good idea. Hey, Hammer. Where's Sheila?"

Hammer said, "I don't know. I thought you sent her home."

Gruf said, "Fuck. When was the last time you saw her?"

"I don't know. I think she was in the waitress station right before I went out to empty the grease."

Gruf said, "Well, it's not my problem now. Let the cops handle it."

He slid into a booth and ran his fingers through his black hair. I sat at the next table, stretched my legs out in front of me, and closed my eyes.

Hammer said, "Who do you think did it?"

I looked over at him. He was sitting in the booth across from Gruf, leaning on his elbows.

"Must've been a robbery," Gruf said. His voice was muffled because he had put his head down on his arms.

Hammer said, "Right in our own parking lot? I doubt it."

Gruf looked up at him, irritated. "Who knows who did it? That's for the cops to figure out, okay? Just shut up for once, would ya?"

After a while the big gray-haired cop came in and motioned Hammer out of the booth and over to the table across from me. Hammer grabbed his coffee and scrambled out of the way. The cop slid into the booth where Hammer had been. I poured him a cup and he said thanks.

"How's your dad, Joey?" he said to Gruf. "I've been so busy I haven't stopped in the bar for, jeez, more than a week, I guess."

Gruf said, "Same as always, Alan."

Alan nodded. "Where's your waitress?"

"We don't know. I never told her she could go. She was just gone."

"Did she clock out?"

"I'll check the computer." He went to the waitresses' computer on the coffee counter and punched some keys. "No, she didn't log out."

Alan said, "What time did she go missing?"

"Musta been, maybe eleven forty-five? Twelve?"

Gruf looked at me. I shrugged and nodded. "I saw her in the waitress station around that time. She had a big bug up her ass about something."

Alan said, "Gimme her address. I'll send somebody over to check on her."

"That's probably who did it," Hammer piped up, excitement in his voice. "Her or her husband or her boyfriend."

Alan's head jerked in Hammer's direction.

Gruf muttered, "Oh, jeez, Hammer."

"What makes you say that, son?"

"Because, like, she's got this noodle husband and a big crazy-lookin' boyfriend."

Gruf interrupted him. "Hammer, shut up. This is no time to be running your mouth."

Alan gave Gruf a cold look. "Have there been words between this girl's male friends and the dead boy out there?"

Gruf said, "No. Not that I know about."

Another cop came into the dining room. "Forensic's here," he told Alan.

Alan took off his glasses and held them up to the light. "That was fast." He pulled a napkin out of the holder and began to rub the right lens.

"Yeah. They were having some kind of emergency readiness meeting up at the library."

"That's right. I saw the memo. Okay, good. Hey, send in Cooper and, uh, Bell, I guess. I need some people picked up." The officer hurried out. Alan told Gruf, "I need that waitress's address. We'll wanna ask her some questions."

Gruf gave Hammer a look, then went back to the office, shaking his head. He came back in a minute with a piece of paper and handed it to Alan. By this time two other cops had come in and were standing there, waiting.

Alan handed the paper to them. "Get her and her husband. There's a boyfriend, too. Find out from the girl where he lives and pick him up. Take 'em all in, and keep 'em separated."

Gruf said, "Hey, Brian?"

One of the cops turned back and smiled. "Gruf."

I thought, Does Gruf know every cop in this town on a first-name basis?

Gruf said, "Can you do me a favor? That waitress Sheila? I was gonna fire her at the end of shift tonight. Can you tell her I said not to come in tomorrow?"

Brian nodded and bounced his eyebrows at the other cop as they left.

Alan took a small notebook out of his shirt pocket and thumbed through a couple of pages. "Okay, Joey. His wallet was still in his pants pocket, so we've got his address. We didn't find the murder weapon. Any of you guys see a knife out there?"

We all shook our heads.

"Anybody remember maybe kicking something? Tripping on something?"

We shook our heads no.

He grimaced. "And you say he should've had a money bag?"

Gruf said, "The drivers wear fanny packs buckled around their waists. His isn't there. At least we didn't see—"

"No, it's not there. Okay. Has he been in any disputes with anyone the last few days?"

Hammer said, "Everybody hated him."

"Hammer, shut up. He means if anyone wanted him dead," Gruf said crossly.

"Everybody did. Jackson's brothers threatened him. And you, Terry." Hammer looked at me now, the little shit. "Remember the other night, when you put his head in the sink? And you, Gruf. I heard *you* say you were gonna kill him tonight. I said it myself the other night."

Gruf looked at Alan. "That's just people talking." His voice was flat. Sad. "You know how they do. I was gonna fire him, yeah, but I didn't mean it when I said—"

"But you were mad at him tonight?" Alan said softly.

"Yeah, when he didn't come back from his last delivery. At least, I thought he wasn't back."

"You didn't know his car was up front?"

"No. You can't see that front corner unless you're

over by the side windows. Terry saw it later, after we'd called you guys, when I was calling Kenny Carlo."

Alan sipped his coffee. "Who was the last driver in before the dead boy?"

"I was," I said.

He put the cup down and looked hard at me. "Did you stop your car in the same spot where his car is now?"

"Yeah, I did."

"Was there any sign of him or his car when you pulled in there?"

"No."

"When did you move your car?"

Gruf said, "Terry came in the front door. Brought in his empty bags. I told him there weren't any more deliveries, and he pulled his car around back. Then . . ."

"I parked it, logged it back in, and locked it up."

Gruf said, "Yeah. I saw Terry pull around back, and I was in the back when he came in. From then on, we were all working together inside, cleaning and closing the place. No one went back outside until maybe an hour, hour and a half later, when Hammer went out to dump his grease. That's when he found the body."

"Nobody saw the dead boy park the car out there?"

"No," Gruf said. "We all thought he was still out on his delivery. That's why I was mad. He'd been gone, like, two hours, and the delivery shouldn't have taken more than forty-five minutes, tops. I called the customer and they said he'd been there."

Alan asked about that last delivery, what time the Witness had gone out, and the address of the customer. Gruf punched it up on the computer, copied the address onto an order pad, tore off the sheet, and gave it to him.

"All right, guys," Alan said. "I gotta go outside for a minute, get some people searching the Dumpsters, visit with the forensic boys. Wait here."

Once he was gone, I had to ask. "Dude, how do you know that guy? Is he related or something?"

Gruf sighed. "He might as well be. He and my dad have been buds since kindergarten."

About half an hour later Kenny Carlo came walking in the back hall with his lawyer. I was surprised to see that his lawyer was Bud Hanratty.

Bud grinned at me and said, "Hey, Terry. Kenny, this is the guy who's gonna build me my deck."

Bud was wearing a yellow and white running suit. It looked like it'd never been worn before, and the gut pushing out through the silky material bore out that theory.

Kenny Carlo is a tall, tan, rich-looking guy, with black hair going to gray.

He wore a heavy white T-shirt with a Carlo's logo on the pocket and a pair of black jeans. He grinned at me and I saw about a mouth and a half full of white teeth.

Kenny Carlo said, "No shit? Huh. I've been thinking about a deck. . . ."

"Well, then, this here's your man," Bud told him. Then he said to me, "I was over at Bump's earlier tonight. His deck is lookin' good. He says it's gonna have lights set into the railings? That'll look sharp."

"Yeah. It's a nice effect. Hey, if you're gonna be home Sunday, I could come over and give you your estimate."

"Shit, I don't need an estimate. I know what you're charging Bump. But you can come and measure, or whatever you need to do to get started. I'm ready to go."

"Great," I said.

While he wrote out his address for me and gave me directions, I stood there thinking how weird it was to be talking business when there was a dead kid lying in a pool of blood outside. He asked if I could come early, like around ten, because he wanted to go up to the marina and take his boat out in the afternoon. To me ten was late, practically lunchtime, but I said ten would be fine.

Bud looked at his wristwatch. "Lord love a duck, it's two-thirty in the a.m. Somebody pour me a cup of that coffee." Gruf was on it, getting cups for Bud and Kenny.

"Thanks," Bud said. "Have the cops talked to you boys yet?"

"Alan Bushnell asked us some questions," Gruf said.

"All right, lemme go visit with Alan a minute, see if we can all go home. By the way, none a you did it, didya?" And with that he fixed each of us in turn with the most penetrating stare I've ever been on the receiving end of in my life. Including that time my grandmother caught me in bed with my brother's *Playboy* when I was nine.

We all said no.

Bud said, "Who do you think did?" This question he aimed at Gruf.

Gruf said, "No idea. I guess it was a robbery."

Bud said, "Right here in the parking lot? I doubt it."

"That's exactly what *I* said," Hammer said triumphantly.

"Didya now?" Bud said, and flashed him a smile. "Bright boy."

Hammer turned to Gruf and gloated.

Chapter 9

The next morning I had trouble dragging the bones out of bed. I hit snooze twice on my new clock radio, but I had to wake up so much just to find the damn snooze button that the third time I just kept rolling until I was standing under a very hot shower.

Danny and I were getting our first cups of coffee in Brewster's, talking about the murder in hushed voices, when I was surprised to see Gruf walk in. He looked tired.

"Fuck are *you* doin' here?" I slid over to make room for him.

"Thought I'd tag along today and watch you work. If you don't mind."

It was strange seeing Gruf in something other than his black Carlo's T-shirt. He was wearing a very cool T-shirt in a strange stone-washed red color. The fabric was a little heavier than what you usually see in T-shirts. It looked expensive. I like my plaid flannels, but it was a nice-looking shirt.

I said, " 'Course you can. But I might put you to work."

"That's okay with me."

About that time, I heard a rumbling sound and looked out the front windows in time to see Bump's Harley roll into a spot next to my truck.

He came in and slid in next to Danny. He told us

he'd heard the news on his radio. He was furious. Sputtering. He nodded when Mary held up the coffeepot.

He wanted to hear what had happened. Every detail. While Gruf told him, he fixed up his coffee, blew across its surface, and sipped carefully, all the while making a visible effort to calm himself down. When Gruf was finished, Bump set the cup down and said tightly, "Somebody thinks they can come in here and do one of *my* boys?"

His words were garbled because he was so mad, but I understood exactly what he meant. It was personal for him. I felt some of that, too, even though I hadn't been working for Carlo's nearly as long as he had. Who thought they could come to Carlo's, where *we* worked, and rob and kill somebody? Even if it was only the Witness, who nobody really knew and nobody really liked, he still wore the black Carlo's T-shirt. He was still one of *ours*.

Gruf said, "I swear to God, I'm gonna get whoever did it. Even if I get fired, which I probably will . . ."

Bump said, "Why would Kenny fire you? It's not like *you* had any control over it."

Gruf raked his fingers through his hair. "Come on. I thought he'd fire me after Carrie's accident, or whatever it was. But he will now for sure. If I was him, I would. But really, that's not important. What's important is, maybe I coulda done something to keep that kid from getting killed. If I'd seen his car through the side windows. If I'd checked sooner . . ."

Bump said, "That's bullshit. What're you supposed to do, stand at those side windows all night?" Bump leaned forward. "Listen. If it was a robbery, they coulda dragged him out of his car when he opened the door. Drag him back to the Dumpster, rip off the fanny pack, cut his throat, and they're gone. Coulda been done in less than a minute. Nobody expects you to be standing at the side windows every minute of the night. Gimme a break!"

I said, "What time did you finally get outa there last night?"

"Not long after you did. I just finished up my paperwork. Kenny and the lawyer were still there when I left."

I said, "Oh, yeah, Bump. Guess who Kenny Carlo's lawyer is."

Bump nodded. "Bud Hanratty. Yeah, I know."

After breakfast, Gruf rode with me over to Bump's house. On the way we stopped at a convenience store called Petey's and I bought a couple sixes of Coke to stash in Bump's refrigerator. Gruf liked my truck. He drove an old puke-green Jeep which he claimed to love, even though it had no heater and no windows to speak of.

Bump apologized for taking off right away, but said he had business to take care of. He loaded some stuff from his garage into his truck and left. I continued framing up the deck and Gruf stayed right with me, watching to see how everything was done and asking questions. You could tell he was preoccupied with the murder, but he paid attention to what I was doing, and whenever he could anticipate what I was gonna do, he jumped in and helped. He seemed to pick things up fast.

Bump came back with his truck loaded with different stuff than what he'd left with. He unloaded it into the garage and had just enough time to shower and get dressed for work. Once he'd left for Carlo's, Gruf and I broke for lunch.

Gruf had brought tuna-salad sandwiches and a bag of chips. I had a couple ham and cheeses and a bag of Doritos. I brought us each out a Coke.

Gruf said, "I *knew* I'd like this kind of work. I wanna learn it. I wanna keep coming, okay?"

I said, "No problem. You can be my manual laborer." I grinned at him.

He stopped chewing and laughed. "Manual laborer," he repeated, laughing.

He looked at me, thinking it over. "Yeah. I'll be your manual laborer. I've always wanted to learn how to do stuff like this. It'll be my backup, in case Kenny fires me. Okay?"

I said, "All good. I already have another job lined up for after this one. For that lawyer, Bud Hanratty. I can't pay you much . . ."

He waved his hand and grinned. "I'm not *worth* much. Don't start paying me now, anyway. I don't know what I'm doing. You can pay me a little when we start on Hanratty's deck. By then I'll be able to help."

I thought about mentioning that you don't learn carpentry by working one little deck job, but I let it go. He was smart. He'd find out for himself if he didn't already know it.

We were just finishing our lunches when a black-and-white came crawling up Bump's driveway. I saw that Crown Vic and my stomach started to go into a knot, but Gruf said, "Hey, it's Alan. Maybe they've caught the killer already." He got up off the woodpile we were sitting on and walked toward the car. I had a feeling what was about to happen, so I stayed where I was.

The two cops said hi to Gruf, but their eyes stayed on me. I stood slowly, keeping my hands out away from my body so no one could make any mistakes about what my intentions were.

Alan Bushnell and the other cop came toward me. Alan stopped right in front of me. Sunlight glinted off the right lens of his wire-rimmed glasses. He said, "Hi, Terry. We'd like you to take a little ride with us. You're not gonna give us any trouble, are you?"

Gruf said, "What are you *doing*, Alan? What's going on?"

I said, "Gruf. Back off." I made eye contact with Alan. "No trouble at all. I'm the friendliest guy you'll ever meet."

Alan said, "Glad to hear it. Then I won't need these." He looped the dangling pair of cuffs he held back onto his belt.

Gruf looked stunned. He said, "Alan . . ."

I said, "Gruf. My keys are in the truck. Go ahead and take off. I'll catch ya later."

Alan said, "Yeah. I wouldn't wait if I were you, Gruf." Then he motioned me toward the black-and-white. He opened the back door for me and I folded myself into the backseat.

At the Spencer police station, Alan pulled open a door to a little interrogation room and motioned me inside. "Go ahead and take a seat there, Terry. I'll be right with ya." He watched until I sat down at the little beat-up table. Then he did something with the doorknob, stepped outside, and pushed the door closed.

I ran my eyes over the beige concrete block walls, the shitty green tile floor, the smeared one-way mirror, and the scarred wooden table. I wondered what he'd done with the doorknob. Whether he'd fixed it so it would lock me in. After a few minutes, my curiosity got the better of me. I got up, took the two steps to the door, gently turned the knob, and gently pushed. It opened. I leaned my head against the door and let it open enough so I could see down the hall.

Alan Bushnell was out in the big main room, standing at a desk sideways to me. He was trying to load a tape into an ancient-looking tape recorder. A movement in the distance caught my eye. I just had time to catch a glimpse of Gruf standing out in the lobby, looking through the dispatcher's window, before an officer stepped up to talk to him.

I looked back at Alan. He gave the tape recorder a slap. Then he brought a hand up to rub his forehead like he had a headache. I gently closed the door and tried to get comfortable at the table. I had a feeling this was going to be tedious.

After a few more minutes, Alan came in with his tape recorder and a file folder with some papers stuffed inside. He set the recorder on the table, plugged it in, and positioned the mike. Then he took a seat opposite me and made a show of lining the folder up straight with the edge of the table. He turned the recorder on and did the usual for-the-record bullshit. When he was done, he looked up at me.

"Terry, Terry, Terry."

I leaned back on the chair, my arms folded across my chest, and watched the reels on the tape recorder. The way the thing was built, the reels were enclosed in casing, which put them in shadow, so I couldn't really see them clearly. But it didn't look to me like they were turning. It looked to me like they were just sitting there.

"Terry. Been out of jail what? A month now?"

I shrugged. "Give or take."

"Kind of a *violent* guy, aren't ya?"

"I wouldn't say that."

He opened the file folder and looked at the top page. "Got a problem with substances. Heavy drinker. Drug abuser."

I said, "I *used* to have a problem with substances. I don't anymore."

He smirked. "That's what you told Nelma Wolfert."
He looked up at me. "She likes you, by the way.
Nelma. She thinks you're gonna straighten yourself
out."

I said, "She's right."

"Uh-huh." He thumbed through some papers,
found something, seemed to be reading. "Ed Hanus
was a little prick, wasn't he? Got himself up a lot of
people's noses."

I considered. "He had his problems."

He let a little time go by. Then he slapped the
folder closed and looked me in the eye. "Look, Terry.
I know you've got a bad problem with alcohol. You
drink too much. And I know you use drugs. And when
you get high and stoned, you get violent. Things happen that you can't really control. Like last night. That
wouldn't have happened if you'd been sober. Things
just got a little out of hand."

I said, "Cut the crap. I haven't had a drop of alcohol
or a molecule of any controlled substance since that
night in that bar. Ask anyone who knows me. They'll
tell you."

"You own a knife, Terry?"

I had to stop and think. "I *used* to have one. My
brother P.J. stole it from me. Right before he got engaged. That was, jeez, ten years ago. Matter of fact,
I'm glad you reminded me. Now that I think about it,
I'd like to press charges."

He almost laughed. He covered it by coughing. He
muttered, "Everybody's a comedian today. First the
King brothers and now you." He looked up at me. "This
isn't a good time to be a comedian, Terry. Things don't
look good for you, you know. You're still on probation
for that other thing, that bar thing, and now this."

He watched me. I sat there and waited. His remark

about the King brothers didn't hit me until later, when I remembered *Jackson's* last name was King.

"Look, Terry. What you need to do now is let me help you. I *can* help you. And I will. But you've got to be completely honest with me. Right now. Okay?"

I nodded. "Okay."

"Okay. Good. So tell me what happened last night."

"Somebody murdered Ed Hanus."

He frowned. "Somebody? Come on, Terry. You can do better than that."

I said, "No, Alan, I can't."

He stiffened. "You don't call me Alan. You call me *Sergeant* Bushnell. And it's time for you to wise up. We *know* you did this."

"Is that right."

"Yeah, that *is* right. I've got some bad news for ya, kid. We've got a witness, and we've got solid forensic evidence. Your ass is grass. It's time for you to tell me the truth."

I was trying not to get steamed, but my heart was pounding way too much blood to my head. "Here's the truth. *General.* You don't have a witness against me, and you don't have any evidence, either, because I didn't do it. When you looked up my record, you musta thought it was your lucky day, but you were wrong. You're wasting your time."

We had a staring contest. Then he reached over and turned off the tape recorder (which it had never been on. I was sure about that now), scooped up his file folder, and left the room.

A few minutes later, another cop stuck his head in the door and said curtly, "Saltz. You're free to go. Don't leave Grand County."

Well, damn. What about my big dream holiday in Cancun? I stepped out into the hallway. There was no sign of Alan. I walked across the big, open, desk-filled room toward the front, stopped to wait for the dispatcher to buzz me through, pulled open the heavy door, and stepped out into the lobby.

Gruf stood up and grinned.

"I was about to call down to Carlo's. Ask Bump for Bud Hanratty's home number."

He followed me through the front door, out onto the sidewalk. He flipped me my keys and motioned down the street to our right. I saw the roof of my truck sticking up above the other parked cars. We stood on the sidewalk for a few minutes watching the traffic. I used the time to settle myself down. Every once in a while I sensed Gruf glancing at me.

Finally I said, "Well, that was interesting."

"Alan came out and asked me if I'd ever seen you drink or use drugs. I told him I know for a fact that you haven't used anything stronger than coffee and Marlboros since you got out of jail."

"Thanks."

He shrugged and let go with a nervous chuckle. "You know, Alan was probably a dickhead to you in there, but once this thing's over and you get to know him, he's not that bad of a guy."

I wasn't sure about that, but I said, "Can't really blame him. As soon as he saw my record . . . Well, fuck it. Let's get back to work."

Gruf and I put in a few more hours at Bump's. When we got to Carlo's, the day crew told us the place'd been wild since they'd opened that morning. There'd even been TV news crews there in the afternoon. I was glad I hadn't been around. Everybody'd heard about the Witness by that time, and it was all anyone talked about. The employees, the customers in the dining room, and the delivery customers were all talking about it in low whispery voices.

Instead of sitting out in the dining room drinking coffee before shift change, Gruf went back in the office to type up some notices for the employees.

He posted them in the back room and on the back door. The one on the back door said:

THIS DOOR IS TO BE KEPT CLOSED AFTER DARK UNTIL FURTHER NOTICE. NO ONE IS TO GO INTO THE BACK PARKING LOT AFTER DARK FOR ANY REASON UNLESS ACCOMPANIED BY EITHER GRUF OR TERRY. DRIVERS ARE TO USE THE FRONT ENTRANCE ONLY. PARK ALL CARS IN THE FRONT PARKING LOT. EMPLOYEES LEAVING THE PREMISES AFTER WORK MUST BE ACCOMPANIED TO THEIR CARS.

The sign in the back room, right above the car logs, said:

DRIVERS: BE AWARE OF YOUR SURROUNDINGS AT ALL TIMES WHILE MAKING DELIVERIES. IF YOU SEE ANY SUSPICIOUS PERSON OR ACTIVITY, OR SUSPECT YOU ARE BEING FOLLOWED, DRIVE DIRECTLY BACK TO THE STORE AND REPORT TO GRUF. CUSTOMERS ARE BEING TOLD TO HAVE ALL OUTSIDE LIGHTS ON. IF YOU GO TO A HOUSE THAT DOES NOT HAVE OUTDOOR LIGHTS ON, DO NOT LEAVE YOUR CAR. GO ON TO YOUR NEXT DELIVERY. IF ANYTHING DOESN'T SEEM RIGHT WHILE YOU ARE AWAY FROM THE STORE, TURN AROUND AND COME DIRECTLY BACK IN. USE THE FRONT PARKING LOT AND THE FRONT DOOR ONLY. BE AWARE. STAY SAFE.

All the employees were edgy. It seemed like every few minutes somebody dropped a glass or a plate. Each time, Gruf yelled, "I hope it was *dirty!*" to lighten the mood, but all the crashes and clatters made everybody even jumpier. There were little irritable flare-ups all night.

On my deliveries, it took some ingenuity to keep from getting trapped in question-and-answer sessions at every front door. I developed a technique where I gave an all-knowing half smile and said, "We've been told not to talk about it." People nodded wisely and let me go when I said that. Tips were great.

The only thing that lightened the atmosphere for me all night was that one of the times I came in to drop off empty bags and get a new delivery, Hammer was standing in Gruf's place at the front counter.

I said. "Where's Gruf?"

"He's in the shitter. He said for you to take these." He pushed a couple of orders to me. He gave me a huge grin, twinkled his fingers at me, and said loudly, "Fly like the wind, Muzzy."

The front girls, who were still hustling around making pizzas, taking phone orders, slicing and box-ing pizzas, and doing all the other stuff they did, burst out laughing. Debby, who was standing at the jukebox punching numbers, also burst out laughing. She turned around to look at me, laughing, but she had a look on her face like she half expected me to be mad.

I had no idea what Muzzy meant. I'd never heard the word before. My best guess was that it had some-thing to do with my flannel shirts, ponytail, and ap-preciation for the vocal and instrumental stylings of Mr. Pink and Mr. Floyd. Or maybe it had something to do with my criminal past. But it struck me that everybody else had a nickname, and Muzzy sounded like as good a one as any. I thought, Lemme just goof on these guys and see if I can get anybody calling me Muzzy. Before I checked out later that night, I crossed out Terry on the schedule and wrote in Muzzy. Now I was aka Muzzy Saltz.

We managed to get into closing without any drivers going missing. Debby got her waitress station closed fast. She was ready to go while we were still putting away dishes. Gruf walked her to her car.

While we were cleaning, Gruf said, "Hey. You know that guy who was in here earlier? He was standing at the front counter when you came in from that last run north. I introduced you to him."

"Oh, yeah. What about him?"

"He was Tiffany's dad." He shoved a tray of dirties into the dishwasher.

I said, "Who's Tiffany?"

"Front girl. Short, plump, short curly hair?"

I shrugged. I usually didn't bother learning the front girls' names. They were usually gone by the time I finished deliveries.

I said, "So? What about her?"

"Her dad wanted to take her home. He'd told her she had to quit. He got home from work, found out she came in anyway, and went ballistic. Because of the murder."

I said, "Oh, boy."

He said, "Yeah. I brought him back here and showed him the signs on the wall, and I told him no employees were allowed outside after dark without you or me. You walked in just as we got back up front. I pointed you out to him. He was impressed that we're big guys. He said we looked like we could handle ourselves if there was any trouble."

"What does he think? We're gonna get attacked by a gang or something?"

Gruf laughed. "Who knows? But he went home without Tiffany."

"Well, that's good."

He said, "Yeah. But some of those families know each other. They talk."

"What families?"

"The front girls' families. Their parents. I hope this thing gets cleared up fast. Because I have a feeling, if one 'em quits, they're all going to."

Chapter 10

Thursday, Friday, and Saturday went by in a blur of tension and hard work. The grim reality of the Witness's murder settled in hard. On top of that, Gruf was on edge because he expected any minute he was gonna get a call from Kenny Carlo, telling him his services were no longer needed, and I kept expecting Alan to show up and want another chat.

Gruf and I busted our butts at Bump's house, and we managed to get his deck finished Saturday. We threw the breakers, and all the lights and power came on just like they were supposed to do. Bump turned the taps on the hot tub, and the water flowed just like it was supposed to do. I crawled down underneath to make sure nothing was dripping. Everything was nice and tight. Bump was giddy with happiness. I love it when a plan comes together.

Bump paid me the rest of what he owed me for the job. Gruf refused the money I offered him, saying that I could start paying him when we started on Bud's deck. We left as the happy homeowner watched his hot tub fill up with water.

I'd been working at Carlo's seven days a week almost since I started there, so Gruf didn't give me much of an argument when I told him I wanted that Sunday off. All I had to do that Sunday was go measure for Bud's deck. Then I could loaf.

Gruf wanted to come along when I did Bud's estimate. I told him I'd be at Brewster's around eight-
thirty. I got there at eight thirty-five. He was already
in the booth, and my coffee was already poured for
me. We gave our orders to a little dark-haired waitress
whose name tag said Tina. She seemed a little spacey
to me. Not at all like Mary, who mostly only worked
weekdays. So I lowered my expectations.

I noticed Gruf was wearing another one of his cool
T-shirts. This one was a shade of lavender, I think
you'd call it. It was a great-looking shirt. I wondered
again where you get a shirt like that, and I was about
to ask him when Alan Bushnell came walking in with
another cop. They looked ominous in their black uni-
forms. Gruf saw them and waved them over to the
table.

Alan slid in next to me. He's a big guy. Between
the two of us, we pretty much filled up that side of
the booth. His thick leather gun belt creaked loudly
every time he moved. His arm kept bumping me. I
didn't like it.

Alan said, "I saw your vehicles parked out front.
Thought we'd stop in for a cup of coffee. Joey, do
you know John Garvey?"

"Don't think I do," Gruf said.

I thought, How 'bout that? There *is* a cop in this
town he doesn't know. Gruf turned to the younger
cop, who had slid in beside him. "Joe Ridolfi, but
everyone calls me Gruf." They tucked in their elbows
and shook hands.

Alan turned to me. "Terry."

I said, "General." My heart was hammering in my
chest.

Alan said to John, "And this is Terry."

"Terry Saltz," I told the new cop, and reached

across the table to shake hands. Then, for some reason, I said, "But you can call me Muzzy."

Gruf gave me a funny look.

Alan said, "John's new, right out of highway patrol school. Comes from Indiana. Hasn't even found a place to live yet. He's staying over at Hollister's."

Gruf and I grimaced. Spencer only has one motel. Hollister's. It's a rathole. I don't know if it actually has any four-legged rats, but I'd delivered pizza there a few times to some pretty seedy-looking two-legged ones. Who didn't tip.

Alan said, "So, if you know anyone who has an apartment for rent, call the station. We gotta get the boy outa that dump."

"I've got an extra bedroom in my trailer," I said, thinking, See? Nothing to hide here. "Until you find a place." And immediately thought, What the hell are you *doing*? Your roommate smokes pot nonstop every night.

Gruf was looking at me like I'd grown a new penis out the middle of my forehead. But it was too late.

John said, "You do?"

"Sure," I said. "It's not furnished . . ."

"That's no problem," Alan said. "We'll just go see Bump Bellini."

I wrote down the phone number and address on the corner of my place mat, tore it off, and gave it to John.

I said, "We're gonna be busy for a couple hours, but if you call after two or so, I should be home. If you wanna come over and look at it."

Gruf said, "He's renting the trailer from Bump."

Alan said, "That trailer Bump bought off Les Kinzie?"

Gruf nodded.

I thought again about how everybody in this town

seemed to know everybody else and everything *about* everybody else.

Alan said, "I know that trailer. I busted Les Kinzie in it." He chuckled like it was a fond memory and gave me a look I didn't like. He said to John, "It's nice. We'll get you a mattress and all that shit from Bump, and you'll be able to move in this afternoon." He looked back to me. "If that's okay with you."

I shrugged, feeling a little sick about the whole thing. "Sure."

"Gosh, I sure appreciate this," John said. "Terry, is it?"

"Muzzy."

He nodded. "Anyway. Thank you."

"Not a problem," I said, even though I was pretty sure it was gonna be.

We left Gruf's Jeep in the Brewster's parking lot and took my truck. I stopped by the trailer first, to let Danny know the terrible thing I had done. He reacted about like I expected ("Holy shit! What were you *thinking*?"). Then we went to look for Bud's house.

Gruf read off Bud's directions and told me where to turn. We found the right street and came to a stop in front of the house.

"You reading that number right?" I said. "This can't be it."

Gruf double-checked. "This is it. It's not exactly what I expected."

"Me, either."

We sat there looking up the hillful of ugly overgrown bushes and weeds at the ratty yellow bungalow. It was good sized, sprawling actually, but it was just how you say, plug ugly.

"Putting one of our beautiful decks on this thing

would be like putting a thong bikini on Sheila Werbel," Gruf observed.

I had to agree. "But maybe he's decided to fix the place up. Maybe the deck's the first step." I put the truck into first and turned into the gravel driveway.

"Maybe," Gruf said. "What the fuck, as long as his check clears."

Laughing, we climbed onto the falling-down back porch and knocked on the lopsided screen door. We had a long wait. Obviously we woke him up. He eventually came padding barefoot to the door, still tying on a sad-looking navy terry-cloth robe. What hair he had was a mess.

"Fuckin' hellshit!" he said, blinking at us. "What the puking time is it?"

I took a second to admire his swearage, then said, "It's ten, Bud. We can come back if you want."

"No, no." He held the door open. "Come on. Lemme just get some tonic in me and I'll be right with you."

We followed him around a breakfast island and into his kitchen, which had three garbage bags spilling all over one corner and stuff piled on every surface. The stuff included garbage, dirty dishes, groceries, and all manner of what looked like legal files, mail, magazines, newspapers, and articles of clothing.

It wasn't all that shocking to me. In fact, from then on, I never thought of Bud as a guy in a suit again. You know? You can't help liking a guy who lives like that. And in fact, Bud's mess was a lot like what I'd grown up with. But Gruf looked horrified.

Bud got a can of tomato juice out of his refrigerator and stood at a counter with his back to us. He got busy pouring stuff into a blender. I saw Tabasco and ReaLemon and vodka. There might have been pepper involved. He pushed the button and the concoction turned the inside of the pitcher red. When it was done, he tossed the lid in the sink, turned around, and drank a slug right out of the pitcher.

"Ach!" he cried, and gave his head a sharp shake. "Hey. Terry. I hear Alan Bushnell rousted you the other day."

"Yeah."

"Don't let him do it again. Lemme find you a card."

He began to rummage around through the piles of crap on his counters, then the piles on his little kitchen table. Eventually he came up with what he was looking for, a business card, which he flipped it over and wrote a couple of phone numbers on the back.

He said, "If he wants to talk to you again, you call *me*. Got it?"

I nodded.

He said, "Okay! Where were we? Yeah, the magazine picture." He searched the pile on his kitchen table again and came up with a magazine picture of exactly what he wanted his deck to look like. It wasn't anything like Bump's deck, but that was okay. I explained that the built-in barbeque and benches, and the two levels, were gonna cost him a lot more, and he said he didn't care what it cost. That was what he wanted.

We left Bud drinking his foul tonic in the kitchen and went out to take our measurements. I showed Gruf how I figured out my materials list. When it was finished, I asked Bud if I could use the phone to check current prices on the wood, brick, and electrical.

I figured out my labor, explaining it to Gruf as I did it, and I gave the figures to Bud. I told him I needed to check in with my plumber buddy and see what kind of a break he could get me on the hot tub. But he didn't happen to be home that morning, or at least he wasn't answering the phone.

Bud was dressed and wide-awake now, and happy as a little kid. He wrote me out a check for the whole thing—materials, labor, everything—on the spot. I couldn't believe it. He said when I got the rest of the prices, or anything else I needed, just let him know. It was the most money I'd ever had in my life. I tucked the check carefully into my wallet.

I asked if I could take the magazine picture with me, so I could plan out the project. I told him that if Bump could get me the backhoe again, we'd be back in the morning to tear off the old porch and grade and dig the footers, unless it rained. He was thrilled. Delirious uh.

We stopped at Bump's. Alan and John hadn't been there yet, but they had called, and Bump was expecting them anytime. Bump was happy about selling the new cop a bedroom suite. I asked him if he could get me the backhoe again, and he said he'd drop it at Bud's later that day.

"Want some lunch?" Gruf asked as I backed out of Bump's driveway.

"Sure. Where you wanna go?"

"Let's go to the bar. My dad has French dip for the lunch special."

I had no idea what bar he was talking about or what French dip was, but I said, "Great."

The bar turned out to be Smitty's Bar, over on Third in the next block from Carlo's. Smitty turned out to be Smitty Ridolfi, Gruf's dad, who looked just like his son except his face was wrinkled and his long, wavy hair was snow-white.

French dip turned out to be the most bodacious roast-beef sandwich I ever had, on a buttered, toasted bun, with roast-beef juice on the side to dip in. The rest of the plate was filled with a side order of crispy, tasty, seasoned potato wedges.

Gruf had a High Life. I had an iced tea, which tasted fresh brewed. With a wedge of nice fresh lemon, too. And it was all on the house. Smitty leaned on the bar and watched us eat. He called his son Joey. Apparently Gruf's nickname hadn't caught on with the old man.

Smitty said, "Joey, Alan was in here a while ago. He said they searched that waitress's apartment this morning."

Gruf said, "Sheila Werbel's? What were they looking for at *her* place?"

Smitty rubbed his handsome chin. "The murder weapon—the knife—and, uh, something else. Uh, I know he said . . ."

I said, "Probably the fanny pack the kid was wearing."

Smitty snapped his fingers. "Right. The fanny pack. But they didn't find anything."

Gruf said, "What else did he say? What else are they doing?"

"They were going to search some other guy's apartment and the Dumpsters at both places. That's about all he told me."

Gruf said, "Probably that other guy, Sheila's ugly boyfriend."

Smitty shrugged. He leaned on the bar. We chewed.

Smitty said to me, "Joey's been telling us about the deck building."

I had just gnawed off a giant bite of roast-beef sandwich, so I could only nod as the juice ran down my chin. I'm a filthy animal.

Smitty said, "Joey's trying to talk me into adding a big deck onto the back of the bar. And a volleyball pit."

"That'd be pretty cool," I said around my mouthful of sandwich.

Smitty watched me chew. "I'm considering it."

After lunch I dropped Gruf off at his Jeep and headed reluctantly out to the trailer. It was time to face the music with my pissed-off roommate.

Danny rose from his La-Z-Boy and gave me a cold look when I walked in.

He said, "A *cop*?" He looked really disgusted with me.

"I know. I'm sorry. I was thinking it'd make me look less like a suspect."

"A *cop!*" he said again, grimacing and nodding his head at me.

"It's only until he can find a place. It's not like he's gonna live with us forever."

He turned on his heel, walked back to his bedroom, and slammed the door. I felt bad.

They came, Alan driving Bump's truck, which was loaded with John's new bedroom furniture. John followed in a black Geo. Danny's bedroom door stayed shut. Alan, John, and I unloaded the truck and got John's bed all set up. Alan took a long look around the trailer before he finally left.

John carried two grocery bags in from his car and set them on the kitchen counter. "I stopped off at the store," he said as he started stashing groceries in the refrigerator. "I haven't had a chance to cook in months. Mind if I cook supper tonight? If you and your roommate don't already have plans?"

"That'd be cool," I said. "About all we know how to do is steak."

He laughed. "My dad's a chef, so I practically grew up in the kitchen. While other kids were playing with LEGOs, I was learning to make white sauce. Hey, listen." He opened cabinets until he found the one that held two cans of green beans. He lined up several boxes of pasta on the lower shelf.

"If you guys smoke weed, I mean, I used to burn a bowl myself now and then. I can't now, of course. The department has random drug testing. But you guys go ahead if you want to, as long as you don't tell me where you got it. I'll just go in my bedroom, so I don't get the secondary. If you do other stuff, don't do it while I'm around, but I got no problem with weed."

With that, Danny's bedroom door flew open and he strolled out, smiling. "Hi. I'm Danny."

My jaw dropped and I turned around to look at him.

Danny gave me a stern look. "You shoulda told me he was here. You shoulda woke me up."

I just stared at him.

"I woulda helped move him in," he continued shamelessly.

I pulled it together and made the introductions. They shook hands.

Danny said, "So. What's for supper?"

John grinned. "How does shrimp fettuccine sound?"

Danny said, "Awesome."

John folded up the last empty grocery bag. I took it from him, folded it with the other one, and tucked them onto the top shelf of the broom closet. Then he said he wanted to carry the rest of his stuff in and get everything put away, and hurried outside.

Me and Danny stood in the kitchen, him grinning at me and me shaking my head at him. Then we bounced our eyebrows a couple of times and went out to help carry. We carried all John's stuff in and he stowed everything away. Then he got busy in the kitchen.

Danny and I loitered while he cooked, awkwardly answering his awkward questions about where we were from, how long we'd been in Spencer, what we did for a living. That kind of thing. Guys getting acquainted.

At supper, after Danny and I made a big fuss over how good everything was, John said he felt like he'd moved right into the middle of the department's hottest case, having me for a roommate.

I was caught with a large mouthful of fettuccine, and I choked for a second, because I thought he was telling me I was still the prime suspect. I struggled to finish swallowing, and stared at him.

"Dude. I didn't kill that kid."

He waved his hand at me. "No, no. That wasn't what I meant. I meant you were one of the ones that found his body. Weren't you?"

I said, "Oh. Yeah," and laughed it off, but I was beginning to feel like I had a big red arrow hanging in the air above me, pointing at my head.

Danny said, "All the girls over at Carlo's are scared shitless."

I looked at him in surprise. He shrugged. "I talk to them when I go in to eat. Those little girls that work in front, answering the phones and making the pizzas? I'm surprised they haven't all quit so they can stay home safe with their mommies and daddies. The only thing that's keeping them working is they all have the hots for Gruf."

John nodded. "I don't blame them for being scared. I know Alan Bushnell's frustrated. From what I hear, the folks they're most interested in won't even answer any questions. One's a waitress?"

Danny said wisely, "Ah. Sheila Werbel."

The way he said it made me laugh. Like he was a cagey old palm reader or something.

John said, "That's right. You guys know her. Well, they're trying to get information from her and some people she's involved with, but they aren't getting anywhere."

The wise old fortune teller said, "Hmm."

I said, "So they're pretty sure it was one of them?"

John said, "They're making themselves look mighty suspicious by being so evasive. I can tell you who Alan hopes *didn't* do it."

I said, "Who's that?"

"Some John Doe who out of the blue said, 'Hey, I think I'll rob me a pizza driver.' If it was someone like that, they might never find him. If it was something like that, Alan's got nothing."

After supper, Danny and John watched TV for a while. Then Danny went back to his room for half an hour and I detected the faint skunky smell of weed. I sat at the kitchen table, drawing out plans for Bud's deck, getting it all staged out the way I like to do.

Danny drifted back to his La-Z-Boy and settled in for some mellow TV viewage. John said something about the lack of available apartments in town. Danny said, "Fuck. Just stay here. There's plenty of room. Huh, Terry."

I tried not to laugh at him. "Yeah. We'd have to be crazy to throw out a guy who can cook like you."

John said, "If you guys are sure . . ."

"Hell yeah," Danny said.

"Okay, then, gosh. That'd be great."

Chapter 11

The bedrooms Danny and John slept in were at one end of the trailer. Mine was at the other end. John liked to go outside and run before his shower, while Danny sleepwalked to his shower straight from bed, like I did. John and Danny had no problem with sharing the bathroom at their end.

John was all good with eating breakfast at Brewster's, so that first workday morning we made us a little convoy into town, John all spiffed up in his black cop uniform and following our trucks in his little black Geo.

Gruf was already there. This morning his T-shirt was a light pumpkin color. Those awesome T-shirts of his were killing me, but once again I didn't get around to asking him where he got them, because Bump came sauntering in right after us. Alan Bushnell came in right behind Bump.

Alan gave me a nod, then said, "Hey. Why don't we push some tables together so there's room for everybody?"

We abandoned our booth and pushed three tables together. Alan settled in at one end and opened out his newspaper. I wondered with a sinking feeling if Alan intended to make himself a regular breakfast companion.

Gruf, who was sitting near him, said, "Alan. Can I see the sports?"

Mary moved around the tables taking orders and pouring coffee. We all sat there in silence for what felt like a long time. I sure as hell didn't feel chatty with Alan sitting there. I guessed the others didn't, either.

Alan had just finished his shift. John was just about to start, being assigned to first shift while he trained.

John refolded his newspaper and said, "Quiet night, Alan?"

"Had a domestic over on Washington. Drunk hubby, married to a fire-breathing witch. He's sleeping it off in jail. A few kids drinking over in Bennett's Park. That's about it."

Gruf said, "Fuckin' Tribe. Scored seven runs in the bottom of the ninth to break the Twins' hearts." He folded the paper. "What's going on about the murder, Alan? Got a suspect?"

Alan glanced my way as he sipped his coffee. Little hairs crawled around on the back of my neck. He said, "*Every*body's a suspect. No standouts yet."

Gruf said, "What happened when you questioned Sheila Werbel? Why'd she leave Carlo's so fast that night?"

Alan said, "No comment."

Gruf hooted. "Oh, jeez, Alan. This isn't exactly national security stuff I'm asking about. I wanna know what's goin' on."

Alan folded up his newspaper and tucked it under his coffee saucer. He gave Gruf a long, thoughtful stare and glanced around to make sure no one was trying to eavesdrop. Then he leaned in and said quietly, "She said she heard Boyd Chesnik . . . you call him what?"

I said, "Hammer."

"Hammer. Right. Said she heard Hammer calling the police and got scared. Doesn't really hold up in my opinion. If you're scared, do you go running out alone across a dark empty parking lot? Said her husband, Lenny, wasn't there when she got home. He wasn't there when the boys picked her up. They found him sitting in Taco Bell."

Taco Bell was over on Third, less than a block from Carlo's. Gruf said, "Was the boyfriend home?"

Alan shook his head. "Claims he was drinking in Smitty's until closing, but nobody remembers him being there. We picked him up the next morning."

"Man. This coffee hits the spot," Danny said to me. I nodded.

"What's the boyfriend's name?" Bump asked.

Alan pulled out his little notebook and thumbed pages. "Fred Oatley."

Mary came out balancing a tray loaded with half our breakfasts. Another waitress followed with the rest.

Bump nodded. "He *looks* like a Fred Oatley."

"Who does?" Mary asked, setting my number four in front of me.

"Fred Oatley," Bump said.

She said, "Okay, *don't* tell me," and went back for another coffeepot.

I looked over my three eggs, corned beef hash, hash browns, sausage, and Texas toast, and my mouth watered.

Gruf said, "If Fred Oatley was in the bar until closing that night, someone would remember. Hell, they'd all remember."

"That's the way I see it," Alan said.

John said, "Do any of them have criminal records?"

Alan said, "All three of 'em do."

"For what?" Bump asked.

"She's got a shoplifting. So does the husband. The

boyfriend has a juvie stolen car, which I busted him for, and an assault."

We all looked at each other around the table. I thought, well, thank God there are some other outlaws besides *me* in this mix. Then I got busy with my food like a healthy growing boy. Mary came around with the coffee.

Bump said, "Well, what's their story? How do they explain everything?"

Alan shook his head. "They don't. They aren't explaining anything. The three of them are obviously hiding something, but damned if I know what."

Everybody ate quietly for a while. I began to think about Sheila Werbel. In my mind, I found myself calling her Repuda. Repuda the Beauta. I wondered why she'd been so uptight that night, right before we found the Witness. When she was all smoking and chewing on her thumbnail.

Bump was sitting next to me. He nudged me. "I got your backhoe delivered out to Bud's for ya, Terry."

I said, "Great. Thanks. Same machine as last time?"

He nodded.

I said, "I guess I oughtta think about buying one of my own, if I keep getting new deck customers."

He nodded and shoveled another bite of French toast in past his mustache.

I had a sudden thought. "Matter fact, that one you have would be perfect." I slurped coffee.

He nodded. "I left the trailer out there."

I looked at him. "Uh. The trailer?"

"For hauling the backhoe around."

"Oh. Oh, okay." I studied him. He sure was interested in his French toast.

"Whose backhoe *is* that, anyway?"

He looked at me, his green eyes all business. "Mine now. *Yours* when you pay me for it."

I laughed. I love that guy. "Bump, you rat bastard, you got a sale. Can you work out a payment plan for me?"

"Sure," he said. "Pay me when you get the money. That enough of a plan for you?"

Me and Gruf left first. I was anxious to get away from Alan, and we were both anxious to get to work.

Nobody was home at Bud's. On the back door was a note with the back door key taped to it. It said, basically, Howdy, make ourselves at home. I put my six of Coke in Bud's refrigerator.

It took a while to tear off the old back porch because of the warped boards, bent nails, stripped screws, and all that sort of thing. It was tedious. I drove a big-ass splinter into the heel of my hand. There was swearing involved. We finally got the porch loose from the house; then we took it apart and piled it out by the front curb. After that we went to work on the footers, me driving the backhoe and Gruf shaping the footer holes with a shovel.

After a bit he wanted to play with the backhoe, so I let him do some grading while I framed the footers up. Then we sat down to eat a late lunch and wait for the cement truck.

Billy Grabowski was the cement-truck driver again. We made quick work of getting the footers poured all nice and neat. When we were done, Billy and Gruf shared a bowl and we shot the shit for a while.

Billy let go a lungful and passed the bowl to Gruf. "There was something on the news about Spencer. Some pizza driver got murdered or something."

Gruf and I looked at each other. Gruf scraped the edges of the bowl with his thumbnail, then tamped it down and relit.

I said, "Dude worked at Carlo's. So do we."

Billy said, "No shit! You guys *knew* him?"

We nodded.

Billy said, "Wow! Did they get the guy that did it?"

Gruf said, "Not yet."

Billy shook his head. "Man! That'd freak me out. I bet everybody in the place is freaking."

Gruf passed the bowl back to Billy. "I know *I* am."

I looked at him. "You are?"

He said, "Shit, yeah. Aren't you? I keep dreaming that the back parking lot's full of bodies, and there's murderers hiding in the walk-in waiting to pick my employees off. Don't try to tell me *you* don't jump at every little noise when you walk people out to their cars at night."

I just shrugged. I realized guiltily that I'd been a little too wrapped up in my own worries and hadn't noticed how worried Gruf was. Billy left and we went back to work, but I kept on thinking about the murder. I found myself wondering about Mr. and Mrs. Sheila Werbel and good ol' Fred Oatley.

When we broke for a smoke, I said, "I've been thinking about Sheila. Does she have a final paycheck coming?"

He looked over. "Yeah. It's sitting in the office safe."

I said, "Well, I was thinking. Sheila and her husband and her boyfriend won't talk to the cops, but maybe she'll talk to us. You and me. If you pour on some of that Ridolfi charm."

He grinned. "Tell her to come in for her check? Try asking her a few questions?"

"That's what I was thinking."

He rubbed his chin. "That's an idea. What've we got to lose? I'll get the number from Barb and call her."

He went inside and came out a few minutes later. Grimacing.

I said, "You look like you just ate something very, very bad."

He shook his head. "It sure doesn't take much to get *her* going. Yech! Anyway, I asked her to come in for her check. She said she'll come in tomorrow night around closing time. I know *I'll* be counting the seconds."

Carlo's was pretty busy for a Monday night. When I came in from my first delivery after supper break, Hammer was standing at the front counter all excited. "Some babe was just in here askin' for you. Man, was she *hot*!"

I stood there staring at him, thinking. Then I groaned. Marylou. It had to be her. Who else *could* it be?

"I told her you were out on delivery. She said she'd come back."

What the hell did the Bitch want with me now? How did she even know where to find me? Oh, shit. It was the note I'd left for my brother P.J. When I burgled his house for my power tools, I'd left a note telling him he could reach me through Carlo's. But I'd specifically said not to tell anyone else, especially the Bitch, where I was. Note to self: Beat crap out of P. J. first opportunity.

"Well?" Hammer was practically drooling. "Who is she, Muzzy?"

"If she comes back, tell her I don't work here anymore. Are those deliveries for me?"

But when I came back in, her little blue Honda was parked in front, so I pulled around to the back and snuck in the back door. I peeked into the kitchen. Hammer was pulling an order of chicken out of the deep fryer.

I said, "Why's she still out there? Didn't you tell her?"

"Of course I told her! But she said she saw your truck parked outside and she got all nasty with me."

Gruf came into the kitchen from the front counter area. "That's the Bitch out there, huh?"

"Yes, it is, and I don't want anything to do with her."

Hammer said, "But she's so *hot!* If you're done with her, can I have her?"

I burst out laughing.

Gruf thumped Hammer on the head. "Get that chicken on a plate, dude."

Gruf turned to me. "All right. You keep sneaking in and out through the back door the rest of the night, and we'll keep pouring her coffee and telling her we don't know where you are. She can sit in the dining room till she gets tired of it."

"Thanks, man. This feels like high school."

"A man has to do what a man has to do," Hammer said wisely, setting the chicken plate up on the pass-through window to the waitress station.

Marylou waited in the dining room for an hour. I came in from a trip just after she left. I headed for the waitress station for a cup of iced tea. Debby walked in after me and stood there with her hands on her hips.

"Well?" she said.

I said, "Well, what?"

She said, "Well, what's the deal with you and your wife?"

I had to laugh at her. At the way things were at Carlo's. It was like, nobody was allowed to have a private life, or even a secret. Everyone felt absolutely entitled to butt into everybody else's business. And yet, I realized I sorta liked it. If my truck broke down in the middle of the night (it wouldn't, of course, not my Tacoma, but just say it did), I knew I could call any number of people who would gladly get out of bed and help me. Bump, Gruf, Danny, and John, of course. Jackson, Hammer, and yes, Debby, too. You bet, Debby.

"*Ex*-wife, Debby. All right. I was married to her. She screwed me over pretty bad. She's divorcing me—"

"No," she interrupted me.

"Huh?"

"No. She's not divorcing you."

"Yes, she is. Wanna see the papers?"

"She may have *been* divorcing you, and you may have some papers, but that woman is not divorcing you *now*. I know what a woman who's divorcing somebody looks like, and I know what a woman who wants her man back looks like. That woman wants her man back."

"You're full of shit. She wants to borrow money, or something."

She smiled and nodded at me. Her big silver hoop earrings bounced and sparkled. "Yeah, okay, we'll just see who's full of shit and who's not."

We stayed busy. By the time I came in from a trip at a little past ten, I already had twenty deliveries. That's a lot. There was a guy walking toward the front door at the same time I was, so I opened it and stepped back to let him go in ahead of me. He walked up to the counter. I stepped up next to him.

Gruf looked up from the computer. "Be right with ya, Terry. Yes, sir. Can I help you?"

"Uh, I *think* so."

I looked over at the guy. He stood a few inches shorter than me, was probably four, five years younger, and wore his hair in a style I always think of as English Prep School or American Soccer Player. Short at the bottom, very long and straight on top.

Side part. It was blond, but he'd streaked it white. With his tan, it looked good. He was a good-looking kid. Athletic, healthy, cocky. He wore a pale green T-shirt, cutoffs, and sandals. Preppy. As I watched him, he shuffled a little bit, and something about the way he did it made me think maybe he was a little nervous.

Gruf looked at him and waited. Looking at his profile, I saw the skin crinkle at the corner of his mouth and knew he was flashing Gruf a grin. The guy said, "Uh, see, I was a friend of Ed Hanus."

Gruf wrinkled his forehead and shook his head. "Ed?"

"The guy who was, uh, murdered?"

"Oh! The Witness. I didn't connect the name at first. We always called him by his nickname. Oh, you were a—a *friend* of his?" His voice got skeptical, which was just how I felt. How could a guy who looked like this be friends with a loser like the Witness? We both studied this guy closely, curiously.

I said, "You were a friend of *his?* You look so *normal.*"

He turned to me and grinned. "He was sort of odd. I know. But see, we practically grew up together. I live right across the street from him. Our mothers are friends. When we were little, they used to put us in the same playpen while they gabbed."

Me and Gruf nodded. You could sorta see how a friendship would develop, even when they were so different.

He said, "Yeah, I know everybody thought he was so weird." He laughed uneasily. "Some days when we were in school, it seemed like I spent all day keeping him out of trouble. Stopping people picking on him. He was like my weird little brother or something."

I said, "You're older than him?"

"Only by a year."

Gruf nodded. "So. What can we do for ya?"

"Well, I guess this'll sound odd, but I haven't heard anything at all about the investigation. I don't feel like I can ask his parents. Can't really call the cops and ask. I guess I just wanted to see where he worked. Talk to some of the people who knew him here. See if you guys know what's going on." He ran his fingers through his hair. "I've just felt so damn *bad* about the whole thing."

Gruf said, "Yeah." A phone started ringing. One of the front girls picked it up. Then another one started ringing. Gruf said, "I'll tell you what. I can't talk to you right now, but if you wanna sit in the dining room, have something to drink, wait until things settle down, maybe I can come out and talk in a bit."

"Oh, would you? That'd be great. Yeah, I'll wait."

Gruf answered the phone, took the order, dispatched me, and I headed back out again. Hammer sent me out on the next run. When I came back in, we were about done with deliveries for the night. I headed through the dining room to go back and start cleaning. Gruf was setting a glass of Coke in front of the Witness's friend, who was sitting in the end booth. Debby was already done with her closing work. She sat across from the guy, smoking.

"And this is Terry Saltz," Gruf told him. "You met him when you first came in."

"Yeah." The guy stuck out his hand and I shook it. "Brandon Tercek. Good to know you."

"Brandon's gonna hang around a little while after closing. There hasn't really been much time to talk. Debby's been keeping him entertained." Gruf grinned at Debby. She made a grab at his crotch, but he danced out of the way.

Gruf made for the jukebox and I went down the

back hall. We went into closing mode. Jackson was off that night. I closed with the new driver, the old lady. I still hadn't learned her name.

As busy as we'd been, the back wasn't too bad. The old lady was turning out to be a pretty good worker, and we got the closing work done in forty minutes or so of furious activity.

As soon as the old lady and I had gone out and pulled our cars around back and Gruf had checked us out, I walked her out to her car. Then I got a cup of coffee and went out to the darkened dining room and slouched into the booth next to Debby, who was telling the Witness's friend biker stories.

Some of Debby's stories seemed to feature Jackson's brothers. The King boys were bikers, apparently. I was unpleasantly surprised to hear this. The things I'd heard about them, Hammer saying they'd threatened the Witness and Alan saying he'd questioned them, came back to me. Now, hearing they were bikers, I got a bad feeling about them, because I liked Jackson so much. I was afraid maybe they'd had something to do with the murder. Well, *I* wasn't gonna be the one to bring it up.

Hammer came out a few minutes later with a Coke and collapsed into a chair at the nearest table. A few minutes after that, done with his closing paper work, Gruf came out and sat down across from Hammer.

Brandon Tercek said, "This would be a cool place to work. I can see why Ed liked it."

Gruf and I looked at each other. What would Ed have liked about Carlo's? No one liked him. No one was nice to him.

Gruf said, "What do you do, Brandon?"

"I manage an Arthur Treacher's in Fairfield. It's okay. Lotsa headaches. I'm sure *you* know."

Gruf nodded.

Brandon said, "I just wanted to meet you all. Ask what you've heard. Whether the cops have turned up anything."

Gruf shook his head. "Not that we know of."

"Nothing solid yet?"

Gruf shook his head, sighed, and got up to pour himself a cup of coffee. "Anybody need anything?" Nobody did.

"I don't know," Brandon said again. "I just feel so damn *bad*."

"Have the cops talked to *you*?" Hammer asked.

Brandon turned to him. "Why would they talk to me?"

"Well, maybe it was someone who knew him from school, or someone from the neighborhood."

He shrugged. "Maybe. No, they haven't talked to me. I mean, if they wanted to, I'd want to do anything I could to help."

At this point, Debby elbowed me. "Move, Muzzy."

I was delighted to hear myself called by my new nickname for the first time by someone other than Hammer. I slid from the booth to let her out.

"It's been fun, girls," she said, "but I gotta cruise on home if I wanna get any tonight."

Hammer choked on a mouthful of Coke.

Gruf followed her out the back to walk her to her car.

"She's nice," Brandon said.

Hammer said proudly, "I'm pretty sure she's not."

We only stayed a few minutes longer ourselves. Brandon told us that the Witness had often talked about the girls at Carlo's, how cute they were, and about one in particular who liked him. Brandon wanted to know who she was. We looked at each other, baffled.

"Can't help you there," Gruf said.

"Unless it was Sheila," Hammer said.

"He said he took this girl to the movies," Brandon said. "He said she was really cute."

"You couldn't call Sheila cute by *any* stretch of the imagination," I said.

"And he never went out with her, as far as I know," Gruf said. "Or with anyone else from here."

"He was probably bullshitting you," Hammer said.

Brandon shook his head. He seemed offended. "No, he wouldn't have done that."

"Well," Gruf said, standing up. "Maybe you just misunderstood him. Let's close this pop stand, boys. I'm beat."

I drove home thinking about what Brandon had said. If the Witness had been talking to Brandon about a girl, that girl had to be Sheila Werbel. A kid like the Witness couldn't have enjoyed many tender moments like the one I'd interrupted while he and Sheila sat in his Jeep after work that one night. If he was talking to Brandon about a girl, that girl had to be the one who'd given him what was almost certainly the only blow job of his young life. Sheila.

As I thought about it, I got more curious about just what had been going on between Sheila and all her various menfolk. It seemed to me that the murder *had* to have been a result of Sheila's tangled social life and her troublemaking skills. But even if Sheila, or her husband, or that ugly Neanderthal boyfriend hadn't actually done the deed, there was a pretty good chance Sheila might know who did.

Over the course of the day, it had slipped my mind that she was coming in at closing time the next night to get her final paycheck. I remembered it now, and I was glad Gruf and I had gone ahead and set that up. Maybe we'd get lucky and get some answers.

Chapter 12

Tuesday morning, me, Danny, and John walked into Brewster's to find that the three tables from yesterday were already pushed together and there was a big vase of red and yellow snapdragons or something sitting in the middle. Mary came toward us, coffeepot in hand, as we sat down.

I pointed to the snapdragons and looked at her with my eyebrows up. "What's this, Mary?"

She smiled. That woman has the sweetest smile you ever saw. "Just wanted to make pretty for my favorite breakfast boys."

Danny threw his arm around her hips and hugged her awkwardly. "You're the best, you know that?"

"Watch it! You'll make me spill all over you!" She finished pouring coffee and walked away, laughing.

I glanced out the front window. Alan Bushnell was out there dropping a coin into the newspaper vending machine. Gruf was there, too. Chatting with him. They walked in together. Bump came in right behind them.

". . . so he himself was probably a criminal waiting to happen," Alan was saying quietly as he and Gruf and Bump found places along the table. "And it's no wonder, with a couple of squirrels for parents like that kid had."

"Who wha?" John said.

"That Ed Hanus kid that was murdered over at Carlo's the other night. I was telling Joey we turned over a nasty rock up in Fairfield last night."

"Fairfield?" Bump said.

"Yeah. The victim lived with his parents in Fairfield. And what a pair those two are."

"Oh. I didn't know that." Bump smiled up at Mary as she poured his coffee.

"Mary put flowers on our table this morning," Danny told Bump. "Wasn't that nice?"

"Mary's a good woman," Bump said, still looking up at her. "She oughtta get rid of that deadbeat husband of hers and give one of us upstanding young men a chance."

She turned tomato red and hurried away. We all watched her go. I looked around the table wondering if she really did have a deadbeat husband and if everybody but me knew all about it. Well, John wouldn't know, being new to town, and Danny wouldn't. But everybody else.

Bump cleared his throat, got up, and sauntered back toward the waitress station. He stood close beside Mary with his hands behind his back and talked to her while she loaded one of the big coffee machines. After a while she looked up, stuck her tongue out at him, and shooed him away. He sauntered back to the tables, grinning, and sat down.

"So what was under the nasty rock?" Bump asked Alan.

"Oh, up in Fairfield, you mean?" Alan stopped and looked around the table. "Listen. I've decided to talk to you guys about this case more than I normally would. I've decided I'm gonna trust you to keep anything I say to yourselves. All right?"

It was less a question than an order. We all nodded.

"I think if I keep you up on things, maybe something will ring a bell. Maybe one of you knows something that you don't realize is important . . ."

We all glanced at each other.

". . . and I'm thinking, if you know where the case is going, maybe you'll all be a little safer."

I thought about this. I thought about my friends not being safe.

Bump said, "Okay. We get it. So under that nasty rock in Fairfield?"

"Some funny business between your driver and a little neighbor boy. Allegedly. According to one of the other neighbors."

Everybody made disgusted noises. Gruf said, "Sexual?"

Alan said, "Not as far as I can tell. More like sadistic shit. Bullying, threatening. Knock the kid off his bike, then take him for ice cream. I'm trying to get a better handle on it. Got a psychologist gonna do some sessions with him, find out the exact nature. It's like, if the kid told you about one incident by itself, you'd sorta go, 'So what?' But there were a lot of incidents. There was a pattern there."

Mary came back and began taking our breakfast orders. I waited for my turn, thinking about the sick drawings on the Witness's Styrofoam cups. I don't know why I didn't mention it right then and there.

"You've pretty much ruled out the possibility it was a robbery?" Gruf asked.

"I didn't say that," Alan said. "Nothing's ruled out. Anything's possible." There wasn't much more to say after that. We finished breakfast with a lot of small talk about the Tribe and the weather.

Gruf and I went straight from Brewster's up to Bud's, but then I had to leave right away to go for my weekly meeting with Nelma. I had just enough time to show Gruf how I wanted him to finish sorting and stacking the wood.

Driving back into town, I found myself thinking about the previous week, when Nelma and I had gone over to the coffee shop, and I remembered what flavor of cappuccino she'd ordered that day. So, in spite of worrying she'd think I was trying to brownnose her or something, I ran into the coffee shop and bought us each a cappuccino and carried them carefully across the street into her building.

Today Nelma was wearing some kind of huge yellow flowery muumuu or something. She gave me a big smile when I stuck my head in the door, and a bigger one when she saw what I was carrying. "Oh, my stars? No, you did *not*!"

"Okay, if you don't want it . . ."

"Just set that thing down right here and stop talking crazy!"

As I settled in, she blew lightly across the surface of her cappuccino and said, "You had an awful thing happen down at Carlo's, huh? Was the victim a friend of yours?"

I shook my head. "I barely knew him. I don't think anyone at Carlo's knew him. He was the kind of kid everybody ignores, unless he pisses you off."

She frowned. "He must've really annoyed *some*body."

I shrugged.

"I heard you and Joey Ridolfi found the body."

I nodded.

"I heard Alan Bushnell took you in for questioning."

I caught her eyes and held them. "I didn't do it, Nelma."

She snorted. "I know that. But are you okay? I

mean, here you are, trying so hard to stay off the booze and drugs . . ."

I shook my head. "It's not all that hard. I've always known there're some guys that just can't drink, plain and simple. For them, alcohol's poison. Now I understand *I'm* one of those guys. And I'll tell you what. I like being sober. Everything goes smoother."

She smiled. "You keep talking like that and I might have to stop worrying about you."

I laughed. "I don't think either one of us has to worry about *me* anymore."

She thought about that. "But some things can shake a person's resolve. Like when you saw the body . . ."

I shrugged. "Yeah, that was the first time I ever saw anybody dead. But it's not like I've never seen blood before. I've seen guys run nails through their feet. I've seen guys fall off ladders. I once saw a guy get stapled to a roof. I saw a guy cut off two of his fingers, and I waited in the emergency room while he got 'em sewed back on. I mean, you can't work on a construction site and not know all about blood and broken bones."

She nodded. "I talked to Alan yesterday. It sounds like they're having a tough time with their investigation."

I shrugged. "They'll catch him, whoever it was. They always do."

She nodded. After a minute, she went down her checklist: still in the same residence; I showed her a pay stub from Carlo's; I showed her a receipt from making a payment on my court costs and fines; no, I had not had a drink or a hit.

I told her about finishing Bump's deck and that I'd started Bud Hanratty's deck, which seemed to impress her. I also told her that Bud had gotten me my truck back, and that I'd hired a "manual laborer," and I told her about John moving in with us. I even mentioned breakfast time at Brewster's.

"Nelma, yesterday we had to push three tables together, just to fit everybody in. Today Mary pushed them together before we got there so they were ready for us. And she brought flowers in."

Don't tell anybody, but suddenly, to my horror, I got choked up and had to stop talking.

She looked at me closely. "Danny, Bump, Gruf. This new roommate, John. Even Mary, the waitress. They mean a lot to you, don't they?"

I swallowed hard. "I feel like I've known 'em all my life. The people I knew in my old life, before I went to jail, they were all pretty mean hearted. But *these* people, Nelma. They're the best. They bring out the best in me. I'd do anything for any one of 'em."

Gruf had finished sorting the wood and was eating an early lunch when I got back to Bud's. By that time, dark clouds were billowing in. The air was stirring and we could smell rain in it. Working as fast as we could, we set up the sawhorses to make the work surface the way I like to have it; then we did all the preassembly we could before the skies opened up around two. As the first raindrops hit, we scrambled to cover the woodpiles and pack the tools.

I dropped Gruf off at his Jeep in the Brewster's parking lot, then decided to have a little visit with my brother P.J. about giving out my personal information to my ex-wife.

I drove south down to P.J.'s house with my windshield wipers on high. The rain hissed and spit as it struck the hot asphalt. Steam swirled and streaked above the highway's surface.

I expected P.J. to be off because of the rain, same

as me. But he wasn't at home, so I headed south again for another five miles to the office and yard of Perkins Construction. When I stepped into the office trailer, Red's fireplug of a secretary, Linda, looked up from a pile of paperwork and blinked at me.

"Terry? What are *you* doing here?"

"Hi, Linda. How's it going?"

She grimaced and took off her thick-lensed glasses. She blew on each lens and put the glasses back on. Poor kid. The office stayed so dusty from the trucks racing through the yard all the time, she pretty much spent her days working in a sand cloud.

She pushed back from her desk, grabbed a stained coffee cup with a big yellow sunflower on the side, and waddled over to the coffeepot.

She said, "Want some coffee, hon? Red's not here, but he may be back before too long."

"No, thanks. I'm not here to see Red. I need to talk to P.J. Where's he working at today?"

"Ooh, that's good. I was afraid you were gonna ask Red for your job back."

"No, Linda. I definitely do *not* want to work for Red anymore."

"Well, that's good, because he won't hire you back and he'd love to get to tell you that." She turned to look at me, screwed up her nose, and sniffed through it.

"So, if you could just tell me where P.J.'s working today?"

"Him and Ralphie are building a garage over in Hudson. Hang on, I'll get you the address."

All you have to do to find a Perkins Construction job is get on the right street. Red's crews all drive red trucks with the company name in huge white letters along the side panels. He makes you back your truck into the driveway, unload, then pull all the way down to the curb, so traffic passing by can't miss seeing the logo parked there. He places a lot of emphasis on this.

Red cares more about how his trucks are parked than he does about things like right angles. I think you carpenters out there know what I mean when I say this. So once I got on Quailridge Parkway, I didn't even have to check addresses. The truck was parked right where Red wanted it parked.

The doors on the new garage weren't hung yet. I put my arm over my head and ran through the rain up the driveway. P.J. and Ralphie were putting up shelving. P.J. drove his nail with two whacks and spotted me.

He said, "Hey, bumblefuck. What're *you* doin' here?" It was the first time I'd seen my big brother since before I went to jail. No, he did not exactly bust his ass bringing me any care packages.

He dropped his hammer and scratched under his flannel shirt in the general region of his armpit as he walked toward me, then stuck out the same hand to shake mine. I shook. What the fuck. He's my brother. He's in his mid-thirties and still has acne on his nose and chin. Fuckin' P.J.

I said, "I went over to the house. I thought you'd be off 'cause of the rain."

"Hell, no. I'm goin' up to Canada in two weeks. Don't wanna miss any pay *now*."

"Hunting or gambling?"

He grinned. "Both." And then, of course, he had to slap me on the cheek, because that's his thing, proving to Ralphie I'm still the kid brother and he can still smack me whenever he wants to. Even if I *am* six inches taller and have a good thirty pounds on him.

Ralphie chuckled. "How was jail, asswipe?"

"Fabulous, Ralphie. Thanks for caring."

"So, what're you doing here?" P.J. asked suspiciously. "I thought you were with Danny up in Spencer. You're *not* moving in with me and Marcy."

Marcy. That whiny bitch. The thought of living anywhere near her makes my teeth hurt. "Did I *ask* to move in with you?"

"What, then?"

"Marylou came walking into my work last night, dude. I wasn't happy she knew where I was."

He roped his eyebrows together. "So? *Dude*?"

"So, you're the only one who knew I was working at Carlo's. I purposely didn't tell anyone else. I purposely haven't even called anyone else since I got out."

"I didn't tell her. Hell, I haven't even talked to— aw shit. Marcy."

Marcy. Of course.

He took off his Perkins Construction baseball cap, wiped his black hair back off his sweaty forehead, and stuck the hat back on.

"I think Marcy said she had lunch with Marylou last week sometime."

Yeah. Marcy doesn't miss many lunches. "How did *Marcy* know where I am?"

"Fuck. I probably left your note lying around."

"Nice."

"So what? All of a sudden you can't handle Marylou?"

"She's trouble. You yourself used to tell me that fifty times a day. I don't want anything to do with her."

He held up a hand. "All right. *All right*. What the fuck."

"All right. Please. Don't tell her anything about me. If Marcy's getting thick with her, don't tell Marcy anything about me. Please. Okay?"

"Jeez, Terry. It's not like you're the only thing any of us talks about."

I glared at him. "I wanna give you my phone number, in case you have to get in touch. But keep it in your wallet, huh?"

He laughed. "Like it's safe from Marcy in my wallet? Get real."

I pulled a scrap of paper and a pen from my shirt pocket. "Okay, I won't write my name. Here, I'll put, uh, I know. I'll put my new nickname on it. Muzzy. There. Now if she finds it she won't know . . ."

"*Muzzy*? The *fuck* kind of nickname is Muzzy? What's it mean?"

I shrugged. "Some kid gave it to me at work."

P.J. looked at Ralphie. "Muzzy." He looked back at me. "Whatever."

I handed him my phone number and said, "Heard from the old man?"

P.J. snorted.

"Well, if you do, can you give him my phone number?"

"Like he's gonna call you? Go catch Father-Son Day at the ballpark?" He laughed sarcastically.

"Just give him the number if you hear from him, huh?"

"Sure thing. You bet."

I've got a bunch of brothers. The funny thing is, compared to the rest of them, P.J. is a prince. I was really happy to turn my truck back toward Spencer.

As things wound down at Carlo's that night, Gruf and I started watching the door for Sheila Werbel. She'd said she'd come in to get her paycheck and we were gonna try to get some answers from her. But the minutes ticked by and we were beginning to think she'd stood us up. Gruf was cashing me out by the time she walked in the front door. Everybody else was long gone by that time.

We'd just finished pulling out the fryers in the kitchen and scouring the greasy walls and floors. We were standing at the computer at the front counter. We both looked up sharply at the sound of the front door opening.

Gruf said, "Hey, Sheila." He managed a nice smile. She walked up to the counter, leaned her elbows on it, and smiled.

"Busy night?"

Gruf said, "Always. Give us a minute to finish up Terry's cash-out."

She waved a pudgy red-nailed hand and smiled brightly. "Take your time."

Once we were done, Gruf led the way back to the office. He said, "Well, let me get your check."

He knelt in front of the safe so his body was blocking the dial from sight and began to turn it. I leaned on the office doorjamb and smiled at Sheila, because we were supposed to be softening her up so she'd talk to us. But behind the phony smile, I was analyzing why she looked so repulsive to me.

She was wearing a short-sleeved denim work shirt and short denim cutoffs. The cutoffs were gross. There oughtta be a law against a girl like Sheila exposing that much thigh oatmeal to public view. But I decided the main turnoff was the way she held her upper lip pulled up off her front teeth in that double sneer.

I studied her more closely. It seemed to be the two little muscles on either side of her nose that did it. She seemed to keep them almost permanently retracted. She was busy watching Gruf fiddle with the safe dial, so I tried to imitate the expression. I could lift my upper lip, but I couldn't hold it steady. Everything wanted to twitch. I decided an expression like that probably took years and years of practice.

Then Gruf said, "Shit! I hate this fucking safe. I

stopped at the wrong number. Now the timer won't let me try again for ten minutes." He looked around at Sheila and gave her his sexiest smile. "I guess you're stuck here with us for a while."

She grinned and patted her stiff platinum hair.

Gruf said, "Well, we might as well get comfortable. Let's sit out in the dining room. Something to drink, Sheila? Coke? Iced tea?"

Gruf and Sheila sat across from each other in the employees' booth of choice. I sat at the next table with my legs stretched out in front of me. Once we were all settled with beverages in front of us and our cigarettes lit, Gruf leaned across the table and put a hand on her arm.

"Sheila, I'm glad you could stop in tonight. I've wanted to talk to you, ever since that night the Witness was murdered. I owe you an apology."

She screwed up her lip even more. "For what?"

"It was cold, having the cops tell you not to come in anymore. I've really felt bad about it."

She didn't react. She just sat there watching his fingers stroke her arm.

He said, "I should have told you, face-to-face. Explained. I was so freaked about the Witness I didn't stop to think."

She waved her cigarette hand. "Forget about it."

He shook his head. "No. I'm really sorry. I'm sorry how I did it, and I'm sorry I had to fire you. The thing was, it was either you or Hammer, and I can't fire Hammer. No one can run the kitchen during rush but Hammer. He's faster than *I* am. He's even faster than Jackson. He's the fastest cook we've ever had here. So it had to be you."

Now she looked up and smiled. "It's okay. Don't worry about it."

Gruf heaved a sigh of relief. "Well, that's really nice of you. You're a nice person."

She tipped her head, smiled, and blinked at him. "Hey, maybe the three of us could party tonight, huh? Get a little messed up, do like the doggies do. Huh?"

Gruf's head jerked. "Oh. Uh, jeez. Uh, we have to get up early. Huh, Terry?"

"Yeah." *Gah!* "But getting back to what you were saying, Gruf. You weren't the only one that was upset. Everybody was. And now it's even worse. At least, it is for me. The cops are all over me."

Sheila's eyes jerked to mine.

I said, "Because of my record. You know I have a record?"

She nodded.

Gruf said, "I guess they've questioned you, too, huh, Sheila? You and your husband?"

She nodded. "Me, Lenny, and everybody else I know, seems like."

Gruf said, "Lenny. That's your husband?"

She nodded. "Lenny Werbel. Been married six years."

Gruf said, "I guess you and Lenny want this thing cleared up like we all do. Get things back to normal."

That was the end of the eye contact. She stubbed out her cigarette, took a hefty swig of her Coke, and got interested in Gruf's hand again. He gave her arm a final pat, leaned back against the booth, and stretched his arms over his head.

I said, "I guess you and Lenny told the cops everything you know. . . ."

She let out a large "Hah! We're not telling 'em *notheen*!"

Gruf said, "Why not? The sooner this thing gets cleared up, the sooner—"

She said, "Bull*shit!* Fuckeen cops." She shook her head forcefully enough to make her stiff hair sway. "We're not telling 'em notheen!"

I said, "What *could* you tell 'em that you're *not* telling 'em?"

Big mistake. I could almost see her face slam shut. Her eyes jumped to the wall clock. She adjusted her weight impatiently on the booth bench. The quiet dining room was filled with the farting noise of her big, bare sweaty thighs pulling free from the screaming vinyl.

She said, "I think it's been ten minutes. You wanna try that safe again?"

There was no way to get her to relax after that. Gruf tried a few times, but she was finished with us. There was nothing to do but get her check and let her out the back door. Gruf and me walked back to the dining room for a final cigarette.

I said, "That went well. Sorry, dude. I fucked it up."

He shook his head. "She woulda clammed up no matter how we went at it. She's hiding something."

"Oh, no doubt."

"You think one of them really did it?"

I shrugged. "She's got *me* wondering."

We puffed in silence.

I said, "I didn't know there was a timer on the safe."

He grinned at me. "There isn't."

Chapter 13

Wednesday turned out to be chick day for me. A double chick whammy. Good chick, bad chick.

There was a little silver BMW roadster parked to one side of the garage when we got to Bud's Wednesday morning. I pulled my truck up beside it so I wouldn't be blocking it. It was the first time we'd seen a vehicle there, other than Bud's Caddy. I'd meant to ask Bump if Bud had a family, but had never gotten around to it.

Anyway, there were no signs of life outside the house except the AC was on for the first time that I'd noticed. The heat pump just around the back corner of the house was roaring and rattling.

When I went inside, I was surprised to see that the kitchen was clean. I stood there with my six-pack of Cokes dangling from my hand and looked around. All the counters and the table had been cleared off and washed, the floor had been waxed, the sink and faucet were shiny, there was no trash to be found anywhere, and everything smelled like some kind of cinnamon potpourri shit, or something. I went ahead and put our Cokes in the refrigerator, which had also been cleaned.

Once we got to work, I forgot the car was even there. So it gave me a start when I heard the screen door being pushed open. Me and Gruf were sitting side by side on the edge of the deck eating our lunch, our backs to the house.

The door swung open. As we cranked our necks around to see who it was, the most beautiful girl I've ever seen in real life came walking out in a tiny silver bikini. She popped the top on a can of Coke, spread the white towel she carried, and sat down close beside Gruf like she'd been there many times before.

She squinted up at the sky. "It's gonna be a hot one today, isn't it?"

She had shoulder-length black hair, all thick and soft and swingy. She had big dark eyes, round cheeks, a little rosebud mouth, and a body that'd keep *you* up all night, Weezer. She had three, four little silver rings on the long, graceful, pink-nailed fingers of each hand, and a little silver ankle bracelet that, when I saw it hugging against her tan leg, nearly made me howl.

We sat there a while, me and Gruf frozen in two different stages of raising our sandwiches to our mouths, and her sipping on her Coke. I breathed in the exotic scent of the sunscreen she'd used. A drop of aluminum sweat fell off the bottom of the can and landed on her upper thigh. I quickly looked away and tried to think about something else for a minute.

She said, "I'm glad you guys went ahead and fixed that screen door. That thing was about ready to fall off."

We both laughed quite a bit. We wouldn't have laughed at all if an ugly girl had said it.

She said, "I'm Mike. Who're you?"

Gruf said who I was and who he was. She said, "Who bought the Cokes?"

Gruf told her that I did. She leaned around Gruf and looked at me. "Thanks."

I nodded.

Somehow we managed to finish eating. We wadded up our wrappers into the brown bags. Gruf wadded my bag into his bag and tossed it through the truck window. I went over to the sawhorses and picked up my circular saw. We went back to work.

After a few minutes, she spread out her towel in the backyard weeds and stretched out facedown on it. The bikini was a thong. Gruf and I looked at each other, and he grabbed his crotch and did a bump, grinning.

About an hour went by and she didn't move. Finally, Gruf said, *"Hey! Mike!* You fall asleep over there?" She jumped, then turned to look at us. Her eyes were droopy. That was exactly what she had done, in spite of the saws and hammering and drilling.

"You're gonna get burned," he warned her.

"Yeah. Thanks." She got up, tossed her hair, and stretched. I had to look away. She picked up her towel, came over, and hoisted herself onto the deck.

"Yell if you need anything," she told us, and went inside.

I coulda yelled all day.

About an hour later, the door swung open again and she came out wearing a short little white skirt, tan heels that almost matched her skin color, and a tight little tan belly shirt. She was wearing Jessica McClintock perfume. I recognized it because Marylou likes that one. Mike wears it a hell of a lot better than the Bitch does, though.

She smiled at us and said, "Gotta go. Have a good one." She eased herself down into her little car, started it up, and backed out of sight down the driveway.

Gruf said, "Whad'ya think? Daughter or girlfriend?"

I had just assumed she was Bud's daughter. It hadn't occurred to me she might be his girlfriend. I chewed on the question the rest of the afternoon.

I smelled that Jessica McClintock perfume again around nine, nine-thirty that night, but it wasn't on Mike. It was on Marylou. I pulled up to the front corner of Carlo's and ran in the front door without looking around, just thinking about how I was hungry and hoping for a meal break. I didn't notice her car sitting there. She was standing right inside the front door.

I pulled up short and stared at her. She had her blond hair all back combed up into giant mall hair, and she was wearing way too much makeup. I made her wear her hair more natural and go much lighter on the makeup when we were together. Obviously now that she was back on her own, she was going through the hair spray and makeup like gangbusters again.

She *is* a good-looking woman. She's tall, five-ten, built like a model. She does aerobics faithfully every day. Under the blusher she has a pretty face. Under the eyeliner and black mascara she has pretty blue eyes.

She's plenty good-looking. My problem with her doesn't have anything to do with her looks. It's that she was a spoiled child and she has grown up into a very spoiled woman, and nobody has ever taught her that there's anything more to life than her own countless and never-ending needs. In the early days, it was sort of fun trying to meet her vast assortment of needs each and every waking hour.

She said, "Hi, Terry."

"Marylou," I said, and walked on past her to the

counter. I piled my empty delivery bags on top of the counter and made eye contact with Gruf, who looked from me to her and back at me again.

"Want a meal break?" he asked, quietly, so she wouldn't hear.

"Yeah, I guess. I guess I might as well get this over with."

"Whad'ya wanna eat?"

I turned around to Marylou. "You hungry?"

She said, "I already ate."

"Okay." I turned back to Gruf. "Spaghetti. Three meatballs. Blue cheese on the salad."

He punched my order into the computer. I turned around to Marylou. "Go get us a booth. I gotta pull the car around." Actually, I wasn't supposed to pull the car around. Gruf's safety signs were still plastered all over the back. I just wanted a minute to breathe, get my head together.

She was dialing through the jukebox pages when I slid into the booth across from her a minute later. I set a glass of Coke in front of her and sipped my Coke from my Styrofoam cup.

"So, what's up?" I asked her, and I know my voice couldn't have sounded anything like friendly, or even interested. Debby came out with a tray of food for a nearby table and winked at me as she walked by.

Marylou used her long, curling, white-polished fingernails to dig four quarters from her little purse. She dropped them into the jukebox and punched in numbers. Michael Bolton started singing something.

Across the room, I heard Debby groan and say, "Who played *that*? Dude, did you play that?" The guy at the table laughed and loudly denied it.

Marylou gave no sign she heard the criticism. She batted her reinforced eyelashes at me and said, "Why are you working *here*?" Her voice was whiny. I tried to remember when I'd heard her say something that *didn't* sound whiny.

I said, "The county's making me. Community service."

She nodded and said, "Oh."

Like it seemed entirely possible to her that Grand County would be making me work at Carlo's. I swear, you can tell that woman just about anything, and as long as you keep a straight face, she'll go, "Oh." It's not that she's stupid. I think what it is, she doesn't pay attention. Her mind's already skipping ahead, thinking what *she's* gonna say next.

I realized I was bouncing my knee under the table, and stopped. Pictures flashed in my brain of all those years of her flirting with my friends, holding out her hand for more money, going into one of her tantrums and flouncing away, blurting out embarrassing things at the wrong times, in the wrong places. Not to mention the cold-hearted way she bailed on me when I got into my trouble.

"So," I said. "Just in the neighborhood? Or what?"

She drew in breath a couple of times as if she was going to unload whatever burden she was carrying, but no go. Hammer came out carrying my spaghetti and stuff. This was completely unnecessary. I mean, for him to carry it out. Debby would have done it. He just wanted a close-up look at Marylou. I chuckled at him. He stood there an extra minute, waiting for something, then turned around and went back into his little kitchen cave.

I knew I was supposed to sit there and keep saying stuff like, "What's wrong? *Tell* me," so that she could finally let it be dragged out of her, whatever it was she was here to say. But I wasn't playing that game. I was perfectly happy to sit there shoveling spaghetti and salad into my mouth. I was thinking how surprised she'd be if she hadn't spoken up by the time I was done, because when I was done, I was going back to work, whether she'd had her say or not.

But maybe some sixth sense told her she didn't have all night, because after a while she finally said, "Terry."

I looked up at her. Her pink lipstick had caked a little bit. There were hairlines spreading across her lower lip.

She took a deep breath. "Okay, Terry. I was mad at you. I really was. But now I miss you. You can come home now."

The knife I was about to butter my second piece of garlic bread with paused in midair. I really had thought she was there to ask me for money. I said, "What?"

She smiled. "I canceled the divorce. We can stay married. You can come home." She said this like it was some kind of wonderful announcement.

I burst out laughing. "No. We can*not* stay married."

She smiled indulgently. "Yes, we can. I'm not mad anymore."

"I don't care if you're mad, glad, or indifferent. We're not gonna stay married."

She blinked at me. "I don't understand."

"Try to focus, Marylou. I want you to *un*cancel the divorce. I don't wanna be married to you."

Debby happened to be walking by as I said it. She walked on a few steps until she was behind Marylou, turned around, and mouthed "I told you!" I grimaced at her and she went on into the back hall.

"But Terry . . ."

I folded the last of my garlic bread in half and used it to mop up the last of the spaghetti sauce. I slurped the last of my Coke. "I gotta get back to work."

She straightened, insulted. "Just like that? Can't we discuss this?"

I snorted like Bump does. "I don't have time." I stood up, gathered up my meal mess, and pointed at her Coke glass. "Done with that? Or ya want more."

"Terry . . ."

I shrugged. "Whatever. See ya 'round."

I don't know if she sat there a while or left right away, but when I came in from my next trip she was gone.

Chapter 14

The rest of that week was a bear. Hard work in the hot sun all day at Bud's, and fast-paced pizza delivery all night at Carlo's. Debby Duncan was doing a great job of waitressing, so that eased some of the stress on Gruf. He had also found another new night driver, a guy named Jeff White, so he told me I could drop back to five nights a week if I wanted to. Boy howdy.

I chose Sundays and Mondays as my nights off. When Sunday finally rolled around, I slept until noon. I got up feeling stiff and sore. I walked out to the kitchen for a glass of water and met Danny coming from his end of the trailer. The same barking dog had gotten us both out of bed.

We couldn't decide whether we wanted to go over to Brewster's for breakfast or just scrounge something at home. Danny suggested we should go for a walk through the trailer park to wake ourselves up and work the kinks out.

It was a good idea. There was a sweet, clean-smelling breeze, and the summer sun was hot. The sky was a rich, deep color of blue. I felt hap-hap-happy to be alive. We walked along, talking about old times.

Danny stopped to cradle his lighter in the breeze. "Remember that time you knocked Red's ladder over?"

"And while P.J. was yelling at us, Red stapled P.J.'s thumb to the subroof?"

"P.J.'s up there screaming, *'Pull it out! Pull it out!'* "

"And Ralphie goes, 'That's what *she* said!' "

We howled.

He drew on his smoke to get it well lit and we began to walk again. "God!" He exhaled. "Why didn't one of 'em murder us? I would've."

I shook my head. "Thank God P.J.'s thumb hurt so bad, or he woulda beaten me to death. It seems like a long time ago."

"That it does."

We walked a while in silence, watching the kids and dogs and cats that seemed to be swarming all over the trailer park in the warm sunshine. Kids on bikes, kids on skateboards, kids on foot. I wondered how all those kids and animals fit into the trailers at night.

Danny said, "Let's invite Bump over for supper tonight."

I looked at him. "What brought that on?"

"I think he's funny. I never get to talk to him that much."

"That's true. Everything's been so crazy this past week that I haven't talked to him much, either. Okay. I'm off from Carlo's. Maybe John would wanna cook."

"That'll make four of us. After supper we could play some cards."

"We can ask him."

John was all good with the plan, and said he was gonna make beef Stroganoff. Dude loved to cook, and the idea of an extra mouth to cook for tickled him silly. Bump, when I called him, sounded pretty happy with the idea. He said he loved beef Stroganoff. That impressed me. I had no idea what beef Stroganoff was. I was just glad everybody was so fucking happy.

Bump's Harley rumbled to a stop in front of the

trailer around six. When he came in the front door, Danny woke up from the nap he was taking in his La-Z-Boy and gave him a groggy "Whassup?"

I said, "Bump, beer?"

Bump said, "I don't drink. Coke's fine."

I handed him a Coke and we sprawled on the sofa while John chopped stuff in the kitchen. On the tube, Nascar racers roared around a track somewhere.

Bump said, "Gruf's pissed he has to work tonight. But he's coming over after closing."

Carlo's closed early on Sunday nights. Cutoff for delivery orders was ten. A lot of times on Sunday nights, we were closed and out of there by ten-thirty.

I said, "Oh. That's cool."

He nodded. "How's Bud's deck coming? I haven't had a chance to get up there since you started."

"Good. We dropped in the hot tub yesterday. Get it roughed in tomorrow."

"Sweet." He snickered. "I bet the new deck makes the rest of his place look even more like a rathole."

"You got that right. Why does Bud live like that? He can afford to fix it up and get a maid in there a couple times a week, can't he?"

"He can afford to do about anything he wants to do, at this point. I guess he just doesn't care what it looks like. You should see his boat, though. That thing's tits and ass."

"Hey. There was a girl there Wednesday. Mike. She his daughter?"

"She's my sister."

I stared at him. *"Your sister?"*

He laughed at me. "Nice lookin', huh?"

"That doesn't even begin to cover it."

"She liked you and Gruf, too." He sipped his Coke with a smug look on his face.

"What was she doing at Bud's?"

He grinned. "She thinks she's everybody's little mommy, or something. She goes up there once a week or so to yell at him for his drinking and clean his place and cook him a meal or two. She tries to do it to me, too, but I won't let her."

"How come Gruf doesn't know her? I thought you guys all grew up together."

He shook his head. "We went to Catholic school. I didn't know Gruf until he started working at Carlo's."

"Where does she live?"

"Next door to me."

I tried to visualize the houses on either side of his, but I couldn't. I hadn't paid any attention to much of anything outside his yard. "She's got her own house, too?"

"Her and my brother have it together. It works for them, 'cause they work different shifts, so someone's usually there with the dogs."

I vaguely remembered hearing dogs barking on the other side of a barrier fence that ran down the south side of his backyard.

"What's she do for a living?"

"Nurse," he said. "Emergency-room nurse. Cleveland Clinic. They both are." He turned toward the kitchen. "Hey, John. How long till dinner? I'm starvin' to death over here."

"Twenty minutes. Here, I'll get the salad made."

Salad led into the Stroganoff, which became my all-time favorite meal with the first taste, which led to cheesecake and coffee, which led to all of us leaned back from the table and unhooked our jeans. John started to get up and clear.

"Siddown, Martha Stewart," I said. "Me and Danny got cleanup." Bump started to get up. "You sit, too. You're company." Bump leaned back in his chair, grinning, and clasped his hands behind his head.

Me and Danny got everything washed up. I knew

Danny wanted to make a little trip back to his bedroom for some mood adjustment. I told him to go on and I finished putting stuff away myself. After a minute or so the faint skunky smell of pot drifted out from the direction of Danny's bedroom.

I caught John looking over his shoulder a couple of times, making sure I put everything where it belonged, but he was smart enough not to comment if he saw mistakes. Danny came back out, topped off Bump's Coke, and got beers for himself and John. Bump started shuffling cards.

We started off playing spades. Danny and I won the first game by a mile because we'd played spades as partners a time or two before. Then Bump changed places with me and things were more even. Bump and Danny won the second game.

After that, Bump started shuffling the cards. "Let's play something easier. I'd rather talk than concentrate on cards. Here. Let's try this one."

He dealt out all the cards, then explained that during your turn you discard sevens, then build up and down from the sevens following suit. If you can't play, you pass. Last one holding cards loses.

As we played, we started to see there could be some strategy involved, but not much. It was pretty fun and, like he said, it took no concentration.

After the first game was over, Danny said, "Yeah, I like that. What's the name of it?"

Bump said, "Fuck if I know."

Danny dealt.

"How'd you get the nickname Bump?" John asked.

"Motorcycle accident."

"Yeah? Explain?" Danny threw the jack of diamonds on the ten.

"I was in a semicoma a while. All I would say was Bump."

"Why were you saying Bump?" I threw my queen on Danny's jack.

"How would I know? I wasn't there at the time." He laughed. "No, but when I was coming out of it, the doctor asked me if I remembered what happened, and I said I hit a bump. See, it was funny because what I hit was a telephone pole."

John said, "On a bike? That'll leave a mark."

"Yeah. I was pretty messed up for a while."

Danny said, "A while, like how long?"

"I was in the hospital a few months." Bump threw down the ten of clubs.

"You'd never know to look at you now. How old were you at the time?" John threw the jack.

"Thirteen."

"*Thirteen?* What were you riding?"

"BSA 650."

John looked at him. "A thirteen-year-old can't handle a bike like that."

"Duh." Bump grinned at him. "Anyways, that's why my nickname's Bump, and that's why I don't drink or do drugs."

"Because you like to be in control of yourself?" John asked, throwing the four of hearts.

"Because I was stoned and drunk at the time."

John said dryly, "Thirteen, stoned and drunk, riding a BSA 650. So, like, what caused the accident?"

Bump grinned and shrugged. "What can I tell ya?"

We went around the table a time or two, discarding. Then Bump said to John, "Dude, what's going on in the murder investigation?"

John said, "Well, let's see. They've made a big effort trying to find the knife and the fanny pack. I think they've searched about every Dumpster in town. They're desperate for some kind of physical evidence."

"So this thing could drag on for a long time?" Danny said.

"Forever?" Bump said.

John shrugged. "From what I hear, without either the fanny pack or the knife, they're not very hopeful. They don't have anything solid on anybody."

I said, "Me and Gruf tried to see if we could get anything out of Sheila Werbel last week. When she came in for her final paycheck."

John gave me a disapproving look. "Don't go interfering in the case, Terry."

I said, "Muzzy. We weren't interfering. Not really. We just thought she might talk to us. But we were wrong. She wouldn't talk about it at all. She's definitely hiding something."

Bump said, "Well, alls I'm saying is, I want the thing cleared up."

John pursed his lips and tossed the three of hearts. "Everybody wants it cleared up."

I said, "Except whoever did it."

"Yeah," John agreed. "Except them."

Gruf came in just after ten-thirty. I hooked him up with a beer while Bump explained the game of FuckifIknow. Danny dealt.

Bump said, "Terry, what you said a while ago has me thinking."

I said, "Muzzy. What did I say?"

He said, "About you and Gruf questioning Sheila Werbel. That got me thinking. You know, somebody's gotta just come out and say it. This murder investigation's going nowhere. It's bugging the hell outa me. Somebody's gotta do something."

I stared at him. John shook his head.

Gruf said, "Like who? Like what?"

"Like *we* get involved."

Gruf laughed. "If Terry told you about us and

Sheila Werbel, then you know we went down in flames."

I said, "Yeah. It was pathetic. What're *we* gonna do?"

Bump said, "Some investigating of our own."

John said, "Oh, no. No, you're *not*."

Gruf snorted. "We don't know anything about investigating a murder. Terry and I proved that. If cops who're trained to do that sort of thing can't get anywhere, what makes you think *we* can?"

Bump spread his hands. "Just listen, okay? Just listen, John. I think we could find out some things. Like, we could sniff around the Witness's neighborhood in Fairfield. That kid he supposedly was whomping on. Maybe there was a little more to that. Maybe we need to see what's what with that kid's daddy. If I had a kid, and I found out somebody was messing around with him . . . I mean, if it was bad enough, *I'd* think about killing him. Right?"

We shrugged.

Bump said, "I think where you guys went wrong with Sheila Werbel, you took the direct approach. Naturally, if she's got something to hide, she's gonna clam up if you go at her directly. I'm thinking, dog that kid's daddy. Find a way to see what's what with him."

I looked at Gruf. He shrugged. "How would we even *find* him?"

Bump said, "You told me about that dude who came down to the store the other night, said he was friends with the Witness? You said he lives across the street from the Witness. He can prolly tell us who that little kid's family is."

Bump snapped his fingers, searching for the right words. "I don't know how to explain what I'm thinking, exactly. I'm thinking, we get in close to him and get him talking. Like, he doesn't even know it has anything to do the Witness. You know? See what we can find out."

Gruf shook his head. "We'd be wasting our time. Plus, we could really screw things up and get Alan Bushnell on our backs. Alan would be really pissed off if we messed around like this."

John gave Gruf a look of gratitude. He said, "You got *that* right."

But Bump had me thinking. "Maybe Bump's right, though. We can't let this thing drag on and on. Think about *this*. Remember Carrie Hall? What if she was telling the truth? What if somebody really *did* run her into that ditch on purpose? What if that and the Witness's murder are connected? That could mean it's not over. Somebody else could get hurt. Jackson, or one of the other drivers, or one of your little front girls."

Gruf said, "Oh my God."

Bump nodded. "See? And I don't think it *is* over. And just so everybody understands. I'm doing this. With or without you guys."

I said to Gruf, "I don't want him going ahead on his own. Do you?"

Gruf frowned. "No."

John didn't look too happy. He got up without saying anything and got himself another Bud. He held up the can with the door still open and said, "Anybody else?"

Everybody was ready. He handed over cans of beer and Coke. Then he sat heavily and glared around the table. He said tightly, "Can I talk now? That be all right with you, Bump?"

Bump nodded.

"Don't you yay-hoos think the department's got enough pressure on it without having a bunch of amateurs running around screwing things up?"

Gruf said, "Hang on a minute. How do you think we would screw anything up?"

Bump said, "What is there to screw up? You guys got nothin'."

John said, "You don't know *what* Alan and his guys have so far. Neither do I. You won't know if you're messing him up or not."

Gruf said, "I heard that Alan's shorthanded because of vacation schedules. And because there's some kind of tri-county drug task force operating."

Danny sat up straight.

John saw Danny's reaction and laughed. "I don't think they're after pot smokers, Danny. The focus is more on cocaine and heroin, from what I hear."

Bump said, "I don't see what the problem is, John. Think about it. I don't see how we could be screwing up anything Alan's working on. We're just sniffing around the edges a little bit. It can't hurt anything. It might even help."

Everybody was quiet a minute, letting John think things over. I lit a cigarette.

Finally, John said, "Really, I should go to Alan and tell him about this. If he ever found out that I heard you guys talking about messing around like this and didn't tell him, I'd be history."

Bump said, "How's he gonna find out? *We're* not gonna tell him."

Gruf, Danny, and I all said, pretty much in unison, "Fuck no."

Bump said, "I don't think we're gonna do anything that Alan will ever need to hear about. We'll just get next to that kid's daddy somehow, strike up a little conversation . . ."

I said, ". . . and if he happens to give us a little information that might be useful to you courageous boys in blue . . ."

Danny said, "Black. They wear black."

John said, "And hardworking. Courageous and *hardworking* boys in blue."

Bump grinned at him. "That goes without saying."

John sighed. "I always wanted to be a cop. Always. And now I finally have a job in a department with guys I really like, in a town I really love . . ."

Bump said, "Dude. Nobody is ever gonna know you knew about this. Now. The Witness's friend. What was his name?" He reached back to the breakfast bar for the phone book.

It took me and Gruf a minute to come up with Brandon Tercek's name. Bump thumbed back to the Ts. "Shit. There's about a million Terceks up in Fairfield."

Gruf said, "Hang on. He said he lives right across the street from the Witness. Lemme see the book."

Bump passed it over. Gruf ran his finger down the column. "Middlewood. This is it. How're we gonna do this?"

"Call him and ask him where the little kid lives."

Brandon's mom said he was at work. Bump looked up the number for the Fairfield Arthur Treacher's, and a minute later Gruf had Brandon on the phone.

It took a few minutes to explain what we wanted. Then it seemed to take some thought on Brandon's part to come up with what little kid it might have been that the Witness was involving himself with, but finally Gruf was writing down a description of the house and its location. He hung up, smiling.

Bump took the directions from Gruf, folded the paper up and stuck it in his vest pocket. "Here's what I'm gonna do. I'm gonna go home and get my truck.

Then I'm gonna drive up to Fairfield tonight and find
the house and stake it out. We need to find a way to
get close to the dad, and to do that, we need to know
when he works, where he works, and what he does
after work."

Bump gave John a questioning look. John grimaced,
then gave a reluctant nod.

"How are you gonna sit up there all night and then
be at work tomorrow at eleven?" Gruf asked.

"Fuck. I don't need much sleep."

"We'll sleep when we die?" I thought I remembered hearing a tough guy say that in a movie, or
somewhere.

Bump said, "Exactly."

Gruf glanced over at him. "And what if he hasn't
left the house by the time you have to leave in the
morning?"

"I'll have my cell phone with me." He gave out the
number. "You guys call me from Brewster's, or I'll
call you at Bud's. If he hasn't left yet, one of you'll
have to come up and take over the stakeout."

Gruf glanced at me, but didn't say anything. I knew
he was still lukewarm on the whole idea.

Bump said, "Come on, guys. This isn't gonna take
a lot of time. First chance we get, we'll move in on
him and see what we can do. Okay?"

Nobody said anything. Bump went off. "Fuck! We
got Carrie Hall maybe run off the road and coulda
been killed, and we got the Witness *dead.* What does
Alan Bushnell do about it? Hauls *Terry's* ass in for
questioning. *Please!* What's it gonna take for you guys
to get off your asses and *do* something?"

I made up my mind. "Okay. Let's do it. Gruf, if
you don't mind, you take the day watch, 'cause that
way I can keep working on Bud's deck. If we don't

have anything by midafternoon, I'll come up and relieve you in time for you to get back to Carlo's."

Gruf said. "Okay."

Bump said, "That's what *I'm* talkin' about. When Gruf comes up, I'll hand off the cell phone to him. Terry, when you come up, get the phone from Gruf. I don't want anyone up there without the phone. This is a murderer we're looking for."

"And," John said, fixing each of us with a hard look, "before anything has a chance to go wrong, you guys call the station. If things start to get hairy, do *not* try to handle it yourselves."

"Yeah."

"Okay."

John groaned. "I've got a terrible feeling about this."

When I finally went to bed that night, I couldn't fall asleep. Somebody's dog was barking. The thing barked and barked. At first I thought any minute the owner would get his leash and take him out. Then I realized he must have been left home alone. Because who could sit there doing nothing while his own dog barked like that?

I didn't feel good about Bump sitting up on some dark street in Fairfield all night in his truck. I couldn't sleep. I called him twice. Both times everything was quiet. Both times he told me he appreciated me calling him. Both times he said Gruf had just called him, too.

Chapter 15

Five minutes before my alarm went off Monday morning, the phone rang. It was Gruf. He was calling on Bump's cell phone. He said he had decided to go up and relieve Bump early. Bump was on his way home to get some sleep. I told Gruf I'd call him when I got to Bud's.

I did. He said, "They're up and moving around in the house." I could tell by the excitement in his voice that he was warming up to this stakeout business. "I moved my Jeep down to the end of the block. They won't notice me, but I'll see when a car leaves the driveway."

"Okay. I'm leaving Bud's door open so I can hear the phone. You need me for any reason, I'm there in fifteen minutes." As I heard myself say it, fifteen minutes sounded like a long time. I wondered if it did to him, too. "You got Bud's number?"

"No. Give it to me."

I did. I said, "I'll call you back in an hour or so."

Gruf said, "Ten-four," in a sissy voice. We laughed and hung up.

The condition of Bud's kitchen had deteriorated since Wednesday. An empty Carlo's pizza box sat on the table, along with a full ashtray and a big pile of mail. A couple of empty beer bottles and some dirty glasses and cups sat on the sink counter. Fuckin' Bud.

I worked my ass off for the next hour trying to get the plumbing roughed in. I was surprised at how slow and hard it was, working alone. You don't realize how much difference your partner makes until he's not there. I called him back after an hour or so.

"I'm sitting a ways down from the entrance to the Perry Nuclear Power Plant," he told me in an excited voice. "I followed the guy here just a few minutes ago. What time is it, anyway?"

"Ah . . ." I had to take a few steps toward the clock on Bud's stove to read it in the glare of the sunlight streaming through the kitchen window. "It's a little before ten. Ten of. That'd put him starting work at ten, huh?"

"Yeah."

"Assuming he works an eight-hour shift with an hour for lunch, that'd mean he gets off at seven."

"*Can* we assume that, though? Ten o'clock's an odd hour to start a shift."

"Yeah. I guess we'll have to sit there till he comes out."

"Yeah."

"Are you real obvious, parked there? Nuke plants have hellfire security, don't they?"

"I parked down quite a ways. I pulled into a little unused driveway-looking thing, I guess you'd call it."

"Listen. I'm gonna bust ass here until eleven-thirty or so. Then I'll come up. I'll bring you some lunch."

"Cool."

"Tell me how to find you."

Two and a half hours later, I turned my truck off the road and parked beside Gruf's Jeep. He got out and climbed into my truck.

I'd bought food at a Wendy's in Painesville. We ate silently for a while. The cell phone rang while we were polishing off our fries. Gruf answered. I went on eating and watching. After a few minutes, Gruf snapped the cell phone closed and said, "Bump can't stand being left out. Business at Carlo's is slow today anyway, so Flute's gonna finish the shift alone and Bump's coming up here in an hour or so."

We were sitting in a little clearing, weeds growing up through a thin layer of gravel. It was a hot day, but after we repositioned the truck to catch the lake breeze, it wasn't bad. The Lake Erie shore was just north of us, on the other side of the woods we were backed into. We could hear and smell the lake and feel the breeze, but we couldn't see it. We listened for a while to the birds and other chirping, croaking things all around us.

There'd been some outgoing lunch-hour-type traffic earlier, and now there was some ingoing lunch-hour-type traffic, but our boy didn't show. Gruf picked up the phone again. "I'm gonna call Jackson and tell her she's in charge tonight. I don't wanna miss anything here."

Not long afterward, Bump's truck came rolling up next to mine. He came walking up to my window. He said, "Who's leaving and who's staying?"

Gruf and I looked at each other. I turned back to Bump. "I think we're both staying."

Bump grinned. "Figured. Okay, we gotta stash two of these vehicles. There's a little shopping center back a ways. Let's do it fast and get back here."

We parked the two trucks in the shopping center parking lot. I ran into the little grocery store and bought some beverages, a Styrofoam cooler, a bag of ice, and some snackage. We hurried back toward the nuke plant and parked the Jeep nose out, well back into the weeds.

Gruf wanted the backseat so he could shut his eyes for a few minutes. He told us the car we were looking for was a little red Saturn, pointed out the piece of paper stuck in his visor with the license plate number scrawled on it, and described the guy. He told Bump there was a pair of binoculars under the driver's seat. Then he flopped on his back with his legs folded up in about four places and a minute later we heard him snoring.

Bump and I sat there talking quietly for a while; then Gruf woke up and climbed out to take a leak. There was a fairly steady parade of cars and delivery trucks going by now, so we had to pay pretty close attention. That got tedious, so we took turns being the one to pay attention. The other two could climb out and stretch, or lean back and rest, or eat.

Myself, I did a lot of eating. Among the other crap, I had bought a bag of pork rinds and a bottle of green Tabasco sauce to drip on them. Gruf was disgusted with the whole idea. Bump tried it and liked it.

The sun was getting low. I was the one on watch. I glanced down at my watch, saw that it was almost seven, and looked back up in time to see a little red Saturn roll by.

"Uh-oh," I said. "It's show time."

By this time Gruf was back in the driver's seat. He'd seen it, too. He started the motor and we pulled out. He set a pace well back from the car.

"Did you see the driver?" Bump asked, leaning over the back of the front seat. "Is it our guy?"

"It's our guy," Gruf said happily. We followed him along Route 20 right through the heart of Painesville, where the heavy traffic made it easy to keep him from spotting us. Once he had passed through the main business areas of Painesville, though, the traffic thinned out considerably. Gruf fell back. He passed me the binoculars so if the guy turned, I could spot where.

Almost on the Fairfield-Painesville line, the guy turned into a little bar. The sign said O'CONNOR'S. Gruf slowed down. By the time we pulled into the parking lot, the guy was walking in the door. We parked at the other end of the nearly empty parking lot from the red Saturn.

Bump was freaking. "This is *perfect*! This is fuckin' *perfect!*"

"How we gonna do this?" Gruf asked.

"Okay, lemme see. We need a scam." Bump leaned over the seat between us, working his hands in the air between our shoulders.

"One of us is drunk," Gruf said. "That'll be me, since you guys don't drink. Get me sitting right next to him."

"Okay," I said. "Your two buddies have taken you out to get you drunk."

"Yeah, good." Bump said. "Because it's a bad day for you. . . ."

"It's an anniversary. . . ." I helped the story along.

We sat there another ten minutes, reworking and polishing our story, and then we went in.

Gruf was supposed to be wasted. He lurched as we came through the door, and I grabbed him by the elbow and straightened him up. Bump and me grimaced at each other and grinned. Gruf righted himself with great dignity and found his way to an empty stool next to our man, who was wearing a faded blue industrial uniform and a red Perry Nuclear Power Plant cap.

There were only two other patrons in the bar, and they sat hunched over their beers on the opposite side from our boy, with about five empty stools between them.

Our boy adjusted himself away from Gruf and carefully avoided eye contact. The bartender watched Gruf center himself on the stool and looked at me, frowning. "I think you boys've already had enough. I can't serve you."

I leaned across the bar to him, smiling. "Me and him aren't drinking," I said, jerking my thumb at Bump. I saw in my peripheral when the guy in the red cap looked over at us. "We're just looking out for our friend, so he can get trashed. It's a bad day for him."

The bartender eyed us, but the frown wasn't as pronounced. "Bad day, huh?"

Bump climbed on a stool. "Bad, uh, anniversary, I guess you'd call it."

Gruf squared his shoulders, eyed the bartender, and spoke in careful syllables. "My little brother would have been twenty-one today."

The bartender blinked. We had him curious. He said, "Would have? What happened?"

Me and Bump looked protectively at Gruf. "You don't have to talk about it," I told him. I said to the bartender, "Can we get two Cokes, please? What'll it be, kid? Stickin' with the High Life and mescal?"

Gruf rocked back on his stool. "It's served me well so far," he said in a voice just slightly on the loud side. He turned his head to Mr. Red Cap, caught him looking, and gave him a sunny smile. "I don't often get drunk," he told him with great sincerity. "I'll be no trouble whatsoever."

"You're fine," the man said, winking past Gruf at me. "Don't worry about it." He turned his head to face front and played with two quarters and some bills sitting in front of him on the bar.

Meanwhile, Bump laid a twenty on the bar. I climbed onto my stool between Gruf and Bump. In the mirror behind the bar I could clearly see our boy's face. I studied him in quick takes. He was a big guy with short sandy hair, and his face was too red. It was that kind of red face that can be howling with laughter one minute and flaming with rage the next.

The bartender, black Irish if I ever saw one, and I should know, since all my mother's brothers are that breed, set up our drinks and wiped the bar around them. You could tell he wanted to hear the story.

"Another gorgeous day out there today, huh?" he said.

We all nodded. Gruf tossed back his shot and chug-alugged his beer. I reached over in front of him and nudged both glasses toward the bartender. He refilled them and set them back in front of Gruf.

Gruf said, "Thank you, Mr. . . . are you O'Connor?"

"You just call me Connie," the bartender told him warmly, then picked up Bump's twenty and brought back the change, which Bump left lying on the bar.

"Thank you," Gruf said. "I will."

When Bump and me finished our Cokes, Connie promptly refilled our glasses, again taking payment from the money lying in front of Bump. I reached into my pocket and pulled out another twenty, which I added to the top of the little pile of bills. Connie smiled.

Weaving slightly, Gruf looked around. He said, "This is a nice place. Why haven't we ever been here before?"

Bump looked surprised. "I thought you had. You said to turn in here. I thought you knew the place."

I started laughing. "Back in Willoughby, you said there was some place you wanted to go, and you gave us the directions."

The bartender and Red Cap joined in laughing.

I said, "Well, however we got here, it *is* a nice place." I turned to Bump. "Dude, ya see the pool table over there?"

"I saw it," he said. "You think we can leave this drunkard long enough to shoot a game?"

I looked at Gruf. He said, "Go! Go on! I have

everything under control." Swaying slightly, he turned to Red Cap. "Don't I?"

Red Cap grinned. He said, "Looks that way to me."

Bump said to Connie, "Don't let our friend pay for anything. Whatever he wants, take it out of the pile here." He dug some quarters out of his pants pocket and handed them to me. "Money breaks. Rack 'em."

We picked up our Cokes and walked over to the pool table.

From the pool table, Bump and I couldn't hear what was going on at the bar. Somebody had dropped a lot of quarters in the jukebox and all we could hear was back-to-back Loretta Lynn and George Jones. But I'll tell this part like we *could* hear, by splicing in what Gruf told us later.

Once we'd walked away, Gruf knocked back his shot and beer, and Red Cap, who wanted to hear the story of Gruf's little brother as bad as Connie did, said, "The next one's on me. In memory of your little brother."

Gruf turned to him. "He would have been twenty-one today."

Connie quickly refilled the glasses, set them in front of Gruf, and leaned in close for a good heart-to-heart.

Over at the pool table, Bump leaned on the table as I racked the balls. "That bartender doesn't have anything else to do but stand there and mess things up. We gotta get him over here, so Gruf can work the guy alone."

"How we gonna do that?"

"We'll shoot a while and give Gruf some time to set the thing up. When he's ready, I'll try to drop the balls, only the coin carrier'll be jammed." He winked at me.

I said, "We gotta get Gruf over here first. Work out the fine points."

Bump nodded, chalking his stick. "Hey! Drunkard! Com'ere and show me how to do that break you were braggin' about!"

Gruf grinned, slid off the bar stool, and walked carefully over to the table. The three of us stood at the business end of the pool table with our backs to the bar, and Gruf took Bump's stick. We modified the plan while he went through the motions of explaining where to set the cue ball, how to sight the strike, and what kind of English to use.

Gruf said, "Lemme give you a signal when to call the bartender. I'll yell, 'Who's winning?' "

"Gotcha."

Gruf straightened, stepped back to watch Bump break, then, laughing, walked back to his place at the bar. "My little brother was the cutest little kid you ever saw," he said confidentially to Red Cap as he swung a leg over his stool.

"What was his name?" Connie said.

"Casey." Gruf caressed his beer glass, then picked it up and drank a slug.

"But you haven't said what happened to him," Connie said.

Gruf looked up at him. "Murdered. Hey, where's the can?"

Connie pointed toward the back hallway and Connie and Red Cap watched him make his way in that direction. So did we. He was gone quite a while. Connie wiped the bar with his damp white towel, killing time.

A few minutes after he'd settled himself back on his stool, Gruf turned toward us and yelled, "Hey! Who's winning?"

I said, "We're about to be one and one. The next game'll decide it." I dropped the four and one balls and lined up on the eight. Boom. Corner pocket.

"Nice shot," Bump said, and bent to the coin slot. I didn't see what he did, but he got it jammed good. He yelled, "Connie! Little help?"

Connie dropped his towel on the bar and lifted the key to the pool table lockbox off a hook above the register. As he walked to the table, Gruf turned confidentially to Red Cap.

"See, I didn't know what was going on," he said quietly. "If I woulda known, I'da fuckin killed the guy." He pulled on his beer. "Yeah, that's right. I'da killed him. Sure, I'd be in jail now, but it'd be worth it. My little brother'd be out with his friends tonight, celebrating his twenty-first birthday." He gave out a big sigh and swallowed some beer. "But I just didn't know."

He fixed Red Cap with hard eyes and waited.

Red Cap said, "You didn't know what?"

"He never told anyone. We didn't find out until after he was dead. He was afraid to tell."

Red Cap said, "Tell what?"

"About the guy," Gruf said impatiently. He looked at Red Cap. "What the guy was doing to him."

Color drained from Red Cap's ruddy face as he began to realize where the story was going. "The guy that killed him?"

Gruf nodded. "If Casey just woulda told *me*. If I'da known, I'da killed the bastard so fast . . ."

Red Cap said slowly, "Your little brother was being abused and he didn't tell anyone?"

Gruf turned to him. "And then the son of a bitch killed him. There was nothin' I could do about it."

Red Cap, who'd been keeping pace with Gruf on the drinking, only couldn't hold it as well as Gruf could, looked down at his beer.

Over at the table, Connie was on his knees studying the coin slot. "I can't figure out why it's jammed."

Red Cap said quietly, "I just found out someone was messing around with *my* son."

Gruf jerked upright. "No, you didn't!"

"Yeah. I did."

"Who *is* the bastard?" Gruf said vehemently. "I'll help you get him. No, wait. Your son needs his father. I'll get him *for* ya. I will. I'll do him good."

Red Cap shook his head. "Somebody already got him. The little fuck's dead."

Gruf lost his balance a little bit and swayed toward Red Cap, then righted himself. "Seriously? No shit. *You* didn't do him?"

"No. I didn't even know what was going on until after the little bastard was dead. Rotten bastard lived right in our neighborhood. My son was afraid to tell anyone until he knew the shithead was dead 'cause the guy scared him so bad."

"Well, who killed him, then?"

"No idea. Wish I knew. Sure would like to thank him."

Gruf whistled. "You were so fuckin' lucky."

"Tell me about it."

They drank in silence for a minute, while Connie continued to try to solve the puzzle of the jammed coin carrier. Gruf began to plan the best way to get us out of there.

Red Cap said, "You know what I keep thinkin' about, though?"

Gruf said, "What's that?"

"Well, the wife saw on TV that perverts get that way because somebody abused *them*."

"Yeah?"

"Yeah. She says it's whatcha call a cycle. The abused kid grows up to be the abusive adult."

"That how it works?"

"Yeah. So what I wonder about, who abused the son of a bitch who was messin' with my son?"

"Who do you think?"

Red Cap shrugged. "I don't know the bastard's family, but my wife says they're weird. Probably the father. Who knows? Makes ya wonder, though."

"Yeah. I see whatcha mean." Gruf slammed his shot and drained his beer. "What a world! God, I'm tired." He pushed the glasses away and cradled his head on his arms.

Over at the pool table, Bump was down on his knees next to Connie, who had his head bent low to examine the guts of the coin carrier. I saw Gruf's head go down and tapped Bump's shoulder.

"Wait a minute," Bump said. "I think I see something." Connie edged away and Bump stuck his head close to the table. He reached inside and fumbled around a few seconds. "No, I guess it wasn't . . . Well, here. Let's try it now."

Connie placed the quarters into the slot and it slid easily in and out. The coins dropped easily into the box and the balls dropped smoothly onto the tray. Connie said, "Just like new! What did you do?"

Bump said, "Hell if I know. I musta knocked somethin' loose."

Bump and I made pretty fast work out of noticing Gruf was passed out and carrying him out of the bar. Once we were back on the road, and Gruf had miraculously regained consciousness, he was exhilarated. All we'd done was eliminate a suspect, but you'd have thought we broke the case wide open.

Gruf calmed down and said, "I gotta call Jackson. Make sure everything's okay at the store. Then I'll tell you everything."

"Everything," Bump said. "Every fuckin' word."

· Chapter 16

We picked up our trucks from the shopping center near the nuke plant and got back to Carlo's a little after ten. Danny was sitting in the dining room waiting impatiently for us, feeling all left out and miserable.

Jeff and the old lady were the closing drivers. They quickly made the last of the deliveries and Gruf, Jackson, and I started the closing jobs. Danny and Bump sat out in the dining room, Bump with his head down on a table, listening to tunes on the jukebox. Closing went fast with the extra hands. Before long we got the drivers, Debby, and Hammer escorted to their cars. And then, as Gruf liked to say, it was Miller time.

"You shoulda seen this guy!" I said. "What an actor!"

Gruf snorted, but he liked being complimented in front of Jackson.

We all sprawled in the darkened dining room, smoking and drinking coffee, and we told Jackson and Danny what happened in the bar.

Danny laughed his head off. "Dammit! That is *so cool*. I wish I woulda been there. I can't believe I missed it."

Jackson said, "I can't believe you guys got the kid's father to talk to Gruf like that."

I said, "Bump was right. All it takes is a little planning. Jeez, I can't believe how thirsty I am. This coffee isn't making a dent."

Jackson said, "So the kid's dad is eliminated as a suspect. Who's next?"

We looked at each other. Gruf said, "Red Cap said the Witness was probably the victim of an abuser himself. What if he was, and that abuser is still around?"

Jackson said, "Maybe if you find out who that was, you'd have the murderer?"

"Why would the Witness's abuser wanna kill him? He would've been more fun alive," Bump said.

Jackson groaned. "Sick!" She slid out of the booth and went back to the waitress station. When she came back, she was carrying two cups. She set one in front of me. "Try that. It'll cut your thirst."

I gave her a wink and chugged. It wasn't bad.

Danny said, "Anyway, how would you find out who that was?"

Gruf said, "Maybe a relative? His father?"

I said, "Somebody in the neighborhood?"

Gruf said, "If it was someone in the neighborhood, he would've gone after that Brandon guy. He's a lot better looking than the Witness."

"Yeah," I said. "But maybe the Witness *looked* more like a victim. Anyway, if there'd been some predator in the neighborhood while Brandon and the Witness were growing up, wouldn't Brandon have known about it?"

Bump said, "Really, we don't even know if the Witness *was* abused. We have to find that out before we go wasting a lot of time."

Danny said, "How do you find out something like that? The Witness wouldn't have walked around advertising something like that."

I said, "He advertised that he was a disturbed son of a bitch. Those drawings on his Styrofoam cups."

Gruf snapped his finger. "That's right!"

I said, "We gotta get next to the Witness's parents. See what they can tell us."

Bump said, "The cops have already talked to them. They must not've got anything there, or we'd have heard, right?"

Danny said, "Maybe they weren't asking the right questions." He leaned over to stare down into my cup. "Dude, what the hell is that you're drinking?"

Jackson said, "Ice water with lemons squeezed in it."

He wrinkled his nose.

Jackson said, "It's good. Wanna try some?"

He shook his head and tapped his coffee cup. "I'm good."

Gruf said, "We could go up and pay a courtesy call on his parents. I have his last paycheck. His coworkers and boss, coming to say how sorry we are?"

"That'd work. Call 'em right now," Bump said.

Gruf glanced at the clock. "Kinda late . . ."

Bump said, "So apologize. Call 'em. And see what time tomorrow would be convenient."

Gruf made the call. He woke up the Witness's mother. He groveled for a while, then explained about the final paycheck and asked about us coming up to visit them. He grinned broadly as he listened to her answer.

"They'll both be home all day tomorrow. Mr. Hanus has Tuesdays off because he has to work Saturdays. I told her we'd be there around noon."

Gruf said, "Perfect."

"Meanwhile," Jackson said, "I got something for ya."

We all looked at her. She smiled, reached back, and pulled the black scrunchie away from her hair, letting it fall loose. She shook her dark blond hair out and it fell over her shoulders. I coulda sworn I heard Gruf groan.

"You guys aren't the only ones who've been snooping. You know that one guy?" she said. "Sheila's so-called boyfriend? Fred Oatley?"

"Yeah," one or more of us said.

"He's *my* number-one suspect. And I know where he lives, what he does for a living, and what he does for a hobby. Whad'ya think of that?"

Bump said, "So, give."

"Okay." Now she ran her fingers up through her hair, scratched her scalp briskly, and let the hair fall loose again. "He lives in King's Row Apartments, B-302. He drives a delivery van for Spencer Auto Parts, straight days, going around to gas stations and auto-repair places. And he's all about war games. He goes almost every weekend out to Captain's Acres to shoot paintballs at people."

Gruf wasn't happy. "I do *not* want you mixed up in this shit!" he told her a little too forcefully. Jackson's chin came up and her eyes flashed, and anyone could see you weren't really going to get anywhere trying to order her around.

Gruf's voice softened. "I just don't want you to get hurt."

She frowned at him.

"You did good, though," he finished lamely.

"*That's* tellin' 'er," Bump said, chuckling.

Gruf shrugged.

"Where'd you dig all that up?" I asked.

"My brother Chuckie's a paintballer 'cause he doesn't like hunting like the rest of my brothers do. Doesn't like killing stuff. Chuckie's talked to this Fred Oatley guy a few times out there at Cap's. So that's how I know about that. His number's in the phone book, and so is the street address, which I know from delivering pizzas is King's Row Apartments, but the phone book doesn't tell the apartment building and number. So I called Oatley and said I was compiling the new phone book and needed to verify the address, and he gave me the apartment number. It was all very dangerous work." She gave Gruf a dazzling smile.

"Where does he drink?" Bump asked.

"What makes you think he drinks at all?" Gruf said.

Bump said, "He's mixed up with Sheila the Beast, isn't he? Gotta be a drinkin' man."

"Chuckie said he thinks he's seen him out at the Midway a few times."

Bump said, "I doubt it. Anyways, he doesn't go out there Fridays or Saturdays."

This surprised me from my nondrinking friend. "How would *you* know?"

" 'Cause I'm a bouncer out there on the weekends. Work the door, do the carding, collect the cover . . ."

This amazed me.

Gruf was surprised, too. "You work at the Midway?"

Bump nodded.

Gruf said to me, "You ever been to the Midway?" I shook my head.

"It's a total dive. Biker bar. No offense, Bump."

Bump laughed. "None taken. It *is* a dive."

"They charge a cover on the weekends? In that dive?"

"Sure. To pay for the band."

"They have live music out there? I didn't know that. Is the money good?"

Bump snorted. "Hell, no. I just do it because I like it."

"You like what, exactly?" Gruf said.

"I like watching the biker chicks dance. I like the way they hang on me. I like when some hotshot gets outa line and won't leave when I tell him to. I like when some drunk guy won't take no for an answer when the bartenders cut him off." He chuckled warmly.

I had to ask. "What do you do when a guy won't take no for an answer?"

Bump shrugged, grinning. "Take him outside."

"Then what?"

Bump chuckled. "Well, once I get him out the door, if he swings on me, I get to beat the crap out of him." He chuckled again.

I stared at him, finding it way too easy to picture him as a bouncer in a tough-guy bar. I tried to imagine how it would go if Bump and *me* ever tangled. I thought that if I could get in that first punch, I might have a chance against him. But I was pretty sure I'd never get a chance to throw the first one. With Bump, I think what would happen is he'd move so fast, you'd never see it coming. You'd be on your back before you ever even knew what hit you.

I said, "I'm glad you weren't working in the bar I trashed."

He looked at me for a long minute. "So am I."

Jackson sniffed the air. "What's that smell? Oh, I know. Testosterone."

Gruf laughed. "You'd be the expert on that, growing up in that house of yours."

I must've looked puzzled, because Jackson stopped laughing and told me, "He means my brothers."

That reminded me about something I'd been wondering. Something I hadn't wanted to bring up, or even think about, to tell you the truth. "Your brothers are bikers, huh?"

She grimaced. "Among other things."

"Somebody mentioned something about your brothers."

They all looked at me and waited.

"Something to do with your brothers and the Witness."

Gruf said, "I know what it was. The night of the murder, when Hammer was running his mouth. He said something about Jackson's brothers threatening the Witness. I don't know where he got *that*."

Jackson frowned. "I do. There was an incident in the parking lot one night."

She had our full attention. Gruf said, "Did you tell any of your brothers that the Witness was bothering you?"

"*No!* Are you kidding me? I'd *never* do something like that! You know what would have happened if I'd told any of my brothers about the Witness?"

Gruf said quietly, "They'da cut his throat?"

She glared at him. "Don't *even* start wondering if any of my brothers did *that*. If my brothers ever wanted to kill somebody, I guarantee you the body'd never be found. They certainly wouldn't have left it lying right out there in the parking lot."

I said, "Well, tell us what *did* happen."

She said, "The night after you put the Witness's head in the sink? Chuckie and Artie came to pick me up, so I was going out the back door, and the Witness followed me out. He was mad at me. He blamed *me* for that sink thing. He was trying to tell me that I shouldn't have let you do that."

We all shook our heads.

She said, "I was tired and I didn't want to talk to him. I said something over my shoulder and kept walking out the back door. He followed me out and tried to grab my arm, and that made me mad. I guess he didn't notice Chuckie's car sitting there, or he didn't know it was my brothers, or something. Anyway, he grabbed my arm. That was all it took. My brothers were out of the car like a shot. They put the Witness up against the building and explained to him never to grab me again."

I said, "Whew. The Witness had a bad couple of nights there, didn't he?"

She said, "I'll say. But that was it. It happened and it was over. They laughed about it all the way home."

I said, "Did the cops ever talk to them?" I knew the answer to that, but I wanted to hear it from her.

She nodded. "Alan Bushnell took them both in for questioning the day after the murder. Put them in separate rooms and told each one that the other one had confessed and he knew they did it, so they might as well tell him the truth."

"That's more or less what he did to me."

She nodded. "They just laughed at him. After a while he let 'em go."

I looked at the guys and shrugged. "I'm satisfied. But as long as I'm raising questions, here's something else we haven't talked about yet. This Fairfield guy, the Witness's friend . . ."

Gruf said, "Soccer boy?"

I grinned to think that the guy's hair gave Gruf the same image it gave me. "Yeah. Brandon."

Gruf said, "What about him?"

"We haven't really talked about him as a suspect."

Bump said, "Huh."

Gruf picked up his coffee cup, swirled it, and drained it.

I said, "What do you guys think? Could he have done it?"

Jackson said, "I don't know. I haven't met him yet."

Everybody frowned.

Bump said, "*Any*one could have done it."

Gruf said, "I don't like Brandon that much, but to me he's not a suspect. What would've been his reason?"

Bump said, "Yeah. They're friends their whole lives, and then he murders him? Why?"

Gruf said, "Plus, he strikes me as too goody-goody." He shook his head. "Naw. Not the homicidal type. In my opinion."

Jackson said, "Why, Terry? Do you think he's a suspect?"

I shrugged. "Muzzy. I don't know. There's something about him."

Jackson said, "Can we get back to Fred Oatley? He goes out to the Midway Wednesday nights for Slam Night."

"Slam Night?" Gruf said. "What's that, like moshing, or something?"

Her eyes twinkled. "No. It's poetry. Slam poetry."

Bump said, "Oh, wait a minute. I heard something about that. Giselle came up with that idea."

Jackson said, "Supposedly it's sort of a national thing. People doing it in bars all over the country."

Gruf said, "And your brothers go."

She punched his arm. "One or more of my brothers goes to the Midway *every* night. It wouldn't matter if it was Tupperware night."

Bump said, "Yeah, I remember now. Giselle read about slammin' in *Newsweek* or somewhere and she was all like, "Oh, ve got to do dat here!'"

Gruf said, "Who's Giselle?"

Bump said, "Lothar's wife." He pronounced the name like Low-Tar. "They own the place."

I said, "Yeah, but what is it?"

Jackson said, "Poetry reading. You go up to the mike, you say an original poem in, like, three minutes, or something, the crowd cheers or boos, and at the end of it they pick a winner."

Gruf and I looked at each other. "God," I said. "It sounds worse than karaoke."

Bump chuckled. "I bet it's way worse."

Gruf said, "Well, it might be a good atmosphere for pullin' off a scam."

I said, "Are we gonna scam Oatley?"

Their grins answered the question.

Danny said, "I'm coming, too."

I looked at him.

He said, "Wild horses couldn't keep me away. I'll be the Kooky Neighbor."

"Okay," I said, "but I'm telling all of you right now, I'm not standing up in front of a bar and saying any poetry."

Bump said, "Me, either." We looked at each other. Then we looked at Gruf. "You're doin' it," Bump told him. "You're the actor in the family."

Gruf said, "Nobody has to say a poem. We can just sit there and listen. So what's the plan?"

We all began to chew on our lower lips like that would help us think better. A couple of minutes went by and nobody had anything. "I guess this is gonna take some time to figure out," Gruf said.

I said, "If one of them did it, it had something to do with jealousy. All that shit going on between the Witness, Fred Oatley, Sheila, and, what's her husband's name? Lenny? So maybe we set up a three-way, a girl and two guys."

Gruf said, "We'd have a girl there with us?"

Bump said, "Yeah."

Jackson said, "I'll go."

Gruf thumped her on the head. "You're a minor."

Bump said, "I'll tell you what you *can* do to help, though, Jackson. Would you cover for me here tomorrow, while I go with these guys up to the Witness's parents' house? Open for me, just for an hour or so. I'll come in as soon as we get back from Fairfield."

She nodded. "Okay."

Gruf gave her a smile.

Bump said, "I'm thinking about Debby. For the scam. She's got the balls to do it."

Gruf said, "She's, like, the queen of the bikers. Everybody in there would know her."

"Dude," Bump said. "How many bikers do you think go to the Midway on Slam Night?"

Gruf said, "Besides Jackson's brothers? I don't know. Do you?"

Bump shrugged. "I told ya, I've never been there on a Wednesday."

I said, "I think we're gonna have to take a run out there Wednesday night. See what's what."

Bump said, "Yeah, that's a good idea."

Gruf said, "Anyway, Fred Oatley knows Debby from Carlo's. Using her might make him suspicious."

Bump shook his head. "He's not exactly a rocket scientist."

"That's true," I said.

We sat drinking our coffee for a while.

Gruf said, "Yeah."

Chapter 17

The weather was beautiful Tuesday morning. There was a high haze that burned off early and left the sky one of those startling shades of blue that you keep looking up at. Gruf and I took his Jeep to Bud's. I got Gruf started on the wiring for the hot tub. Then I drove the Jeep to Nelma's office for our weekly meeting. Which she cut it short when I told her we were going to pay our condolences to the Witness's parents. I had time to get back to Bud's and check Gruf's connections before Bump came along on his Harley.

The three of us piled into the Jeep for the drive to Fairfield. Gruf, by the way, was wearing another one of his awesome T-shirts that day. This one was dark gray. I started to ask where he got those awesome shirts, but once again the question got away from me.

As we drove, Gruf reminded us that Alan had said the Hanuses were strange people. We wondered what that could mean. Following Bump's directions, Gruf turned off Lake Shore Boulevard, turned again, and we found ourselves in a tightly packed little working-man's neighborhood with screen doors hanging open and rusting pickups parked on the grass. All the houses were little matchbox-looking frame homes on slabs. Bump pointed out Red Cap's house; then half a block farther, he spotted the address we were look-

ing for and pointed to a driveway. Gruf pulled in and
parked. The yard had no bushes or plants in it whatsoever. Just closely trimmed grass right up to the foun-
dation. Obviously no landscaper types living here.

As we walked up to the door, I glanced at the house
directly across the street. Brandon Tercek's house. It
was a little larger and a lot nicer looking than most
of the other houses around it. Landscaped to within
an inch of its life. All the windows had white venetian
blinds in them, and they were all down and tightly
closed.

Gruf knocked.

I said, "What's their last name again?"

"Hanus," Gruf said as the door opened.

A painfully thin, pale little bald guy stood there,
blinking at us through thick glasses. Gruf introduced
us and the man reluctantly opened the door wider and
stepped back to let us in.

"They're here, Mother," he said over his shoulder.

"Oh, see?" said a woman's thin, nervous voice. She
almost sang it. "Oh" ran down the scale and "see"
ran up it. I looked across the dim little living room
toward the little dining room and found her standing
on the near side of the dining room table. As I
stepped into the house, stuffy heat seemed to wrap
around my face like a plastic bag.

Mrs. Hanus was even tinier than Mr. Hanus. She
wore a faded little blue flowered housedress that hung
on her thin bones. Her brown shoulder-length hair
hung limply around her pinched face. There wasn't a
speck of personality in either one of them.

The next half hour was about the most excruciat-
ingly uncomfortable chunk of time I have ever had to
sit through in my life, including my sentencing hearing.
The Hanuses sat side by side on the extreme front
edge of the worn green sofa, her with her hands folded

so tightly in her lap that I imagined I could see her fingers turning blue, him fidgeting like he was sitting on an anthill.

Bump had the armchair because he got to it first. Gruf and I had to sit crammed together on the little green love seat, our shoulders rubbing every time either one of us shifted position and our knees wedged against the short end of the coffee table.

In the uncomfortable silence, Gruf shifted and swung his knees so he could stretch his legs out along the outside edge of the table, but I had nowhere to go with mine. Mrs. Hanus's knees blocked any escape from my corner of the table.

Once we were all settled, I noticed how the four little Hanus eyes bounced around between the three of us but always skidded away from making any sort of actual eye contact.

Gruf said awkwardly, "First, I want to tell you how sorry we all were about, uh, about, you know."

I glanced at Gruf. It was the first time I'd ever seen the silver-tongued devil at a loss for words. "It was a terrible thing," I said quickly to get him off the hook. "We want the cops to get the person that did it."

The Hanuses' faces pinched up even more. Mr. Hanus said, "Thank you."

Mrs. Hanus said, "Yeah, huh?" She spoke in a high, small, baby-talk voice, like she was talking to little kids, or something, and the words ran down and back up the scale again.

Mr. Hanus reached out and rubbed his index finger on a little area of the dark coffee table, like he was trying to remove a spot of something, but I couldn't see anything there. I looked up at the ticking clock on the wall above the portable TV. The clock was one of those black-rimmed $9.98 Kmart specials and it had the loudest tick I've ever heard in my life.

It was so hot and stuffy in there I could hardly breathe. I realized the windows were all closed. I also realized that the TV had not been on when Mr. Hanus had opened the door. I wondered if these two lived in this stuffy little house with the TV off most of the time and the ticking clock the only sound.

Mr. Hanus said, "Can you tell us about that night?"

Gruf cleared his throat again and gave them a summary, leaving out the gory details. When he finished, we all sat there uncomfortably, not knowing what to say.

Finally Mr. Hanus said, "I see."

I tried as hard as I could to picture the Witness in this house, but I couldn't. There wasn't any way in the world I could imagine the Witness in this house. I looked around the room. There was nothing on the white walls at all, except for the clock. There was nothing on the tabletops, either, except for a lamp. A white lamp with a white shade. There were no throw rugs on the wood floor. There was no hutch in the dining room. Just the dark table and three matching dark chairs.

It was weird. Creepy. There were no knickknacks, no family photos, no magazines or mail lying around, no what you call creature comforts, nothing but bare walls and furniture. Like it was moving day and the boxes hadn't come yet.

Mr. Hanus said, "Can you tell us about that night?"

Bump, Gruf, and I looked at each other in alarm.

Bump said, "Aaall righty then," and was ready to stand up and get the hell out of there, but Gruf signaled him to stay where he was.

Mrs. Hanus was looking at her husband. "You already asked them that question, Father."

He said, "Oh, I did?"

She said, "See?" and made as if to pat his hand,

but she didn't actually touch him. She more or less patted the air above his hand.

She looked at us. "When he's upset he repeats himself," she explained.

I said, "Ah!" way too loud, and fought off a sudden urge to giggle. I could feel trickles of sweat running down the sides of my face and the middle of my back.

Gruf said, "Uh, I mentioned that I had Ed's last paycheck." He climbed up out of the love seat, which wasn't easy—we were both sagged way down into it—dug the folded-up check out of his back pocket, and handed it across me to Mrs. Hanus. She set it down on the coffee table, but Mr. Hanus picked it up right away and handed it back to her.

She said, "Oh. Sorry, Father."

He began rubbing with his fingertips at the table where the check had rested, like he was trying to rub away a smudge, or some dirt, or something. She looked at the check lying on her lap and refolded her hands on top of it. Then she looked up and saw us staring. She glanced at her husband, looked back at Gruf, opened her mouth to say something, changed her mind, looked back down at her hands and the check, and clamped her mouth tightly shut.

Bump gave Gruf an annoyed look, like, Why don't we blow this pop stand? Gruf shook his head no. Bump blew air loudly out over his upper lip, the force of which lifted a few scraggly blond hairs off his forehead, and fell back in his chair with a loud groan, resigned to wait it out.

Gruf said, "Uh. Okay. Well, like Terry said, we really want the cops to get the person who did it."

Mrs. Hanus sang, "Yeah, huh?" It was weird how she kept saying this. I wondered if it was an involuntary kind of thing, like a facial tic, only in her speech. I stared at her.

Gruf said, "Yeah." He leaned forward, trying to warm up to the task. "Yeah, in fact, we've been trying to look into the matter in a kind of an amateur way, you know, try to find out anything we can that might help the police investigation?"

Mr. Hanus made a little coughing sound and said, "Can you tell us about that night?"

From the easy chair at the other end of the coffee table, Bump blew air again, loudly, and rolled his eyes to the ceiling. Everyone else just tried to ignore it.

Gruf said, "One thing we've turned up . . ." He looked around at me, eyebrows raised, like, Should I do this? I shrugged and nodded, even though I had no idea what he had in mind. He took a deep breath. "One thing we've turned up is that Ed might've had some, uh, trouble in his childhood."

I thought, Oh, man, here we go. Gruf sat back and waited.

Mrs. Hanus blinked at him. "What sort of trouble would that be, dear?"

Bump sat forward, like he was getting ready for action, and there I was, tightly wedged in between the love seat and the coffee table and Mrs. Hanus's knees.

Gruf said, "There was a suggestion that, in the past, Ed might have been, uh, mistreated. As a child." He just let that hang there.

Mrs. Hanus stared at him. "Mistreated? You mean, like, mistreated?"

Gruf said, "I mean, like, abused."

The word hung in the air like a big poisonous balloon. The silence was suffocating.

Then Mr. Hanus said, *"Abused?"*

All three of us nodded at him. You could see the anger boiling up under the thin blue skin of his face. *"Abused!* That's ridiculous!"

Gruf shook his head. Softly he said, "No, sir. I'm sorry, but the question has been raised whether someone may have abused Ed when he was a child."

"Just what are you trying to suggest?" Mr. Hanus screamed at Gruf. His face was bright red.

Bump leaned over and put a restraining hand on the sputtering little man's shoulder. "Easy there, dude. Don't go postal on us."

Mrs. Hanus said, "Oh, dear. Oh, dear."

I was afraid she was about to bust out crying. Her hands fluttered around in front of her and her husband like she was trying to smooth out wrinkled air.

"I'm sorry to upset you both, I really am," Gruf said. "But if we don't find out the truth about all this, I don't think we can catch the person who killed Ed. See, we think maybe if someone abused him when he was little, that same person might've had something to do with his murder."

"But that is the most outrageous thing I've ever *heard!*" Mr. Hanus said. "What kind of people are you, to come into my house and say a thing like *that?*"

I said, "Please, Mr. Hanus. We're not accusing *you.* We're asking you to help us."

"Help you? Help you *what?* You don't come into my house and . . . You listen to *me*, boy. We have a clean house here. *Clean!* Don't you think we loved our son and took care of him and kept him *clean?*"

This was so odd we all just stared at him. Once again Mrs. Hanus looked up, opened her mouth to say something, then seemed to change her mind. I watched her. She sat wringing her hands in her lap and chewing her lower lip. Then apparently she felt me watching her. She looked up at me.

I said, "What is it, Mrs. Hanus?"

She glanced sideways at her husband, took a deep

breath, and then said, "Father. You'd better go get started on the garage. You're falling way behind schedule."

He gave her an annoyed look, but then he got agitated and seemed to be struggling with a decision. Finally he said, "Yes. All right."

He got up and Bump scrambled up to let him out past the easy chair. Mr. Hanus disappeared through the dining room. We heard the back screen door swing quietly closed.

The rest of us just sat there for a moment. Then Mrs. Hanus said, "Would you children like some juice?" Children? *Juice?* I swear, she was the weirdest woman I've ever met in my life.

We nodded at her, and she went out to the kitchen. A few minutes later she came back carrying a yellow metal tray with three little glasses of orange juice on it. She passed them out, set the tray on the coffee table, and settled back onto the sofa, smoothing the thin blue dress over her knees. "Have you children ever heard of obsessive-compulsive disorder?"

We shrugged. She said, "Well, anyway, Father has it. That's why he said that, about keeping a clean house." She reached forward to adjust the tray so that its edge was exactly parallel to the edge of the coffee table.

She said, "I understand OCD can take many different forms, but for him it means that he has to clean everything all the time. He has to go through the house and the garage and the car, cleaning everything in a certain way, according to a strict schedule. He thinks if he doesn't do it in exactly the right way, at exactly the right time, something bad will happen. Is the juice good?"

We nodded.

Gruf said, "Hits the spot." I looked sideways at him and gave him an evil smirk.

She said, "Father always cleans the garage of a Tuesday. He'll be out there now until after dark."

We nodded as if we understood perfectly and waited. She said, "Do you know what agoraphobia is?"

Bump said, "That's when a person is afraid to leave their house, isn't it?"

She smiled at him. "Yeah, huh? Oh my, do you know someone who has it, dear?"

He said, "No, no. I just heard about it. On *Oprah* or something." I thought, now there was something to try and imagine. Bump watching *Oprah*.

She nodded. "Anyway, I have it. I'm agoraphobic."

I said, "You don't go out of your house at all?"

She said, "No."

Gruf said, "What causes it?"

She shrugged. "A chemical in the brain, maybe. I'm sure I don't know." She looked at Bump. "More juice, dear?"

"No, thanks. I'm good."

She leaned forward, tracing the edge of the tray with her forefinger. "We did love our Eddy, you know," she said softly.

Gruf said, "Of course you did."

She looked up at him, looked right at him, and said, "What makes you think he was abused when he was little?"

Gruf shot me an uncertain look. I said, "Tell her."

He took a deep breath and said, "Mrs. Hanus, this is hard for me to tell you, but, uh, Ed was messing around with a little boy down the street. We know that for sure."

She blinked at him, distressed. "You mean . . . Oh, dear."

"The thing is, that might mean that he was abused himself when he was younger. I guess that's the way these things work."

"Yeah, huh? I've heard that. Oh, see?" She sat there for a long time looking down at her hands. Then she said, "Right when you first said it? I realized I've been wondering about that. I think I suspected something like that. I'm afraid I just never faced it."

Bump said, "What do you mean?"

She said slowly, "Eddy would have bad dreams sometimes. And sometimes he would say and do the strangest things. And he was so accident prone. Really, from the time he was little, I knew something was wrong. I just didn't face it. I was afraid."

She looked at each of us with the saddest expression. I felt sorry for her. I reached over and covered her hands with mine. She blinked away a tear.

Gruf said softly, "Was it his father?"

She shook her head adamantly. "Oh! Dear me, no! I know Father would never have done such a thing!"

She noticed my juice glass was empty. She took it from me and set it in the center of the tray. She stared at it, then said, "Anyway, as I told you, I'm agoraphobic. I never leave the house." She squared her shoulders. "No, I'm quite sure. Nothing like that could have been going on here."

I said, "Times when they were away from the house?"

She shook her head. "Father never goes anywhere. When he's not working, he's here."

Gruf said, "Someone else, then? Is there an uncle, maybe, who spent time with Ed? Another relative?"

She shook her head. "No. We don't have any family."

Bump said, "Someone in the neighborhood, then?"

She shrugged. "Maybe. I have no idea who it could have been. I just can't imagine. I just don't know."

I said, "What about the kid across the street?"

She said, "Brandon?"

I nodded.

She stared at me, confused. "What about him?"

"Well, I mean, could *he* have done it?"

She was astonished. "Brandon? Hurt Eddy? *Never!* He's the sweetest, kindest child. Eddy was lucky to have him for a friend."

Gruf said, "Is there *anything* you can think of that might help us? Anything that comes to mind?"

She shook her head sadly and tears pooled in her eyes. "I wish I could help you, but there's nothing. Nothing at all."

Chapter 18

Once we were back in the car and heading home, Gruf said, "I didn't screw that up, did I? It seemed like the direct approach was about the only way."

Bump said, "No, you did good. At least you were thinking. If it'd been up to me, we'da been outa there in a minute and a half."

Gruf said, "When I was in third grade, I started snapping my fingers all the time. My mom was worried *I* had OCD."

I said, "So, what did she do about it?"

Gruf laughed. "My dad cured me. Rolled up a newspaper, swatted me over the head with it, and said, 'Cut it out. You're worrying your mother.'"

At Bud's, Bump hopped on his Harley and hurried off to relieve Jackson at Carlo's. Gruf and I went back to work on Bud's hot tub. The sun got hotter and hotter and we sweated like pigs. We finished all the plumbing and electrical connections by quitting time. I told Gruf, one more good solid day of work, trimming out, routering, and sanding, and we'd be about done.

. We knocked off around three-thirty and Gruf dropped me off at my truck, which was parked in Brewster's parking lot. I went straight home to my shower and got to Carlo's just before five.

We had a new waitress in Tuesday night, training

with Debby. She was a bodacious, flirtatious, toysy little blond named Cindy, who kept turning up by the front counter area talking to Gruf instead of out in the dining room where she was supposed to be.

Jackson was off that night, so I was gonna be closing with that new driver, the old lady. During a lull, the old lady and I were in the back making meatballs when Cindy came mincing through behind us with a handful of ice. Why she was walking around carrying ice in her hands is beyond me. Anyway, she was acting all girly, squealing, "Ooooo! This ice is cold!"

The old lady said without looking up, "Doesn't it kill you how those crazy laws of physics hold up year after year?"

I laughed my ass off. I was beginning to think maybe this old lady would be okay after all.

A few deliveries later, while Gruf and I stood at the front counter waiting for an order of chicken to come up, he told me Alan Bushnell had just stopped by. Wanting to know how we were all doing. Wanting to know if the Witness had ever talked about being scared of anyone.

I said, "Jeez. That sounds sort of desperate. The cops must not have *anything*."

Gruf nodded. "That's just what I thought."

Then it got busy again and I was on the road until almost closing. One of the times I was in the store, I heard a commotion in the back and Hammer came flying through the front and into the kitchen, yelling, "I can't feel my toes! I can't feel my toes!" for no apparent reason. Customers sitting out in the dining room looked around, grinning. I could hear people laughing in the back room.

The last time I came back in from a delivery, while I was standing at the counter waiting for Gruf to finish taking a phone order, I felt someone behind me and turned around. Brandon Tercek was standing there. I groaned when I saw him. I didn't want to have to hang around after closing. I wanted to go home and go to bed.

Brandon said, "How's it going?"

I said, "Good. You?"

"Good. Hey, there's a green Jeep parked out front. Know whose it is?"

"It's Gruf's. Why?"

Brandon got a puzzled look on his face. "Did he go up to Eddy's house today?"

"Gruf, me, and another guy went up. We took the, uh, Eddy's last paycheck to his parents."

He said, "Ooh."

I said, "How'd *you* know we went up there?"

"I saw the Jeep parked in the Hanuses' driveway. I wondered whose it was."

Gruf got off the phone and smiled. "Hey, Brandon. What's up?"

Brandon shrugged. "Not much. Just thought I'd stop in, see if anything's happening."

"Not really," Gruf said.

Cindy came walking up from the back and stopped close to Gruf, bumping her shoulder against his arm. She was clearly a high-maintenance little thing. She gave Brandon a big wide-eyed smile.

"Hi," she said warmly. "I'm Cindy."

Brandon said, "Hi, Cindy."

I happened to glance at his face. He was staring hard at her.

She saw it, too, and let out a nervous little giggle.

Just then Debby came around the corner from the dining room. "Cindy," she said tightly, "ya wanna getcher ass out here so I can show you how to prep the lettuce for tomorrow?" You could tell she was getting pissed at the way her trainee kept adiosing to the front counter.

Once she was gone, Brandon said, "Maybe it was her, huh?"

We both just looked at him.

"The one Ed liked. That he took to the movies?"

Gruf said, "Dude, Cindy just started working here tonight. She never met Ed."

"Oh."

I said, "We already told ya, he wasn't going out with anyone here, unless Sheila gave him a tumble once, and you said it wasn't her."

"Sheila was the ugly waitress, right?"

"Right," Gruf and I said together.

"No, he definitely said she was really good-looking."

I was anxious to go around and get to work on closing the place. This guy was getting on my nerves.

Gruf said, "What difference does it make now, anyway?"

"Oh, none, really, I guess. I was just curious."

I said, holding out my hand, "Well, give it a rest. I gotta get back to work. See ya." We shook and I escaped.

Gruf didn't let him hang around long after that. By the time I parked my car, logged it in, and locked it, Gruf was at the back counter doing food prep for the morning, and the old lady was at the dishwasher slamming trays through. I went to work taking the trays of clean dishes and putting them away. But I was falling way behind her. She was slamming dishes through so fast that I couldn't keep up.

After a while she started carrying the trays of clean dishes out and setting them on the counters to get them out of her way, and when she ran out of trays, she started helping me put dishes away. Once she had some trays emptied, she went right back to washing without missing a beat.

I came back to the sink area for another trayful and said, "Hey, you know what? I still don't know your name."

She looked up. Her face, as well as the whole front of her shirt, was wet from the sink spray. Little curls of wet brown-and-gray hair were plastered on her forehead. "Halle Mally. You?"

"Terry Saltz. Uh, but you can call me Muzzy. It's my nickname."

She blinked at me. *"Muzzy?"*

"Yeah," I said, and grinned at her.

She said, "Lemme get this straight. Your nickname is Muzzy, and that's what you *wanna* be called?"

"Yeah. Something wrong with that?"

She shrugged. "No, I guess not. Not if you like it. It's just that . . ."

"What?"

"Well, it's just that, did you grow up in Spencer?"

"No. I just moved here a few months ago."

She nodded. "That's what I thought. See, Muzzy is a word that, as far as I know, it's homegrown. It's been in the vocabulary here in Spencer for probably forty years or more. But if you use it anywhere away from Spencer, they don't know what you're talking about."

I nodded. "I never heard it before I moved here."

"Yeah. And, see, it's usually used in a derogatory way. Insulting. The meaning is kind of vague, but it's used for someone who's kind of a druggie type. Low income, dumb. The guys who smoke in the boys' bathroom."

"Oh, okay. I kind of had some of that figured out. At my school they called us Curbies."

She smiled. "Curbies?"

"Because we used to sneak out of school and sit on the curb down at the far end of the student parking lot and smoke weed."

She laughed. "Yeah, same thing. So that's why, when you said you wanted to be called that, I wondered if you knew what it meant." She finished scrubbing the stuck-on cheese off a plate, fitted it into a filled-up tray, pushed the tray into the dishwasher, and punched the button to turn it on.

She shrugged. "Nicknames are funny. They're often kind of insulting or ironic when you think about it. Like I know this guy they call Tiny, and he's enormous. He's the biggest guy I ever saw in person. Stuff like that. Or, say, if my nickname was, like, Princess, or something." She chuckled at the thought of being called Princess. "But hey, if that's what you wanna be called . . ."

I shrugged. "Hammer's the one who gave it to me. It was funny when he said it. Yeah, it'll do, as nicknames go." I picked up the next tray of cleans and started toward the kitchen with it.

Behind me, she said, "Okay, then. Muzzy."

I said over my shoulder, "Thanks, Princess."

Debby finished her closing jobs way before any of the rest of us, as usual. She came into the back room and leaned against the food-prep counter, waiting for me to finish mopping so I could walk her to her car.

She said, "By the way. What does Marylou do?"

"Who?"

She looked at me. "Marylou. Your wife?"

"Ex-wife. Whad'ya mean, what does she do?"

Debby said, "For a living."

I swished the mop in the bucket and gave it a wring. "Oh. Uh, she's a bank teller."

"Ooh. That explains it."

Now she had my attention. "That explains what?"

"How she could transfer."

She said it like I should know what she was talking about. I stared at her. "What are you talking about?"

"That she transferred." I was getting mad now, and she saw it. "Oh, jeez. You don't even know. She was in here tonight."

"Yeah?"

"Yeah. Chatted me up like we were old friends."

"Uh-huh?"

"Yeah. So she said she's moving up here to Spencer. She already transferred her job."

"What? Shit!"

"She said she's getting a town house in Green Meadow."

I groaned.

"Sorry, Terry. I couldn't believe it when she said it. I heard you tell her it was over the last time she was in here. You didn't leave room for any doubt, whatsoever. She must live in a fantasy world."

"She's spoiled, is what it is. She doesn't know what it's like to be told no."

Debby said, "She *doesn't? Seriously?* Well, that's it then, dammit. I'm going *blond.*"

Chapter 19

At Brewster's Wednesday morning, we had one final discussion on whether to call Debby and see if she'd go to the Midway with us. Bump said we shouldn't. That we probably weren't even going to make a move on Fred Oatley this first time. He said this trip was more like a fact-finding mission. I looked at him when he said "fact-finding mission" and wondered if maybe he was watching a little too much television. But the rest of us agreed he was right. We'd call Debby when we had a plan. Then Alan walked in and we couldn't talk about it anymore.

Mary was taking orders. "Number four, Terry?"

"Muzzy," I corrected her. Was anybody ever gonna start calling me by my nickname? "Yes, please."

Bump was sitting across the table from me. He looked at me and shook his head.

I said, "What."

He said, "That Muzzy thing," and shook his head again. He sucked on his cigarette.

I said, "What Muzzy thing? What do you mean?"

He said, "As a nickname. It's not working out."

John nodded. "He's right."

I looked at John. "Huh?"

Danny said, "Muzzy just doesn't get it."

Bump said, "See? It's not gonna catch on."

I said, "No, I don't see. Muzzy's a good nickname. What's the big . . ."

Gruf was sitting next to Bump. He said, "Bump's right. It doesn't work."

I said, "Work?"

Bump said, "It doesn't work."

I said, "But I *like* the nickname Muzzy."

Bump shook his head. "No. I don't think so, dude."

Gruf and me worked like dogs at Bud's that day. It was a race against the clock, but we finished his deck. When we broke for a fast lunch, Gruf called Jackson and confirmed that she was going to run Carlo's that night, as he was going to the Midway with us. At the end of the day, I checked all the connections and did a final once-over while Gruf packed up the tools.

John had invited Bump and Gruf over for dinner, figuring we'd all eat together before we went out to the Midway. Bump and Gruf came in first, and they were congregating around the refrigerator for beverages when Danny came banging in the front door, soaking wet from sweat, and smelling like tar.

He smiled and said hi when he saw Bump and Gruf. They stepped back and he leaned into the refrigerator, pulled out a cold one, and disappeared down the hall to the bathroom. We heard the shower go on.

"Must be hot up on a roof in this weather," Bump said. "They couldn't pay me enough to do that."

I agreed with all my heart and soul. Decks were hot enough. John came in, still looking spiffy in his black cop suit. He was carrying a bag of groceries. He started organizing stuff in the kitchen and got dinner going. He turned around from the open refrigerator. "More Coke, anyone? While I'm in here?"

Bump wanted more. He took his glass over to the counter. "More ice, too," he said. Bump, Gruf, and I settled at the kitchen table and lit smokes. A few minutes later, Danny came padding into the kitchen barefoot. John headed down the hall to shower and change. He came back a few minutes later.

Even barefoot, in shorts and a T-shirt, John still looked like he was in uniform, with his buzz-cut hair and his military posture. He went straight to the stove and started stirring stuff. He got a clean spoon out of the silverware drawer and tasted some sauce, then dropped the spoon in the sink.

He turned around to face us and said, "Do you guys have any idea how much trouble I'd be in if Alan ever found out about this?"

Bump said, "Why? We're just going out to the Midway to hear a little poetry." Danny snickered. Bump finished his thought. "Nobody'd get mad about that, would they?"

John grimaced. "They might, if they find out I was at the Midway *with* you guys."

I said, "*You're* gonna come, too?"

John said, "Well, I can't let you guys go out there on your own. Yeah. I *gotta* go."

I said, "Dude. I can't picture you going into a biker bar with that military haircut. You've got cop written all over you."

Bump said, "Maybe it'd work if we tied a dew rag on him. Scuffed him up a bit. How about that, Johnny? You willing to get dirty for the cause?"

John said, "Whatever it takes. I can't believe I'm doing this. Nobody can *ever* know about this. Everybody understands that?"

We all nodded. John said, "Good. Now get outa the way so I can get the table set."

We straggled into the living room. Bump stretched out on the carpet in front of the TV with his hands up behind his head. He groaned.

Danny said, "Bump. I wanna buy a bedroom set off you."

"Yeah?" Bump squinted over at him. "What kind?"

"Oak. Like John's."

"Okay. I'll find you one. Gimme a couple of weeks. What about you, Terry? You want a headboard and a couple of dressers?"

I shrugged. "Sure, I guess."

"Oak?"

"Yeah. That'd be good."

Bump settled his head back, closed his eyes, and groaned again. "This carpet's so soft. I could sleep for a week." He stretched his legs out straight. "Dudes. Let's just stay here and play cards tonight. I really don't feel like going to hear poetry, if ya know what I'm saying."

Gruf gave him a hard look. "Look who's getting cold feet. You're the one that wanted to do all this shit in the first place."

Bump looked over at him, trying to think of a comeback.

Gruf's voice went to mock mode. "Ooo—we can do some investigating of our own. Uh, uh, we can find out things the cops can't. Oh, no offense, John. I was just quoting Bump a little recent history."

John waved a wooden spoon over his shoulder.

Bump folded his arms across his chest and said nothing.

Gruf said, "And anyway, I spent hours working on my poem. You're sure as hell gonna be there to listen to it."

We all stared at him. John stepped out of the kitchen.

Bump burst out laughing. "This I gotta hear. Lay it on us."

Gruf gave him a smug smile. "Yeah. Like I really wrote a poem."

Bump snorted.

Soon after that, supper was ready. John had made some kind of Chinese thing with chicken, rice, and cashews. It was good. Everybody kicked money over to him like we always did to reimburse him for the groceries. He tried to push it back like he always did, and we wouldn't let him like we always wouldn't.

Gruf said, "We can't all go walking in together. We'll have to go in, like, two groups, or something."

Bump nodded. "Yeah. There probably won't be more than five people in the place, then the five of us walk in?"

John said, "And you four have to be split up. Maybe Gruf goes with Bump, and Danny with Terry."

I said, "Why's that?"

He grinned at me. "Are you kidding? Do you know what the four of you look like, walking together?"

We all looked at each other and back at him. "No. What?"

He laughed. "Well, I mean, you're all so big and bad looking. And your hair. When you guys are walking together, you look like, what was that movie? *Young Guns,* or something? *Silverado,* or something? You're attention getting, is what I'm saying."

I hadn't really thought about this before. I took a minute to enjoy the idea. "Okay, then. How 'bout you three guys go in first, then me and Danny?"

John said, "That'll work."

I rode with Danny in his truck. Bump and John rode in Gruf's Jeep. The last of the purple daylight faded into night as we drove. Danny and I followed them out about halfway; then we turned into a convenience store parking lot and they drove on.

Danny said, "Long as we have to wait here anyway, I'm getting some coffee. You comin'?"

We got coffee inside and stood near the front register for about ten minutes hitting on a nasty little red-headed thirty-something while she filed her fingernails and put on Chap Stick. She asked us where we were going and we told her.

She said, "The Midway? Tonight?"

We nodded yeah.

"Isn't it Slam Night out there tonight?"

We nodded again.

She looked hard at us, then smirked.

I was surprised to see that there were a lot of cars and trucks in the parking lot. Danny had to park around behind the building, a couple of rows back. I got out of the truck and did a double take at the rundown old wooden building in the faint glow of its low-voltage, bug-coated spotlights.

We walked around to the front. I kept staring up at the threatening lean of the walls. The front entrance was a raggedy little built-on. The heavy outer door was open, hanging by one rusty old hinge, and judging by the cement floor, which had a big bulge rising up out of it from years and years of frost heaves, this door hadn't been closed for a long time. The inner door didn't have glass in the window, and it looked like someone had given it a good kick, because the wood in the lower-middle panel was split. At least I hoped it had been a kick that had shattered that wood, and not somebody's head.

Once inside, we had to squeeze through a group of some very scruffy individuals who were clotted around a pool table. Just past them was the bar, with people standing two and three deep waiting to buy drinks. Two bartenders were setting them up as fast as they could. One of them was an old, round, jolly-looking guy. I wondered if he was Lothar.

There wasn't any room to stand and reconnoiter, so we elbowed and pushed our way around the bar toward a large, dark, more sparsely populated room with tables around the perimeter.

On the far side of the room was a small bandstand. A skinny girl with stringy blond hair and cocaine nerves in her voice stood in the anemic glow of a spotlight reading a poem about some guy dumping her. I'm no poetry expert, but I only needed to hear a few words to know it was awful.

Danny elbowed me and I looked where he pointed. Gruf, Bump, and John were sitting at a table up near the bandstand. A thick-looking girl was hanging over Bump. She had tattoos on her biceps and her platinum hair was cut almost in a butch. We turned toward the other side of the room and found a table. Almost immediately, an elderly barmaid turned up to take our orders.

I looked over at the table where the boys were and had to laugh at John. He was wearing one of my most raggedy flannels and we'd tied a dew rag on him. He was trying to look bad, but he'd forgotten our instructions to slouch and look bored. He sat there scanning the room, sitting as straight as some kind of fucking military cadet. He might as well have had a sign hanging around his neck that said, "Hi. I'm a cop."

I didn't notice Marylou until Danny gave me an elbow.

He said, "Guess who's here!" I looked over my shoulder where he was looking and saw her.

I turned back to him. He was grinning.

I said, "What the hell's *she* doing here? Did she see us yet?"

He was laughing at me. "She's got her mirror out of her purse and she's all fluffing her hair up. 'Course she's seen us."

"It's not really that funny."

He made an effort to wipe the smile away. "No. No, of course it's not." Then he burst out laughing again.

The elderly barmaid came with our drinks. She was wearing a lot of rings and her arthritic old knuckles were all swollen above and below them. It looked painful. I wondered if she was Giselle, Lothar's wife and the creative genius behind Slam Night.

I scanned the room. "Well, do you see our boy?"

"I don't know him, remember? Is he the guy Gruf's talking to?"

I looked back to the table where Gruf and the guys were sitting. Gruf was turned around in his chair, talking over his shoulder to Fred Oatley.

I said, "Bingo."

The strung-out girl at the mike finished up with a plaintive "When will it end? When will it end?"

Danny said, "Not till you give your nose a rest, honey." A guy at the next table heard him and snickered.

A guy with a large, new-looking cowboy hat stepped up to the mike. He wore a pair of really uncomfortable-looking high-heeled cowboy boots that made him walk funny. Danny sipped his beer, I sipped my Coke, and we tried to look interested. It was hard. The guy started talking about starry skies, campfires, and soft cattle noises.

Danny said, "Think he's ever actually heard a soft cattle noise?"

I shook my head.

Danny said, "So how long are we gonna have to sit here?"

I looked over at the boys. The short-haired girl had

taken up residence in a chair next to Bump and was rubbing up against him, talking a mile a minute. Bump ignored her. He was watching Gruf and Fred Oatley. He saw me looking and nodded. I saw now that the girl wore black lipstick and had her nose pierced. Gruf was still turned around talking to Fred Oatley. John was listening to the cowboy poet and nodding solemnly. It looked like he was really into it.

Then Gruf leaned across the table and started to say something to Bump. The girl leaned forward to hear. Bump said something to her and waved his hand at her to go away. She started to argue with him, but he waved his hand again and said something stronger. She got up and headed for the front of the bar.

Bump and Gruf talked for a minute. Then Bump picked up his Coke and moseyed over to me and Danny. I noticed that more than one girl around the room watched him walk over. It occurred to me for the first time that the girls like Bump. I don't know why it came as a surprise.

He took the chair between us. "Gruf and me are thinking we can go ahead and scam Oatley tonight. We've got a plan for ol' Fred over there. You in?"

I said, "Tonight? Excellent!"

"Okay. Gruf came up with the idea. We're gonna use your ex. You saw her sitting over there, right?"

I nodded.

"Okay. Start acting upset now while I tell you the scam. Act like I'm telling you something you don't like."

I frowned and kind of jerked my head back like I just got some bad news. It made Bump grin because I'm no actor, but he turned his head so that his expression couldn't be seen from across the room where Fred Oatley was sitting.

"Okay, Gruf was talking to Oatley, and Oatley recognized your ex. He said, wasn't that your wife sitting over there and how come you two weren't together. Terry. Try to look like you're pissed."

I adjusted my face. "How does Oatley know my business? He doesn't know me. Or my wife. Ex-wife."

"I guess he was in Carlo's last night when she was. He heard her telling Debby all about her problems with you."

I shook my head. Fuckin' Marylou. "Okay. So what?"

"So Gruf told Oatley he's got the hots for your old lady and he wants to go over and talk to her. So the scam is, Gruf asked me how you'd feel about him making a move, and I'm telling you about it right now, and you're not liking it. Give me another reaction, and don't ham it up so bad this time."

I frowned again and lowered my head like I was steaming.

Bump said, "Hey, that wasn't bad. I was starting to wonder whether you could pull this off."

I looked up at him, trying to give him a dark scowl. "You just don't be worrying about *me,* my friend. So Gruf goes over to Marylou. What then?"

"Then you and Danny come over to the table where we're sitting; you sit in the chair where Gruf is now, and you start telling Danny how pissed you are that Gruf is moving in on your woman. Give Oatley an earful. Then you turn around and recognize Oatley and include him in on your conversation. Try to suck him in, get him steamed up some, and see what he says."

Danny said, "So then maybe Oatley blurts out something incriminating?"

I said, "That's the idea."

Danny turned and waved his beer bottle in the air,

trying to catch the barmaid's eye. "Can I get another Bud over here?"

I said, "What's John gonna be doing? What's his deal?"

Bump shrugged. "John's an observer. He doesn't wanna be involved any more than he has to be."

Danny said, "I think it's a good plan."

I thought it was pretty good, too, and I liked being the go-to guy, but I was trying to keep an angry face. "Okay, let's do it."

"Okay. Give Gruf a nasty look now."

I did, and Gruf reacted with a surprised and innocent look on his face, then turned around and started talking to Fred Oatley, setting him up for me. Bump got up, slowly stretching out his long body, and sauntered back to the table. I suddenly suspected that his saunter was practiced, that he was aware of the girls watching him, and it almost made me grin until I remembered I was supposed to be mad.

Bump sat down across from Gruf and they started a serious discussion. Gruf turned a little in his chair to include Fred Oatley, and Oatley leaned forward so he could hear better. From time to time, Oatley would put in his two cents' worth and Gruf would nod agreement. They all kept glancing over at me. I lit a cigarette and turned in my chair so I wasn't looking directly at them.

Danny leaned across the table. "I'll act like I'm trying to calm you down, huh? Like, dude, you know she's a hideous pile of shit and will only bring Gruf years of torment and discomfort."

I had to turn my head and put my hand up and act like I was coughing. "Shut the fuck up, Danny. You're making me laugh."

A minute later, Gruf stood up and walked over to

Marylou's table. I watched him go. He stopped beside her and put his hand on her shoulder. She looked up at him, smiling. He asked her something and she answered, and then he motioned to the old barmaid, flashed her his charming smile, and we heard him say, "Another Michelob Light, please? And a High Life?"

The two of them said something to the girl Marylou was sitting with, and she got up and moved down a chair. Gruf turned the vacated chair to face Marylou, sat down with his legs open and stretched out along either side of her knees, and I watched my ex-wife warm up to him.

She looked good that night. In spite of the mall hair. Fuckin' Marylou. I had so many thoughts crashing around in my brain that I couldn't sort them out. It was weird. I turned back to Danny.

Acting like I was saying something a jealous lover would say, I told him, "That's pretty weird."

Danny looked at me. "Weird? What's weird about it?"

"Seeing Gruf putting the moves on the Bitch. Even when you know it's pretend, it's weird. Don't you think it's weird?"

He shrugged. Evidently he didn't. *I* did.

We sat there looking at each other for a few minutes. Then I said, "Show time."

I grabbed my cigarettes and my Coke and walked over to Bump. I stood in front of him, looking down at him in an aggressive way, and said, "What the fuck's he doing? Didn't you tell him I said no?"

Bump didn't move or look up at me or anything. He just said in a low and dangerous voice, "Siddown, dude. I don't like people standing over me."

I stood there another few seconds, like I was thinking maybe I'd like to sort a few things out with *him*. Then I looked around. On the other side of the table,

I slowly pushed in the first vacant chair and settled onto the second one with my elbows on the table. I glared at Bump.

Behind me, I heard Fred Oatley say, "Hi, Terry."

Without looking around at him, I said, "Shut the fuck up."

Danny came walking across the room carrying his beer. He gingerly pulled out the chair I had just pushed in, and sat down.

I looked across the room and sullenly watched Gruf and Marylou. I could feel Oatley's excitement behind me. I could hear his raggedy breathing. Marylou took a slug of her beer, and when she set the bottle back on the table, Gruf reached up and put his hand over hers.

I groaned.

Bump leaned across the table. "Now. Are you calmed down?"

I said, "Oh, yeah. It's real relaxing to watch somebody hitting on my *wife*."

Danny turned to me. "Gruf doesn't mean anything. They're just talking."

Bump said, "He's high on something. He doesn't know what he's doing."

I said, "*She* does. Look at her."

From behind me, Fred Oatley said, "They're just talking."

I swung around on him like I was going to do something rude, then stopped. "Don't I know you?"

His face relaxed into a grin. "Sure. You know me from Carlo's."

I frowned. "You never worked at Carlo's."

"No, man, I used to go in there to see Sheila. Remember? Sheila?"

I said, "Sheila? Oh, yeah. She was a waitress. I remember. You're . . ."

"Fred Oatley." He stuck out a hand and we did an awkward shake over my shoulder.

Next to me, Danny said, "Uh-oh."

I looked across the room. Gruf had moved forward to the edge of his chair and Marylou had an arm draped over one of his shoulders. Up on the stage, the cowboy said something about a guitar-strumming senorita. I had to do a double take at him before I got back into character.

I turned a cold eye on Bump. "You told him how I feel about this." I did a lazy point across the room.

He nodded.

I said, "Just wanted to make sure. Now me and him are gonna need to have a little talk." I acted like I was getting up, and Danny, Bump, and Fred Oatley all put heavy hands on my shoulders.

Danny said, "None of this means anything, Terry."

Bump said, "He's not even gonna remember her in the morning."

I said, "He's gonna remember *me*," and made to get up again, and got the same heavy hands on my shoulders. I sat there fuming for a minute. Then I turned around to Fred Oatley.

I stared at him, his narrow stretch of Neanderthal forehead, his bushy black eyebrows that connected in the middle, his badly cratered skin. His enormous disgusting lips. His big stupid eyes. I stared into his bloodshot eyes and wondered if they were the eyes of a murderer.

I said, "You believe this? These guys are supposed to be my best friends? Not to mention Gruf over there. What the fuck."

Oatley just shook his head, baffled.

I thought, Do it. Now's the time. I could feel my heart pounding.

I said, "These two sit here and they're all, 'It

doesn't mean anything.' I'm supposed to sit here and act like nothing's happening? What do *you* say?"

His face went blank. His eyes got glassy.

I said, "Huh? I wanna know!"

He thought about it. Then he said, "If I was you, I'd get another one."

I thought I had him all fired up. I totally expected him to say, "Kill him. Cut his throat in the parking lot." Blurt out a confession, just like that.

I blinked at him. "Huh?"

He shrugged and grinned. "Get another one. There's plenty more where that one came from."

"Get another girl, you mean? Get another girl?"

He shrugged. "Yeah."

I said, "Uh, yeah. You say that now. That wasn't the way you thought that one night. Remember? When you knocked the newspaper vending machine over? Not so coolheaded when it happened to *you*."

You could almost hear the big ol' rusty wheel in his brain turning around as he tried to remember what I was talking about. When he finally had it, he said, "Oh, yeah. Well, that was different. Sheila was supposed to meet me."

I said, "Whatever. If you'da walked in and found her sitting in a booth with some other guy, you'da been feeling just like me."

But he was shaking his head. "I didn't care who she was with. I just wanted my money."

That brought me up short. "Your *money*?"

"Yeah. She said she'd pay me and she never showed up."

I shook my head. "We're getting way off the subject here. She was your girlfriend. . . ."

"What? She wasn't my girlfriend! Please! You think I'd have something like *that* for my girlfriend?"

I just stared at him, thinking that a guy that ugly would be lucky to have a *goat* for his girlfriend.

I said, "Come on! You were in Carlo's all the time, sitting with her, talking to her. . . ."

He shook his head. "I was just sellin' her pot, for her and her ree-tard husband. Sure, sometimes I'd sit and have a cup of coffee, but I was only there doing deals."

I said, "But that night you got so mad . . ."

He shook his big ugly head again. "No, man. You don't understand. Sheila, she come over my place the night before that vending machine thing. She wants a quarter oh zee and she don't have any money. She wants the weed real bad, because she wants to get it on with that one driver of yours? The one that got killed? She give me this big song and dance, swore she'd meet me the next night and pay me. So I go ahead and give it to her. Then the next night she don't come. I was mad."

We all just stared at him. I said, "Huh?"

Bump said, "Wait a minute."

Danny said, "So, you're saying . . ."

John, who was sitting on the other side of me, and had stayed out of it until now, said, "Wasn't that the night before the driver got murdered?"

Fred Oatley's big head cranked over to stare at John. "Who're you?"

John stuck out his hand and said smoothly, "John Garvey."

Fred Oatley shook his hand and said, "Oh."

John said, "So, I don't understand. Why'd Sheila need to get him high?"

Oatley said, "Because she wanted to get it on with him."

Bump said, "I don't get it. Why'd she have to get him high to do the hot and sweaty?"

Oatley shrugged. "I don't know. She said he was all messed up, or scared, or something. She give me this

big sob story. They already tried to get it on twice.
Once, he drove her home after work and they started
making out in his car and he couldn't get it up. And
then that night, they went out to eat, or the movies,
or something, and they tried again, and nothing. So
she has him bring her by my place, see if I can advance
her a quarter oh zee, see if getting him high will help.
She don't have any money, but she says she'll meet
me at Carlo's the next night and pay me for it. So I
give it to her."

Maybe I was in stupid mode that night, or something, but it wasn't until then that the light came on
for me. Sheila and Oatley had been in the middle of
the pot deal when the Witness got murdered, and that
was why none of them—Sheila, her husband, or Oatley—would answer the cops' questions. Shit!

I said, "So the next night, you came into Carlo's
and she wasn't there, and that was when you knocked
over the vending machine."

He nodded. "Yeah, because I wanted my money
and that dyke waitress of yours got so snotty at me."

John said, "And then the next night, he got
murdered."

He shrugged. "Was it the next night? I don't know.
Anyway, the bitch got herself fired from Carlo's after
that, and she *still* owes me my money."

We all sat there looking around at each other. When
my eyes got back around to Fred Oatley, he said, "So
that stuff with Sheila don't have nothing to do with
you and your wife, but I say, fuck it. Get a new
woman. They all look the same upside down."

We got out of there as soon as we could after that.

We stood in the dark in the back parking lot waiting
for Gruf, who came out last. He walked around the
corner of the building, grinning.

Danny punched his arm. "How'd you get away from the Bitch?"

Gruf laughed. "I told her my cab was here."

Danny said, "What did she say to that?"

Gruf said, "She said, 'Oh.' "

Everybody laughed. There aren't any cab companies within forty, fifty miles of Spencer.

Then Gruf wanted to know what Fred Oatley said. We took turns telling him, sometimes talking over each other. Danny got to deliver the line, "They all look the same upside down." Everybody howled. John laughed as hard as anybody. He pulled off his dew rag and slapped his knees with it. I'd hafta say John had himself a pretty good time.

Gruf looked at Bump and said, "Well, shit. So Oatley wasn't the murderer. What do we do now?"

Bump shrugged. "Beats me. I was sure he was the one."

John said, "When Oatley spoke to you that first time and you said, 'Shut the fuck up!' Ho-lee! You should have seen the look on his face. I thought he was gonna clock you right over the back of the head."

I said, "How about ol' Bump when I walked over to the table. 'Siddown, dude.' Man! Is he Clint Eastwood, or what?"

Danny said, "So, Gruf. What was it like hittin' on Marylou?"

We all waited with great interest for his answer. He looked at me, grinning, and measured his words. "Well, she's not exactly the sharpest knife in the drawer."

Danny hooted. "She's not the sharpest *fork* in the drawer!"

I acted offended. "All right. Go easy. That woman was the mother of my unconceived children."

They laughed. Then we all started to shuffle and

look toward the vehicles and think about how late it was.

Bump said, "So, where are we now? Oatley's off the hook, right?"

Gruf nodded.

I said, "What about Sheila? Her, too?"

John shook his head. "If Ed Hanus couldn't, you know, get it up, she could've taken it personally. She could've been mad. . . ."

I said, "She *was* mad the night of the murder. She was standing in the waitress station, smoking and chewing her thumbnail, and when I told her to put out the cigarette she about took my head off. Ooo. No joke intended there."

Bump said, "But you might be onto something. Maybe she tried to take the *Witness's* head off. . . ."

Gruf said, "Another way to look at it would be, if they spent that much time together, maybe he told her something. Maybe he knew somebody was after him, and talked to her about it?"

I said, "That's something I've wondered about. Sheila told Oatley the Witness was scared. Maybe he told her who he was scared of."

Bump said, "And there's still her little husband. I wonder what kind of temper he has. And what kind of damage he might be able to do if he found out about Sheila's games."

John sighed. "We could stand here speculating all night. Isn't anyone else tired?"

Chapter 20

Thursday morning, we hung around Brewster's after Danny, Alan, and John left. Bump had an idea. He seemed to be getting a lot of those lately.

"I know you guys didn't get anywhere with Sheila when you talked to her before, but I want a crack at her. Let's take another run at it."

Gruf said, "When? Now?"

Bump shrugged. "You got something else to do?"

Gruf and I looked at each other. I was trying hard to think of some excuse, because I really wasn't eager to see Sheila again, but I couldn't think fast enough.

Gruf said, "I don't even know where she lives."

Bump smiled. "I do. I know a guy who knows her husband. I called him this morning." He chuckled. "Good ol' Lenny's all pissed off because Oatley won't sell them any more pot until they pay him for that last quarter ounce. And because Sheila won't get off her lazy ass and go find a new job."

I said, "But I mean, what good would it do to go see *her*? The cops've gotten nowhere with her, and neither did we."

Bump said, "She knows *some*thing. We oughtta try to drag it out of her." He shrugged. "Maybe it'll be a big waste of time. As least we will've tried."

Gruf and I looked at each other. It didn't look like Gruf was up for this, either. But what the fuck.

Sheila lived in a really ratty little motel-looking row of one-story apartments in the block behind Smitty's Bar. The building was made of piss-yellow brick, and the wood of all the doorframes and windows was rotting. Half the numbers had fallen off the doors, but the apartments were numbered consecutively, starting with one and ending with eight, so you didn't really need a rusting numeral on the door to figure out which one was number five.

The overgrown parking lot was nearly empty. There was an old, rusted, red Ford pickup parked in front of number seven, and there was an ancient black VW Beetle that was missing one of its front fenders parked by number three. That was it.

Bump stepped up and pounded. Nothing happened. He pounded again. The picture window beside the door was greasy and filthy, and the dirty venetian blinds that hung across it sagged badly on one side. Bump pounded again. Finally we heard someone fumbling with the night chain, and the door swung open.

It was Sheila. We'd gotten her out of bed. She wore a long white T-shirt that was yellowed around the neck from night sweat. Ech.

Bump said, "Sheila. Got a minute?"

She said, "No," and tried to close the door, but Bump's high-top was in the way. He used his shoulder to open the door wider.

Bump said, "Come on, dude. Give us a minute, huh?"

She sneered at him. Then she sighed, stepped back, and let us walk in. The apartment stank. It smelled like rotten oranges, or something. The rotten citrus fumes were so bad my eyes watered. I gave Bump a dirty look as she led us past some really miserable-looking living room furniture to her kitchen table. I glanced toward the little kitchen, expecting to see bags of trash, but there weren't any. I sat there wondering why the place smelled so bad.

We pulled out chairs and sat, but she didn't. She leaned against the kitchen counter and lit a smoke. "Make it fast. And keep your voices down. You really don't wanna wake up Lenny."

I got a mental picture of her skinny little translucent husband and I had to smile. What was that scrawny little question mark of a human being gonna do about it if we did wake him up? Little did I know.

Bump said, "We've got some questions. About the Witness."

She said tightly, "His name was Eddy. Get it right. You bunch of fuckeen dickless assholes. Think you're so much better than everybody else. His name was *Eddy.*"

I blinked at her. She certainly had a way with words.

Gruf said, "You're right. We *should* be calling him by his name. I apologize. You were close to him. He was your friend."

She listened suspiciously.

"Sheila. That's why we need to talk to you. Did he ever say anything to you about, well, someone threatening him? Scaring him? Did he say anything to you at all that might be a clue to who killed him?"

"What if he did?"

Bump said, "Well, did he or didn't he?"

She gnawed on her lower lip like she was trying to figure out an angle. Trying to figure how she could get something in return for her information.

Gruf said, "Come on, Sheila."

She let a little more time go by. Then she sighed. "Oh, fuck it. He was afraid of somebody, all right. He was scared shitless."

At that second there was a noise from somewhere else in the apartment. It sounded like a drawer slamming closed. Sheila's eyes went toward the living room and *she* looked scared.

She said quietly, "You guys hafta leave. Right now."

Bump said, "Not until . . ."

Her eyes were bouncing back and forth between us and the empty living room. "Right now. *Please*."

"What's going on here?"

We turned in the direction of the nasal, reedy voice. Lenny Werbel had materialized in the middle of the living room. He was shirtless, but he'd pulled on a pair of jeans. The dude was pale, and so skinny you could see all his ribs. His chest actually curved in, like he'd been vacuum sealed or something. But his nearly colorless eyes looked like *he* thought he was a much bigger guy. And the butt of the gun, sticking up out of the waistband of his jeans, backed him up on that idea.

I don't know about guns. I don't like 'em, and I don't know about 'em. But this was one big motherfucker of a gun. It looked like you might need two hands. What I could see of the butt was metal, flat black, and ugly. With that gun sticking up out of his pants, he looked like three or four bigger guys to me.

Sheila said, "Lenny . . ."

Bump said, "Easy there, dude. We just want to ask a few little questions."

Lenny said, "Out."

I wasn't gonna argue. I got up slowly and said, "No problem. We'll go."

Gruf got up, too. Bump got up slower. I wanted to kick him for how slow he got up. Lenny put one hand on the butt of the gun and stepped back toward the little hallway that evidently led to their bedroom, leaving a wide space so we could pass by. I moved toward the door. Gruf was right behind me.

Bump said, "Can't we just . . . ?"

Lenny said, "Out. Now."

We went.

Once we were back in Gruf's Jeep, pulling out of the little weedy parking lot, I said, "Nice, Bump. That was a great idea."

Gruf said, "Yeah. *Now* what do we do, Sherlock?"

Bump said, "Yeah. Gimme a minute."

It rained hard Thursday night. Business was steady. I got soaked. Gruf came out to sit with me when I took my meal break. It was the first time we'd had a chance to talk. He lit up a cigarette while I started in on my Hawaiian pizza.

He said, "Bump called a little while ago."

"Yeah?"

"He's trying to figure out how we can trip up Lenny Werbel. He's pretty sure Lenny must be our guy. He called John this afternoon and asked him to check what kind of car Lenny drives, but John said there's no car at all registered to Lenny *or* Sheila."

" 'Course not. That woulda made it too easy."

"He wants us to question Brandon Tercek one more time and ask if the Witness ever mentioned Lenny to him. Also, to cover all the bases and ask him to think one more time if there's anyone else in Fairfield we should talk to. He asked me to call Brandon, see if we could get him down here tonight and you and me talk to him."

I slurped Coke. My shirt was starting to dry out, but not fast enough. It was cold against my skin.

I said, "Did you get hold of him? Is he coming?"

Gruf nodded. "He *said* he would. I don't know if this weather's gonna stop him."

I shrugged. "We're delivering pizza in it."

He said, "We talked some. Me and Tercek. I told him we're narrowing down our list of suspects, but we want to talk to him one more time about Fairfield. I told him what Bump said. That *somebody* did it, and we're gonna find out who. I told him he's gotta rack his brain and come up with some names for us."

I nodded.

He knocked his ash off in the little metal ashtray. "He's a jerk."

"Who? Brandon?"

"Yeah. He can't get off the idea that the Witness was going out with some good-looking girl down here. He asked me about it again. I was like, What difference does it make, anyway?"

"Yeah. Really."

"Yeah. Then he started to get pissy with me. I couldn't believe it. I was like, Anyway, the only good-looking girl who was even working here at the time was Jackson, and she wouldn't give the Witness the time of day. Hey, Tercek said he's never met Jackson."

I shoved a chunk of crust in my mouth. "Who, Brandon hasn't? As many times as he's been down here?"

"That's what he told me. I guess he hasn't been here that many times. Really, let's see. I think he's only been here twice. It just seems like more."

I shrugged.

"Anyway, I told him, Well, she's working tonight. It's your big chance."

I finished my pizza and chugged Coke. He ground out his cigarette.

He said, "At least the rain's letting up a little."

I looked out the window. He was right.

I said, "Thank God. Maybe I'll be able to dry out the rest of the way."

From the front counter, Hammer yelled, "Driver!"

Gruf said, "You done?"

I nodded.

He said, "I guess you're up, then. I haven't seen any other drivers come in yet."

I carried back my plate and garbage and walked through to the front counter. Hammer dispatched me and I started out the front door. Brandon Tercek was out on the sidewalk, just reaching to pull open the door.

"Hey, Terry."

I said, "How ya doin'? We wondered if you'd come out in this nasty weather."

He shrugged. "It's starting to clear up now."

"Yeah. Well, talk to you later."

I got my run done and carried the empty bags to the front counter. Gruf lifted them over and stashed them underneath. "I just sent Princess out. Jackson's in. I got two trips coming up, but they're gonna be a few minutes."

I headed through the dining room for the waitress station to get a cup of coffee. Brandon Tercek was sitting by himself with a Coke in front of him, in the booth where us employees usually sat. Jackson was just coming out of the waitress station with a cup of her iced lemon water. She was wearing a little black corduroy jacket over her Carlo's T-shirt.

I turned around to Brandon. "Hey. Have you met Jackson yet?"

He was smiling at her. He said, "Yeah, briefly, when I came in."

She slid into the booth across from him. I got my coffee and slid in next to her. She asked him about working at Arthur Treacher's. He asked her about working at Carlo's. It seemed like I barely sat down before Gruf yelled, "Dispatch!"

Jackson said, "That's me. Lemme out."

Brandon and I watched her hurry toward the front

counter. A minute later she headed out the front door carrying a stack of stay-warm bags. A minute later Gruf yelled again and I stood up.

Brandon said, "They really keep you hoppin' around here, don't they?"

I grinned. "It's like this right up until closing. Good tips, though."

During that trip, the rain tapered off, but the air stayed heavy. When I got out away from the town lights, I could see lightning in the distant clouds to the north and to the southwest. It looked and felt like we were going to get pounded again.

I did another trip. Then there was a little lull. Gruf said, "I'll have something for you in just a minute. Might as well wait right here."

I peeked around the room divider into the dining room. The employees' booth was empty. I said, "Where'd Tercek go?"

Gruf grimaced. "He called his store to check in and they had a problem. One of the fryers was leaking, or something. He had to go."

I said, "To tell you the truth, I'm glad. I didn't feel like staying around tonight."

He winked at me. "Me, either. But we do need to talk to him. I asked if he'd come back tomorrow night. He said he'd try."

I said, "You gotta give him credit. He's being a good sport about us calling him all the time."

Gruf shrugged. "The Witness was his friend. He wants this thing solved as much as we do."

After the next trip, I came in the front door and saw Jackson standing at the front counter talking to Gruf. I was surprised to see that they both looked pissed off.

"Maybe I was imagining things," Jackson was saying. "Maybe it was just coincidence."

"No. I don't think so. Hey, Terry."

"What's going on?"

"Somebody was following Jackson."

By reflex, I moved toward the front door. "How long have you been back?"

"I pulled in just ahead of you."

I said, "What color was the car?"

Jackson said, "Light colored. Maybe white."

"Shit." I stood against the wall and leaned to look out the door, trying to scan the parking lot. I couldn't see much of it from inside the door. I hadn't noticed anything unusual when I pulled up, but lightning had been flashing in the sky in all directions and I'd been paying more attention to the bad weather than to the traffic.

"Were you followed into the parking lot?"

"They turned in right behind me. I think they first picked me up as I was going out. I think they must have been parked up toward the Thriftway. I saw a car come from that direction. I think it followed me to my delivery. I wasn't really sure it was the same car, except the right headlight was dimmer than the left one. That's what I kept seeing. Then I thought I saw it again coming back in, and like I said, it turned into the parking lot behind me, but when I got out of my car I didn't see it anymore."

"I'm going around the back," I said, already moving through the dining room. Jackson followed me, and Gruf met us in the back room. Gruf told Jackson to stay inside.

We split up in the back parking lot. Gruf started along the back wall of the businesses, where a dark service driveway continued from our parking lot and ran behind the row of businesses next to our building, all the way down to Brewster's on the opposite end.

I turned right and went up the dark little alley that

ran between Carlo's and the end wall of the business block. In front of Carlo's, I studied the upper parking lot. Nothing. I turned around and went back down the dark alley to meet up with Gruf.

I was about halfway through the alley when I heard the loud sound of a car engine. Gruf yelled *"Hey!"* and then there was the sound of squealing tires. I ran toward the sound. Jackson came running out the back door of Carlo's.

We got down into the driveway in time to see tail-lights disappearing around the Brewster's end of the business block, but we didn't see Gruf. There was a fairly bright flash of lightning and a loud crack of thunder, and the wind picked up. "Gruf! Dude! Where are you?"

By this time we were running along the driveway. When we got to where our service driveway meets the one for the little shopping center downhill of us, we heard Gruf say, "Over here."

He was picking himself up from the asphalt next to the florist's Dumpster. We stopped in front of him, looking around in the darkness. I said, "You okay? What happened?"

"Yeah, fine." He twisted to brush gravel off his pants. "I spooked somebody. He was parked on the other side of the Dumpster. It's so dark down here, I didn't know there was a car there until I was almost on top of him."

"So, he tried to run you down?" I bent over to brush some of the gravel off his lower pant leg. "Dude, you tore your pants. Uh-oh. I think you're bleeding. Did he hit you?"

"I don't think he was trying to hit me. I think he was trying to get away. Shit! I feel it now. He didn't hit me. I think I landed on something."

Jackson had moved back beside the Dumpster. She

said, "Terry. Gimme your lighter." I handed it to her.
She bent over, thumbed it, and ran it along the asphalt. "There's some broken glass here." A big rain-
drop landed on the lighter flame and put it out, and
fat raindrops began to hit all around us.

"Come on, let's go call the cops," Gruf said. All of
a sudden the sky opened up. Gruf didn't need our
help to get back to the building. We all ran for the
back door.

There was one trip ready to go. Gruf gave it to me.
When I got back, Jackson was working the front
counter and Gruf was out on a delivery. He came in
about ten minutes later. We stood in the back room,
looking at each other. It was a little after ten.

Gruf said, "Shit."

"How's your leg? What was it, a cut?"

"Yeah, I musta landed on that glass. Jackson says
it needs stitches, but it's okay. She washed it for me
and put some stuff on it and a Band-Aid."

"Did ya call the cops?"

"Yeah. Alan was at some meeting, but Coop and
Brian Bell came down. I couldn't help them much,
though. It happened too fast. Only thing I saw was the
headlights. They were uneven, like Jackson described
them. And it was a light-colored car. The cops said
they'll patrol us more, or something."

We looked at each other.

"What good's *that* gonna do?"

"That's what *I* said. Big fuckin' deal."

I said, "That *fuckin'* Lenny Werbel. It must be a
stolen car he's driving. Driving it on bogus tags."

"You think it was him?"

"Isn't it obvious? We pay that courtesy call this
morning, and the next thing you know he's after another one of our drivers."

"I want that fucker."

"Tomorrow we gotta drive up and down every street and alley in Spencer. We gotta find where he's stashing that car."

"Good idea. Anyway, at the moment I only have one more run. You take it. Hopefully there won't be any more."

Yeah, I thought. Fat chance. We had a lot of customers who liked to wait until just before cutoff to call in orders, so he didn't get off the hook that easily. A few more orders did come in. Gruf and I split them.

After closing, when Jackson and Hammer were gone, Gruf said, "I don't feel like going home yet. Grab some coffee and let's sit out in the dining room and talk."

We sat across from each other in the end booth in the darkened dining room. Outside, lightning flashed and thunder rumbled and cracked. The parking lot was nearly empty all the way up to the grocery store. The black asphalt was as shiny as cheap leather. Water ran in ropes off the roof and in streams along the side of the building.

I said, "Did you call Bump?"

He nodded. "He said the same thing you did. Werbel's gotta be hiding that car somewhere. Tomorrow we scour this town and find it."

I nodded. I looked at my cup of coffee and belched. "Man. Heartburn. I drink too much coffee."

"Me, too. But I can't think what to drink instead."

"Yeah." So we drank it anyway.

Gruf reached down under the table and I could tell he was rubbing his wound. I said, "Is it hurting?"

"It's okay. Just stiffening up a little."

I said, "Lemme see it."

He said, "I *said* it's okay," but I was already out of the booth and standing over him. He grimaced, irritated, but he lifted his foot onto the bench and wrestled his jeans leg up over the bandage and gingerly pulled one side free.

It was a nasty-looking gash. Jackson had been right. It did need stitches. I said, "Come on. I'm driving you down to the emergency room."

That really irritated him. "Bullshit. I'm not going to the emergency room. It'll heal fine."

"It'll heal a lot better and a lot quicker if you get stitches. Don't be stupid. We're going."

I guess he saw I wasn't taking no for an answer. We locked up, he set the burglar alarm, and we headed for Grand County Memorial Hospital.

Chapter 21

—

We did scour Spencer Friday. We split up and did four hours of scouring. But we couldn't find a single light-colored car that didn't have a very good reason for being where it was. We were frustrated and angry.

Jackson and Gruf had a brief but nasty fight right after shift change Friday night. What started it was, there were three deliveries up almost as soon as I'd clocked in, and Gruf yelled, "Driver, driver, driver."

Jackson, Jeff, and I headed for the front. Ladies first. Jackson stepped up to the counter.

Gruf said, "No, Jackson. You're staying inside tonight. Go back around."

She squared her shoulders. "Oh no I'm not. My job description is driver. I'm *going* to *drive*."

He said, "No, you're not. It's not safe. Now step aside and let me dispatch these orders."

She said, "Gruf. That first delivery is mine. Give it to me." She didn't raise her voice, but there was white-hot anger in it.

"No, Jackson. I can't. It's not safe."

She was quiet for a few seconds. I stepped up to the counter beside her, trying to think of something to say or do to stop the fight that was coming.

Then she said quietly, "How 'bout this: Give me a trip. *Right now*. Or I quit."

He was staggered. "Oh, Jackson. Don't say that."

She said, "I mean it, Gruf." She did, too. You took one look at her face, the way her jaw was set, and you knew that.

"Jackson. Please. You're tearing my heart out."

There was pain in his voice. Italian pain. It was the first time I'd ever seen the Italian in him. I turned sideways, trying to give him some little bit of privacy.

She said, "I'm sorry. I really am. But I'm a *driver* and I want a *trip*. Right now. If you don't give me one, I'm walking."

Gruf caught my eye. I shrugged helplessly. He turned his hurt eyes back to her. "Oh, shit. Will you promise, *promise*, if you see those headlights, or anything suspicious, you'll drive that little Hyundai right back here as fast as it'll go?"

She gave him an electric smile that must've just about put him on his ass. She said sassily, "My *God* but you're an attractive man."

We all burst out in tension-driven laughter. Even Jeff laughed.

The bad weather had continued all day and right on into night. It was about as hard a rain as I've ever seen. I was soaked to the bone and shivering after my first delivery. All of us drivers were. The man at the second house made me stand on the little unprotected slab of concrete that served as his front porch while he wrote out his check, letter by excruciating letter.

When somebody phones in a pizza order, the phone person totals up the bill then and there, and gives the total to the customer. The reason they do that is so the customer can have his check all written out, or the money ready, when the driver comes to the door. So I don't get why people like this guy make you stand there in the pounding rain while they write out the damn check. Sadistic little prick.

Rainwater was running in a cold torrent down my back under my Carlo's shirt by the time he handed me the check. Plus, no tip. My hatred for him was perfect and pure.

On the second trip out, I encountered good-sized branches littering the highway and I had to slow down considerably. Flying leaves got stuck under the wiper blades and flew with the blades back and forth across the windshield. The heat escaping from the stay-warm bags caused the windows to fog up so much that even turning on the defroster full blast didn't help. I cracked my side window a touch. Then the icy rainwater came spitting in across my face. But what the hell, I was already soaked.

Delivery was slow and rough because it was almost impossible to see the house numbers through the rain. In town, I frequently had to park and run up into the dark soggy yards before I could make out the numbers. And once you got out of town, delivery was just as hairy because it was almost impossible to read the numbers on the mailboxes through the fogged-up car windows. During the heavier squalls, I could barely even see the driveways. By the time I got my meal break, the rain was tapering off and I had a punishing headache.

"Pretty nasty out there, huh?" Gruf said sympathetically once I'd given him my meal order.

I just shrugged.

"Well, I got nothing else right now. Jackson's just starting her meal break. You can go around."

I was glad to hear it. I started through the dining room. Brandon Tercek was sitting in the end booth. He said hi. As I turned into the hallway, Jackson came out with her salad and lemon water and slid into the booth across from him.

Princess was already at the dishwasher, running

trays through. There weren't many dirties stacked on
the counter behind her. Jeff was carrying the clean
trays out and putting away the dishes.

Gruf came walking back. "I got nothing whatsoever
up there. Maybe we're gonna actually catch a break
on a Friday night for a change."

I said, "Cool."

He said, "I told Princess and Jeff to go into closing
mode. I gotta get a batch of pizza sauce made up.
You can start cleaning while you wait for your food
to come up."

I said, "Works for me."

Gruf turned to the other driver, Jeff. "I'm gonna
have Jackson cash you out when she's done with her
break."

Jeff nodded.

I looked around for something to do. A wadded-up
piece of trash hanging off one of the shelves in the
back hall caught my eye, and I went back to get it. I
looked over the other shelves and groaned. They were
already filling up with trash again.

I grabbed the wadded-up brown bag and pulled.
The corner of it was stuck to the wood shelf, in under
a stack of pizza boxes. I pulled at the stack of boxes
and found that the bottom box was stuck to the shelf
as well. I pried it up off the shelf, carried the stack to
one of the counters, and went back for the paper bag.

With the boxes gone, I could see the problem. Way
at the back of the shelf there was a Styrofoam cup
lying on its side. It'd been knocked over and the
spilled pop had glued the paper bag and the pizza box
to the wood.

I pulled the Styrofoam cup out. When I got it into
the light, I stared at it. It was one of the Witness's
cups. Maybe his last one. His sick drawings went all

the way around the side. I sighed, walking toward the trash can. Poor sick dead bastard. Then I stopped.

I looked closer at the drawings. Something started to crawl around in my gut. There was something wrong. Something about . . . I studied the drawings, trying to understand.

The thing was, I always had it in my mind that the Witness was imagining himself the *perpetrator* in these drawings. That he was fantasizing that *he* was the one inflicting the pain and suffering. But really, when you looked . . .

I said, "What the fuck?"

Gruf had a big metal tub on the floor and was beginning to pour the makings for pizza sauce into it. He stopped pouring and looked up. "What?"

I said, "One of the Witness's cups. Look at this."

He looked. "Yeah? So?"

I said, "Come here. Look at these figures. The one taking the punishment is shorter and has dark hair. See?"

He stood straight, set the can of tomato sauce on the counter, came over to me, and looked. "So?"

"Look at it. The victim is, well, the victim looks like the Witness. It's the same in all these drawings." I turned the cup around in my hand, showing him. "Like it's the same two figures, over and over again. The one doing all the damage is taller, and look how he draws the hair. You can see how it's long on the top. You can even see the side part. And he just outlines it, like the hair is supposed to be—"

Gruf finished it. "Blond."

We stared at the cup, then at each other. My brain ignited, like when you throw a handful of leaves on a fire. "Oh my God! Oh shit!"

The same thing was happening to Gruf. His eyes were huge. He said, "It can't be."

I said, "It is."

"Brandon Tercek?"

"He's out there right now."

"Shit."

The bottom dropped out of my gut. *"He's out there with Jackson."*

We turned and ran through the hall to the front and stopped dead in our tracks. The booth was empty. I looked around in wild confusion. Debby looked up from the table she was clearing.

She said, "Jeez! What's the matter? You guys look like—"

"Where'd they go?" Gruf yelled.

She looked at him like he was crazy.

I yelled, *"Brandon and Jackson!"*

She said, "They just walked out the front door. He wanted her to show him where Hammer found the body."

We both yelled, "Shit!" and started across the dining room, but I happened to glance back toward the booth and my eye caught movement outside the window. A moving figure, heading down the side alley.

I yelled, "Gruf! The Dumpster!"

I turned around and ran for the back door. I could hear Gruf behind me. I burst out the door and there they were, walking side by side, their backs to us. They were almost to the Dumpster.

They heard the door fly open. They turned toward us. In that instant, I saw Brandon Tercek grab Jackson and step behind her, and I saw a flash of metal in his right hand. I pulled up short, and Gruf came to an abrupt halt beside me.

Brandon had her with his left arm over her shoulder and down across her chest, and his right hand was holding the knife at her throat. He was grinning.

He said, "Don't even move."

Gruf said quietly, "What are you doing, Brandon?
Let her go."

He said, "No. I don't think so. She's the one that
messed up Eddy. Now she's gonna get it."

Gruf said, "Dude, it wasn't her."

He said, "You can't protect her anymore. I've got
her now." His voice was singsongy, weird.

We all stood there, frozen. Jackson was perfectly
still in his grip, but her eyes were huge and bouncing
back and forth between me and Gruf. Beside me, I
could hear Gruf forcing deep breaths, trying to calm
down, and I knew he was trying to think of something
to do.

Princess came out the door. She stepped up between
me and Gruf. I heard voices from inside the back
door. Debby and Hammer, having a whispered but
fierce argument. Hammer wanted to come out. Debby
wouldn't let him.

Tercek said, "I knew if I just kept asking questions,
I'd find the little slut. And now I have." He made a
strange sound. It almost sounded like a hiccup, but I
thought it must be a giggle choked off.

Gruf took a sideways step, and then another. From
the corner of my eye, I could see a space opening
between Gruf and Princess. I began to edge away to
the other side. The space between Gruf and me
opened up to at least eight feet before Tercek
stopped us.

"Hold it! Just stay where you are! Both of you!"

Gruf started talking to him in a low, soothing voice.
"Listen to me, Brandon. What good is it gonna do
you to kill the wrong girl?"

"Oh, she's the right girl. Interfering bitch. She
thought she was smarter than me, but she was *stupid!*
She made me kill Eddy, and now she's gonna pay!"

Gruf said, "No, dude, you've got it all wrong. Ed

had the hots for Jackson at first. But she couldn't stand him. I swear. So he got interested in Sheila. Remember we *told* you about Sheila? We found out more about that. We found out that Ed drove Sheila home from work one night. . . ."

Gruf went on talking, keeping his voice soft and soothing, and I realized he was trying to distract Brandon from me. It was working. Brandon was listening to him, watching him. Gruf continued to explain what we'd learned about Sheila and Ed.

I started edging farther away from Gruf, and I was also moving indirectly toward Jackson and Brandon. Brandon didn't seem to notice. As soon as Gruf got into the part about how Sheila scored some weed to get Ed high, he had Brandon's full attention.

Behind me, I heard Princess begin to speak softly, but loud enough to be heard by Jackson. She said, "God, I hope she doesn't *faint*. You know how she always *faints*. I never saw a girl who *faints* as easily as she does." She kept emphasizing the word faint, saying it over and over.

Jackson was staring at Princess, big-eyed. I thought, Jackson would be the last girl on earth to ever faint, but then I realized that Princess was *telling* her to do it. I looked at Jackson and I saw her figure it out, too. I saw her blink, and then she turned her terrified eyes to me, and I nodded. *Do it, kid. Do it right now. It's the best chance we've got.*

Everything happened at once. Jackson let her legs go out from under her and she slid bonelessly down through Brandon's grip. Startled, he pulled his knife hand away from her throat in order to grab her arm. I saw the knife slice through the skin of her upper arm as he tried to hold her up.

I charged him from the right side, going for his knife hand. Gruf came from the other side, grabbing Jack-

son's shoulders and pulling her free of his grip. I
wrapped both my hands around Brandon's wrist. He
stepped back and away, turning in a circle, trying to
get away from me.

We were spinning, but I managed to get a foot behind him to trip him. I pushed and he went down on
his back. His head hit the wet pavement hard and I
fell hard on top of him, my knees skimming his ribs
on either side and landing on the asphalt.

The impact sent the knife skidding across the parking lot. I landed straddling him. I still had his knife
wrist with both hands. He punched at me with his free
hand, and his body bucked as he tried to throw me
off. I let go with my right hand, grabbed a handful of
his hair, and slammed his head hard on the pavement.
That stunned him for a second, and I was able to get
him by the other wrist, so that I had his hands out at
arm's length, pinned against the asphalt.

I leaned down into his face. We were both gasping
for air. There was a cloud of steam around our heads
from our heavy breathing. At that second there was
nothing in this world I wanted more than to beat him
to death.

"Please keep struggling," I hissed. "I want you to."

The fight went out of him, just like that. He went
still and squeezed his eyes shut. Tears ran from the
corners. I looked up. I was facing the back door now,
from about the middle of the parking lot. Gruf was
sitting on the back step, holding Jackson's wounded
arm and pulling her onto his lap. They were both covered with her blood.

Princess had disappeared. She came running back
out as I looked, carrying a wad of wet paper towels.
Hammer was right behind her. Jeff, the new guy, was
standing in the doorway. Hey, welcome to Carlo's.

Princess gently pulled Jackson's wounded arm,

which was bleeding profusely, away from Gruf. She lifted it up in the air so Jackson's hand rested on her shoulder. Then she pressed the paper towels hard against the wound.

She was reassuring Jackson. "Debby's calling the police and an ambulance, sweetie. You're gonna be okay. I have the wound raised above your heart now and I'm using direct pressure. We'll have the bleeding stopped before the ambulance even gets here, you watch and see. Everything's gonna be just fine. . . ."

Gruf looked over at me as Princess continued to soothe Jackson. "You okay?"

I nodded. "You?"

"Yeah. Why'd he want to hurt Jackson? I don't understand it."

Tercek's eyes had come open. He was staring up into the night sky. I said, "You heard him. Why?"

His eyes focused on my face. "Fuck you."

Pain was shooting up and down my legs from my knees, and I realized I had landed hard on them. And the muscles in my back were knotting in the icy air, because I was straddling him at an awkward angle, leaning over him with my weight on hands that had his wrists pinned. I gritted my teeth. There wasn't any way to change position without giving him a chance to throw me off.

Gruf said, "That was *you* in the alley last night. Has *all* of it been you, Tercek? Did you run Carrie Hall off the road a few weeks ago?"

Brandon jerked. A look of surprise washed over his face.

I said, "That *was* you, wasn't it? Let's see if I can guess why you wanted to hurt Carrie. Your buddy told me he thought she was pretty. He was gonna ask her out, but the *accident* messed up his plans."

A sick smile flickered briefly at the corners of his mouth.

I said, "Let's see if I can figure out the rest of it. Sometime last week, your buddy Ed *did* hook up with a girl. He bragged about it to you, and that made you mad. So you killed him, and then you wanted to kill the girl you thought had stolen him away from you. And you thought it was Jackson."

He closed his eyes.

"Little Eddy had been pretty much your personal property all his life, hadn't he? I bet you could do about anything you wanted to him, and he just took it, because he'd been raised by a couple of nutty parents and he was messed up. Nobody but you would give him any attention at all."

Tercek rolled his head to one side. "Shut up."

"Then all of a sudden, you were losing your grip on your little punching bag, huh? Maybe he even told you, 'Hey, Brandon, I'm not gonna take it anymore. I've got someone else now.' Huh? You piece of crap?"

"Shut up!"

"You couldn't control him anymore. Am I right?"

"Fuck you! Fuck you!" His eyes looked crazy and red and glittery.

"Yeah, you were losing your grip, so you killed him. But it wasn't really *your* fault, was it?"

His head rolled sideways and he let out a sob.

"No, the person to blame for little Eddy's murder was the woman in his life. Right? So you came hunting for her? To punish her?"

There was another deep sigh that came all the way from deep in his gut. I felt it start between my thighs. When he spoke, he said it so quietly I barely heard him. "I—I thought he might have told her. About me, about . . ."

My back was in full spasm now. My hands were going numb. If he tried to throw me off again, I didn't know if I'd be able to do anything about it. I thought, Just keep talking. Keep him scared. Make him think you can back it up.

Gruf said, "About you? Oooh, I see. Even if he told her a little bit of it, she might've figured out you were the one that killed him."

I said, "You're such a bastard. You even tried to run Gruf down."

He shouted, "I wasn't trying to hit him!" Then he clamped his jaw shut and stared up at me, realizing he'd just admitted it.

Gruf said, "What the hell were you doing all the way back there? You can't even see the building from back there."

Tercek rolled his head back and forth on the wet pavement. It came to rest with him looking over in the direction of the dark alley where we'd spooked him that night. "You guys and your faggot long hair. Bunch of *hair farmers.* Bunch of faggoty pizza boys."

We heard sirens. We all heard them at once. Gruf said, "Thank God." Jackson was leaning against him now, her head on his shoulder.

Tercek turned his head to listen and tears ran down his temple. I said, "Hear that, asshole? Just listen to all those sirens!"

Cop cars squealed into the parking lot from every direction. Cops jumped out with their guns drawn and began to run for the building. I was worried about the knife.

I yelled, "Everybody *freeze!*"

They all skidded to a stop, and suddenly all the guns came up and were trained on me.

I swallowed hard. "Okay, now listen. There's a knife lying right over there, about fifteen feet from me. See it? It's probably the same knife this guy used to murder our driver, and it's the knife he used to cut the girl sitting over there. And the girl needs medical attention. And somebody take custody of this shithead. My knees are killing me."

Like magic, somebody was laying police tape in a circle around the knife, and EMTs were kneeling around Jackson and Gruf, and Alan Bushnell was standing beside me.

He said, "Okay, Terry. We'll take him now."

I said, "Good. Great."

He tapped my shoulder. He said, "Okay, then. Get up, buddy. We got him."

The thing was, I couldn't get up. My back wasn't working anymore. I looked up at him.

I said, "You guys are gonna have to *lift* me off. I can't move."

Alan and another guy got on either side of me and lifted me off. Once I was upright again it felt much better. Two other cops rolled Tercek over and cuffed him. They pulled him to his feet. I shook my hands and stamped my feet, trying to get the circulation going again.

Tercek turned around to glare at me as they walked him toward one of the cars.

There weren't gonna be any red geraniums by the front door where he was going. No basketball court, no funny Louie the pothead, like at Grand County Jail. Where Brandon was headed, life was going to be a lot more tedious.

Chapter 22

Alan was trying to ask me questions, but there were
some things I had to take care of before I could start
answering them. The EMTs and Gruf were helping
Jackson walk toward the ambulance. Dodging her
blood puddles, I led Alan through the back door and
into the back room. I had to get the Styrofoam cup
safely into his hands. I stopped, looking at the counter
where I'd tossed it. It wasn't there.

I said, "Shit. Shit! Where is it?" I looked around
wildly.

Princess had followed us in. "What?"

"The Styrofoam cup. With the drawings."

She smiled, pointed behind me. "I picked it up with
a Baggie and set it up there."

There it was, safely stowed in a Baggie on top of
the paper-towel holder.

Alan took it and started in again, trying to ask me
questions, but I had to put him off for another thing.
I ran out the back door again and over to the ambulance. Jackson was inside it now, stretched out on the
cot, and Gruf was sitting at her feet.

Gruf was as white faced as she was, watching as the
EMTs worked on her. It looked like the bleeding had
pretty much stopped, just like Princess had said it
would.

I said, "Hey?"

Gruf looked out at me.

I said, "You go with her. I'll take care of everything here."

He said, "You'll have to call Kenny and—"

I said, "I know. I'll take care of everything. You just worry about Jackson and let me handle everything else."

His eyes got shiny. "Thanks."

They were ready to close the ambulance door. I backed off, then turned toward Alan.

"Dude, let me make two phone calls. Then I'm all yours."

I walked inside to the phone at the front counter and ran my finger down the list of employees' home phone numbers. I was vaguely aware that everybody had followed me up to the counter. I looked around. Princess, Hammer, and Jeff were standing there watching me.

I turned to Princess and put a hand on her arm. "You did great, Princess. I don't know how you thought of that, getting her to pretend to faint."

She shrugged. "I think I saw it in a movie, or something."

I shook my head. "If you hadn't come up with that, he woulda killed her."

She smiled at me. "But he didn't."

"Yeah." I turned back to the phone list.

Hammer stood on one side of me, his hand on my shoulder, shaking like a leaf. Princess was on the other side, her hand on my other shoulder, steady as a rock.

First I called Barb and asked her to come in and help us close up. Then I wanted Bump. Since it was Friday, I called the Midway, but they said he'd already left. So then I tried his cell phone. He answered on the fourth ring. I told him what happened as fast as I could and asked him to call Kenny and Bud.

I hung up the phone and turned around. Debby had joined us. I looked from face to face. I said, "All right, guys. Help's on the way. I guess I gotta go answer some questions. Can you all get this place closed up?"

Debby said, "We're on it. Alan's waiting for you out in the dining room."

As I slid into the booth across from Alan, Debby put a cup of coffee in front of me. Alan already had one. I looked around. She had two fresh pots sitting on the burners. She grinned at me and hurried back to start closing out the waitress station.

Alan sipped his coffee and fixed me with a steady look. "Terry, Terry, Terry. For a while there, I really thought you did it."

I lit a cigarette. I was glad to see that my hand was steady. "I didn't."

He nodded. "I'm prepared to apologize."

"Is that right."

He shrugged. "Yeah."

"Okay. I'm prepared to *accept* your apology."

"Good." He sipped his coffee. "But don't *ever* call me General again."

"I'll try to remember."

He gave me some prompts and I started into the story. Five minutes later, Bump came in and slid into the booth next to me. He sat there smoking, drinking coffee, and listening to me answer questions.

I started out trying to tell Alan as little as possible. But his questions led me deeper and deeper into our activities of the past week. "But how did you know . . . ? But why did you think . . . ?" You give Alan half a chance and he's quite the little interrogator. Things got dicey in some of the parts and Bump had to help out. We did manage to protect John. Bump kept refilling the coffee cups.

Sometime during the questioning, Barb arrived. She came out to the dining room and said hi very solemnly. I gave her my fanny pack so she could cash me out. She disappeared through the back hall. I could hear her and the crew talking quietly, stuff rattling and thumping and sloshing while they worked. After a while she came out and set my tip money on the table in front of me without saying a word.

After the crew finished closing chores and got cashed out, they all came out and sat in the dining room and began giving their own statements to the cops. Then Kenny and Bud walked in, and Bump and I had to pretty much start all over again.

Somewhere along in there, Bud called down to the hospital to check on Jackson. She was in surgery. There'd been some muscle and ligament damage and they were putting her back together.

Bud persuaded somebody he knew to get somebody else to go into the operating room and get the doctor's prognosis as far as any permanent damage, and the word came back that the damage was minor and she should be good as new once she healed.

Bud told whoever he was talking to that Jackson was to have the best of everything, spare no expense. He said that Gruf was there as Kenny Carlo's personal representative and was to be given every consideration. Kenny Carlo was personally picking up the tab.

Everybody stayed long after they were finished answering questions, even Barb and the new guy, Jeff. Alan kept asking Bump and me questions, going back over, back over, wanting to make sure he had it all straight, all the gaps filled in.

Finally, I glanced at the window and saw gray light filtering across the parking lot. I looked at Alan. "Dude, the sun's coming up. We about done here?"

He thumbed through the pages and pages of notes he'd taken. "I guess. I'll probably have some follow-up questions, but I guess they can wait."

Bump slid out of the booth. "Terry. Can I catch a ride with ya? I don't have wheels here."

I looked at him.

He shrugged. "My date dropped me off."

I raised my eyebrows. "Date?"

He grinned. "I have a life."

I filed that away for another time.

I stubbed out my cigarette, climbed stiffly out of the booth, tucked my tip money into the back pocket of my jeans, and picked up my lighter and my Marlboros. I looked around the room. The troops were still all sitting there, watching me like I was gonna break out tap dancing or something.

I said, "Well, guys, we're outa here. Later."

There was a chorus of " 'Bye, Terry. See ya, Bump."

Bump and I went out the front door, and the fresh, clean air made my head feel better right away. I inhaled deeply as we walked up the parking lot toward my truck. I glanced across the wide expanse of empty parking lot in the gloomy slanting sunrise, thinking how different everything would look in an hour or so, when the sun was up and the cars of the Brewster's breakfast crowd and the early Thriftway shoppers started filling the lot up again.

Just then Bump said, "Didn't take *them* long, did it?"

I turned to follow his eyes back past Carlo's. A big white Channel 3 News van was rolling into the lower driveway. As it parked across two spaces in front of Carlo's, we climbed into my truck.

We watched the cameraman slide the side door open, hop out, and start pulling out his gear. Somebody inside the van must have been punching buttons, because the big satellite dish on top of the van began to rotate slowly. A tall blonde in an extremely tailored beige business suit and four-inch heels slid gracefully out of the front passenger seat and stood near the cameraman. As he shouldered his equipment, she bent around the front of the van, trying to peek through Carlo's front windows.

Bump said, "Ooo. Nice ass." He had ducked his head to watch them from his side window. I leaned across him to see. We watched them get their stuff together. I straightened up, grinning, and Bump lit a cigarette.

I said, "I hope they interview Hammer."

He turned to look at me and a wide grin split his face. "*I'd* watch that."

I cranked up the engine and we climbed across the lot toward the far entrance.

I said, "You don't have to work today, do you?"

Bump said, "Naw. Neither do you. Kenny's gonna send staff over from the other stores."

I said, "Well, shit. If nobody has to work tonight, we might as well get up a card game."

He nodded. "Hey, mind stopping at Petey's? I'm almost outa smokes."

I said, "No problem."

So there you have it. That's my story. I pulled out onto the highway, dropped her into second, stepped on the gas, and felt all the big bad horses in my big bad Tacoma go gitty up. Did I mention how much I love my truck?

Ah, the open highway in the early northeastern Ohio morning. Nothing else like it.

Turn the page for a preview
of the next Working Man's Mystery
featuring Terry Saltz—

LIGHTS OUT

Coming soon from Signet

I was sitting in Brewster's one Friday morning in the middle of November, happily mauling my number four breakfast like a healthy growing boy. I was enjoying my friends' goofy small talk and watching the weather out Brewster's big front windows. Lightning ripped through black, boiling storm clouds, and sheets of cold, wicked rain slapped at the vehicles in the big parking lot.

Ah, late autumn in northeastern Ohio. Nothing else like it.

My name's Terry Saltz. I'm a carpenter. Breakfast at Brewster's every weekday morning is sort of a ritual for me and a few friends. Eat. Shoot the shit. Get our natural juices flowing by ragging on each other before we head out in different directions to earn our daily pack of Marlboros. As I sipped my coffee and glanced around that particular morning, I was lazily speculating whether or not to go ahead with a fairly radical plan.

I was thinking about maybe getting a haircut.

My hair's long. I've worn it long since I was thirteen. At first, it got long because my old man wasn't around to spot me the cost of a haircut, and I wasn't willing to hand my hard-earned paper-route money over to a barber. In those days, I was using that paper-route money for food half the time.

My hair grew down over my collar. Teachers started getting on me about it, and I discovered that I liked being a bad boy. When it got longer, the girl I'd been watching for a while suddenly got interested in me. Sometimes after school we'd go stand behind the middle school building and she'd reached up and run her hands through my long black hair and say how silky it was, how good it smelled.

After that, I was enthusiastic about three things: my girlfriend, my long hair, and what kind of shampoo and conditioner smelled best. No shit. I spent the better part of a year sniffing bottles all up and down the shampoo aisle in the drug store.

When I was fifteen, my older brother P. J. got me and my best friend Danny Gillespie jobs as gofers for Red Perkins Construction. P. J. and most of the other carpenters who worked for Red wore their long scraggly hair in ponytails, so me and Danny split a pair of leather shoelaces and tied ours back like theirs. That's how we've had it ever since.

Only recently I'd been thinking about getting it cut. All that long black hair is a lot of trouble. That November morning, while I chewed my Texas toast and watched the rain, I was thinking how much easier it would be if I just got it all chopped off.

The absolute last thing on my mind was my wife Marylou, also known as the Bitch. Which, by that time, she was supposed to be my ex-wife. Except that the divorce she'd so cold-bloodedly initiated six months earlier while I was sitting brokenhearted and forlorn in jail, somehow got canceled once I was out and on my feet again, in a new town, with new friends, new money, and a new outlook on life.

The talk around the table that morning turned to names. Gruf Ridolfi mentioned that if your initials spell a word, it makes you lucky all your life. Danny

Gillespie piped up right away with the information that his initials spell "dig."

I looked at him. "I? What's your middle name?"

He got a look on his face like he'd stepped in something. Which he had.

Bump Bellini grinned at him. "I can't even think of a name that starts with I."

Danny got busy stirring sugar into his third cup of coffee. He said, "Don't even start with me. Everybody has a weird middle name."

John Garvey said, "Mine's Thomas."

Bump said, "Mine's Edward."

Gruf grinned. "Andrew."

I said, "William."

Gruf said, "William? So your initials are T.W.S.? Ouch. Sorry, Terry."

I said, "T.W.S. spells something. It spells Twees."

Bump said, "Nice try."

I said, "Hey, you know? Twees wouldn't be a bad nickname."

Bump groaned. "Here we go."

I said, "No. Really. You guys didn't like Muzzy for my nickname. So let's go with Twees."

I saw them all make eye contact. Four pairs of eyes making connections all around the table. Well, fuck 'em if they can't take a joke.

I said, "Yeah, I'm going with Twees from now on. That's what I wanna be called."

There was a heavy silence. Then Bump turned back to Danny with an evil gleam in his eye. "So where were we? Oh, yeah. What's the I stand for?"

We all watched Danny and waited. He squirmed.

John poked him. "Well?" He was grinning.

Finally, he blurted out, "Okay, it's Ignatius. Happy now?"

I'd have to say we *were* pretty happy. Everybody howled.

And just at that point, Danny glanced toward the front door.

He said, "Uh-oh."

I followed his eyes and there was the Bitch, bearing down on me like a mall surveyor. All up and down the table, my friends saw her coming and got the squirms. It looked like Danny, Gruf, Bump, and John had all suddenly gotten infested by some kind of specialized flea that only enjoyed the rich red blood of mid- to late-twentysomething males.

She walked down the side of the table and stopped behind me. An expensive cloud of Jessica McClintock perfume wrapped itself around my head. I put my fork down and turned to look at her. She smiled down on me, but you could see that behind her eyes, lots was stirring.

She said, "Hi, Terry. Can I talk to you a minute?"

I said, "Shoot."

Her eyes flicked briefly around the table. "In *private*?"

In my brain, I said, Oh shit. I looked mournfully at what was left of my breakfast, picked up my coffee cup and my cigarettes, and looked around. The only open table in the place was a booth right behind the pushed-together tables where me and my friends always sit. That was way too close for comfort, but what was I gonna do?

We slid in across from each other, and she nodded when Mary, the waitress who takes care of all of us every morning as if we're her own family, asked her if she wanted coffee. Mary glanced at me and gently patted my shoulder. I noticed the slight rise in her sweet little eyebrows as she turned away.

She brought the Bitch a cup and topped me off. She said, "Don't you want your plate over here, hon?"

I shook my head. I wasn't hungry anymore.

There were a million thoughts flying around in my brain, but the main two were: How did the Bitch know where to find me, and What did she want? I wanted to say something to her about, Where did she get off bothering me during my leisure hours, then I realized it wouldn't make any sense.

So then I thought, Okay, what I was really feeling was that she must have been spying on me to know where and when I ate breakfast. Because ever since I got out of jail and moved to Spencer, I'd been pretty careful not to let her know how to get in touch with me. I should demand to know where she got off doing that. But I didn't.

I thought about saying that I didn't want her coming around me anywhere, anytime, anymore. I didn't want to always be looking over my shoulder, thinking she might turn up here or there. But I didn't really want to say anything hurtful. That was more in *her* line, if you catch my drift.

I ended up not saying anything. I just sat there looking at her, waiting for her to start, while my friends sat at the next table with their ears sticking out. You could almost see their little pink lobes quivering, waiting to pick up every word.

Oh, jeez, look at that. Bump and Gruf were laughing. Danny, too. Now John was leaning over to Danny. Yeah, Danny had said something to make Bump and Gruf laugh and now he repeated it to John, and they were all laughing behind their hands.

One thing, I knew it wasn't anything mean directed toward me. These friends of mine, they're the loyalest bunch of humanus erectus you could ever find anywhere. I doubted it was anything mean directed toward Marylou, either.

What it was, it was just one of Danny's wry little comments on the situation in general. Danny can come up with some pretty good ones sometimes. But it wouldn't have been mean. Danny doesn't have a mean molecule in his body.

I looked at Marylou, sitting there with her big blond seventies mall hair and her two-fisted makeup covering up all her natural good looks. I lit a cigarette and waited. She took a sip of her coffee. Then she looked up at me through her heavy black mascara, combed out into what looked like millions and millions of long, long lashes.

She smiled like she was flirting with me and said, "You could at least act like you're glad to see me."

I didn't want to say anything hurtful to her, but I wasn't gonna sit there and lie, either.

I said, "Why? I'm not."

She poured it on, turning her head a little and batting those eyelashes. "Not even a little bit?" There was actually self-confidence in her voice.

"Not even a little bit," I said coldly. "What do you want?"

Mary was over at the guys' table with the coffee-pot. She stopped by Bump, bent down to whisper something, and stayed bent down to hear the answer. It looked like he was whispering into a microphone hidden in the red carnation she had pinned on her green waitress dress. I swallowed a chuckle and turned my eyes back to the Bitch, who was busy pushing her cuticles back from her pearly white nail polish.

I said, "Marylou, say what you want and leave, so I can finish my breakfast in peace."

She gave me a hurt face and puckered her lips. "You don't have to be so grumpy."

I drummed my fingers and waited.

She drew breath and said, "Okay. I want you to help me move."

I thought about hauling her out of the booth, pointing her toward the door, giving her a gentle shove, and saying, There. You're moving. Happy now?

Instead I said, "Move. To where?"

But I already knew to where. A few months earlier, she'd been in Carlo's, the little pizza place where I worked nights as a driver, and she'd told Debby the waitress that she was going to sell our trailer down in the southern part of the county and move into a townhouse here in Spencer. I'd been horrified at the news.

She said, "Green Meadow Townhouses."

There it was. It was really gonna happen. Not only that, she wanted me to help her do it. I got pissed.

I said, "I'm not gonna help you move up here. I don't want you up here. Find yourself another sucker."

I reached to pick up my cigarettes and go back to my place at the table, but she put her hand on mine.

She said, "You have to help me."

"No. I don't. Get some of your friends to help you."

"You're my friend."

"No. I'm not."

"But I love you."

"That's your problem."

You're probably thinking, Why does this guy have to be such a hard-ass? Would it kill him to help the poor girl move?

If you're thinking that, Chief, it's because you don't understand women. Or at least, you don't understand *this* woman. Neither did I, back when she and I were together. Which it wasn't even that long ago. Just about a year. But I'd learned a lot about women since then, and I knew for a fact that she wasn't here about moving. She could get plenty of help with moving.

Why she was here, she wanted her and me to get back together. The moving was her excuse. She figured, get me to help her move, wear some Daisy Duke cutoffs, something along those lines. Then the whole time during the move, she'd keep brushing against me, keep posing and giggling, keep saying how much she missed me. Keep saying things about how nice the townhouse was and didn't I think I'd like to live there with her? Look, we could get a recliner and put it right there for me. Wouldn't that be nice?

I could see it all happening right before my eyes. And it would've worked once. But not now.

She tried to work up a tear. Her lower lip even got a slight tremble going.

She said, "You loved me once. It's not my fault if your feelings changed."

Making a conscious effort to keep my voice soft and calm, I said, "Oh, you've wrong there. It's entirely your fault that my feelings changed."

She looked away. "Anyway. We're still married. You have to help me."

This made me laugh. "We're not married anymore. Our marriage was over the day I got your divorce papers in jail."

"But—"

I interrupted, making my voice even quieter. "But there's still a piece of paper in a file cabinet somewhere that says we are married?" I shook my head. "It doesn't mean squat to me. We're not married anymore. Plain and simple."

She looked down into her coffee cup.

I said, "And as far as that piece of paper goes, I

don't care anything about it. It can sit in that file drawer until hell freezes over, for all I care. If it bothers you, you go pay a lawyer to make it disappear."

She said, almost whispering, "I don't understand your attitude, Terry. You make it sound like you almost hate me."

I said, "I don't hate you. I don't feel anything for you at all, except I want you to stay out of my life. Starting now."

Now I did pick up my coffee cup and my cigarettes and move back to my place at the table with my friends. They were looking at me curiously.

I stole a glance at Mary. I studied her kind face like it was my own conscience, but couldn't tell whether she looked sympathetic or disapproving.

Well, whatever. I'd explain it to her later if she didn't understand. Because I was pretty sure I felt great. I'd stood up to the strongest of the old forces that had led me down a self-destructive path that ended in a jail cell, and I'd said no. Loud and clear.

Mary came over with the coffeepot. "More coffee, Terry?" she asked softly.

"Thanks, yeah. Top it off."

I heard a little rustling sound behind me. In peripheral vision I saw a figure moving toward the front door. I turned to watch her go. Her short little black skirt bounced side to side like windshield wipers as she walked away.

All of a sudden, everybody was moving and coughing and talking at once. I looked around, waiting to hear what they thought.

A strand of long, golden hair had escaped from Bump Bellini's ponytail. He tucked it back behind his ear and grinned at me. "Whew! I guess you told her!"

Daniel Ignatius Gillespie gave me a high five. He

was laughing. "No offense, dude, but I really didn't think you had the balls."

They were all grinning and laughing. I started laughing, too. We all sat there, laughing like a bunch of idiots.

Everything would've been different if I'd helped the Bitch move that rainy November morning. Some stuff probably would've still happened, just in a different way. Some other stuff probably wouldn't have happened at all. If I were the kind of guy who sits around thinking about what might've been, I guess I could log some serious hours wondering about this. But I'm not, so I won't.

COMING IN JULY 2003 FROM SIGNET MYSTERY

DEAD GIRLS DON'T WEAR DIAMONDS
A Blackbird Sisters Mystery
by Nancy Martin   0-451-20886-2

When a high society jewel thief winds up drowned at the bottom of a pool with a tacky garden gnome tied to her ankles, Nora must swing into action to save her old flame from a hasty murder charge.

MRS. MALORY AND DEATH IN PRACTICE
by Hazel Holt   0-451-20920-6

The new town veterinarian hardly has any kennel-side manner. His patients squirm and bark in his presence— and the humans don't fancy him either. Even genial Mrs. Malory can't find a redemming bone in his body. So when the vet turns up dead, a whole roster of townspeople are suspects.

**Available wherever books are sold, or
to order call: 1-800-788-6262**

Lawrence Block

TANNER ON ICE
19410-1

Once Evan Tanner was known as the thief who couldn't sleep, carrying out his dangerous duties for a super-secret intelligence agency. Then someone put him on ice—for 25 years. Now Tanner has returned and is about to embark on a new assignment....And he's making up for lost time.

THE THIEF WHO COULDN'T SLEEP
19403-9

A wake-up call is the last thing that Evan Tanner needs. Champion of lost causes and beautiful women, Tanner hasn't slept a wink since the sleep center of his brain was destroyed. And with the FBI keeping tabs on him, the CIA tapping his phone, and a super-secret intelligence agency wanting to recruit him, keeping wide awake is definitely a smart choice.

THE CANCELED CZECH
19404-7

The Canceled Czech finds the sleepless adventurer on a mission to Czechoslovakia to liberate a dying man, who turns out to be a Nazi. For his troubles, he finds himself leaping from a moving train, tangling with an amorous blonde, and playing the role of a neo-Nazi propagandist. Just another typical work day in the life of "the thief who couldn't sleep."

TANNER'S TWELVE SWINGERS
19833-6

Evan Tanner, intrepid spy, is back in the third of his original, hilarious adventures. This time he finds himself up to his neck in a dozen leggy beauties and a life-and-death smuggling assignment out in a cold corner of Russia.